*"Now would be a good time for you to make your first pie crust," said Aunt Clara.*

Maggie bowed to the inevitable. Aunt Clara wanted to pass on the family recipe. "Sure. Let me put this trash out in the Dumpster."

The back door to the shop was stuck. No matter how hard Maggie pushed, it wouldn't open. "I'm going outside to check on this," she told her aunt.

All the little shops in the plaza kept their trash in the back for easy pickup. Maggie threw her bag of trash into the Dumpster and looked to see if a bag of someone else's trash was blocking the back door. She stopped dead once she saw what the problem was.

Lou Goldberg was lying across the back step. His eyes were open as though he were staring at the blue sky.

Except that Lou would never see another blue sky.

# Plum Deadly

Ellie Grant

GALLERY BOOKS

New York London Toronto Sydney New Delhi

Gallery Books
A Division of Simon & Schuster, Inc.
1230 Avenue of the Americas
New York, NY 10020



First Gallery Books trade paperback edition September 2013



*Designed by Leydiana Rodríguez-Ovalles*

Manufactured in the United States of America

10 9 8 7 6 5 4 3 2 1

Library of Congress Cataloging-in-Publication Data

Grant, Ellie.
Plum deadly / Ellie Grant. — First Gallery Books trade paperback edition.
pages cm
1. Bakeries—Fiction. 2. Pies—Fiction. 3. Murder—Investigation—Fiction.
4. Durham (N.C.)—Fiction. 5. Mystery fiction. I. Title.
PS3607.R3638P58 2013
813'.6—dc23 2013011692

ISBN 978-1-4516-8955-6
ISBN 978-1-4516-8957-0 (ebook)

*For our Southern mothers and grandmothers, who had patient, pie-making hands and gentle voices.*

*Thanks for the pecan pie and banana pudding. Thanks for being there.*

# One

"Order up!"

Maggie Grady checked her email one last time. There was still no response from her latest job query, but it had only been an hour since she'd sent it. She had a good feeling about this one.

Unlike the hundreds of impersonal emails she'd sent to faceless hiring agents, she knew Claudia Liggette. Maggie had worked with her—partied with her—years before her life had been unceremoniously dumped in the trash.

"Maggie," her aunt called. "This piece of pie isn't going to grow legs."

"Sorry." Maggie left her laptop with a last, longing look at the screen.

*Come on! Come on!*

Professor Ira Simpson smiled as she brought the big slice of Lotsa Lemon Meringue pie to him. He was a kindly older man with sharp wings of white hair at his temples and a twinkle in his blue eyes. "Any luck today?"

She sighed. Did everyone know she was looking for work? She supposed it was obvious since she was back in Durham, working at her aunt's pie shop. She'd asked her aunt not to spread it around that she'd lost her job. There were too many questions to answer about the last six weeks of her life.

"Not yet," she responded. "But it won't be long now."

"You remind me so much of your mother," he said. "You have her nose and her chin, you know. And those same peculiar green eyes. Your mother was a good student. Of course, so were you!"

Maggie filled his coffee cup. He always said that to her. She glanced at herself in the mirror behind the counter. She knew she favored her mother, but only from old pictures she'd seen of her parents. She couldn't remember them. They'd died when she was very young.

She checked on the other five people, most of them eating the special—Dangerously Damson pie—made from fresh damson plums.

"Cheer up, honey," her aunt said as she cut a Chocoholic Cream pie into four slices. "You've worked hard all your life. People will notice that. You'll be out of here in no time."

Those little pep talks made Maggie feel guilty. She'd

ended up on her aunt's doorstep with one duffel bag when she'd lost her job at the bank. She'd barely been able to scrape together enough money for a bus ticket to get home.

It had been twelve years since she'd left Aunt Clara and Uncle Fred in Durham, North Carolina, where she'd grown up. She'd only come home once during that time, and that was to attend Uncle Fred's funeral. To make matters worse, she only called her family a few times each year.

Maggie blamed it on work—flying around the world for the bank, throwing lavish parties at her loft in Manhattan, wining and dining important financial clients from sheiks to senators. It was the kind of busy, high-powered life she'd always wanted.

Then one rainy Monday morning, she'd been accused of stealing money from an important client and had been escorted from the bank. Her boss, Louis Goldberg, showed her the documents proving her guilt and told her how lucky she was the bank wanted to keep it quiet. They weren't pressing charges.

Her bank accounts had been frozen. The bank officer had told her they'd take what they needed to pay back her debt. A policeman was standing outside her door at home to make sure she didn't take anything valuable with her.

By that afternoon, everything she'd had was gone. She had the clothes on her back and some money to go toward her bus ticket. The Salvation Army had helped her with the rest.

Aunt Clara had smiled when Maggie showed up at her front door. She'd listened to her cry as she told her aunt what had happened. There were no recriminations, no "how the mighty had fallen" speeches. Just a simple, "I'm glad you made it home."

She didn't deserve it. She'd been a poor excuse for a niece and was determined to make it up to Aunt Clara after she got a new job. She was a different person. Her life was going to be better, and so was Aunt Clara's.

Maggie shook herself out of the depression that constantly threatened to engulf her since she was fired. "I'm sorry to be so whiny all the time. And I appreciate you giving me a place to live and work. You're the best, Aunt Clara."

As always, Clara's wrinkled face grew pink with pleasure and embarrassment at her words. "You're my only niece, you know. You're more like my daughter. It's not like I'd want you to be out on the street. I'm glad you came to me. It's what your mother would have wanted you to do."

Aunt Clara and Uncle Fred had raised Maggie after her parents' death in a car crash. They'd been there through high school and college when Maggie had worked right here at Pie in the Sky for spending money, dreaming her big dreams about the future.

"I could use a little more tea," an intense young man with spiky, green-tinged brown hair yelled out.

"I'll get it," Maggie said. "How's that mystery pie coming along? People are waiting for it. I think we've already had a hundred suggestions for names. It's smart to introduce new pies that way. Good marketing."

Aunt Clara shrugged her shoulders. Her unnaturally red hair was a little frizzier than usual. It looked like an orange fringe around her still pretty face. She looked like Maggie's mother with that red hair and green eyes. Maggie had inherited her father's dark brown hair that she'd always worn short.

"It's what I've always done. The kids like it. I never guessed when your uncle and I opened this pie shop forty years ago that I'd be here making pies without him." Aunt Clara sighed. "But then things don't always go the way you plan."

*You got that right.*

Maggie brought another small pot of hot water and a tea bag to the young man's table.

He looked like he was working on something important. He raked his hand through his hair again and spilled Amazing Apple pie on his worn black superhero T-shirt. The table was covered with diagrams and charts.

"What are you working on?" She glanced at the papers, trying to be friendly. It wasn't always easy. It had been different when she'd worked here and known most of the students. Now she felt a lot like their mother.

"None of your business," he barked, protectively covering the documents. "I have tea now. Go away."

"Didn't anyone ever tell you that you catch more flies with honey than with vinegar?"

He stared at her like she'd lost her mind.

*Obviously not.*

Maggie walked behind the counter to check her email again. *Nothing.*

"I can't find that chocolate cream pie," Aunt Clara complained from the small kitchen area at the back of the shop.

"Was that the pie you were just cutting?" Maggie smiled at her aunt's forgetfulness. "I think you put it in the fridge."

Aunt Clara found the pie in the large old refrigerator. "Sometimes I think I'd lose my head if it wasn't connected."

It was a slow afternoon. School had only been in session a few weeks at Duke University. It took a while for the new students to find Pie in the Sky and realize what a great hangout it was. It was the same way every year.

Faculty and almost every fireman and police officer in town came in on a regular basis too. It was a popular place through the school year. Summers were a little slow, but the shop managed to stay open.

"Hi, Maggie!" Handsome attorney Mark Beck sat down with his briefcase, like he did every few days around this time. "How's it going?"

"Okay." She sighed. "What can I get for you?"

"I'll take some sweet tea and some Dangerously Damson pie." He waggled his eyebrows. "Sounds exciting. What makes it dangerous?"

"I think it might only be the intent behind it. And Aunt Clara loves alliteration."

"How can I resist?"

She wrote down his order and came back with the pie and tea a few minutes later.

"How's the job search going?"

"Still going." She put down the plate and glass. "It's not a good job market right now."

He smiled, even white teeth against tanned skin. "You'll find something. You have banking experience and you're good with numbers. Something will come along."

*Yes,* she thought darkly, *everyone knows I'm out of work.*

At least they don't know *why*.

Maggie decided to clean up the pie case and stack some dishes in the dishwasher while her customers were busy eating and talking.

She and her friends had loved to study there. That tradition hadn't changed. They could usually count on a full house from 4:00 to 6:00 p.m. on weekdays.

Two young women came in the door together and Maggie took their orders. They went to sit down while she went back for two pieces of Popular Peach pie and two Diet Cokes.

It was hard not to think about those carefree days when she'd been at Duke. She wouldn't have been able to afford school there, but she was a third generation of Duke University graduates, including her mother and Aunt Clara. Maggie had been a special case, maybe a hard luck story, since she'd lost her parents early on in life.

She'd never felt that way, though. She enjoyed her time at Duke and had moved to New York, full of confidence. She'd planned on taking the world by storm. And for a while, she felt like she had.

"Could I get some milk over here?" the guy with the charts and diagrams said sharply.

Maggie got a little pitcher of milk for him. "Would you like another piece of pie?"

"Do I look like I want another piece of pie?" he snarled at her. "Leave me alone."

"Maggie!" Aunt Clara called from the kitchen. "Come quick! I think we're having trouble with the dishwasher."

She looked down at the rude young man and snarled back at him, "You'd better be in a friendlier mood when I get back or this chair better be empty."

Maybe it wasn't good business practice, but she could take only so much.

Maggie went back to the kitchen and stared at all the soap bubbles that were spreading across the floor, bulging from the dishwasher. "What happened? I didn't start it."

"No, honey, I did. I think that new soap might be bad. Get the mop, will you?"

Maggie passed the box of soap that was still open on the cabinet. "Is this what you used? No wonder it's foaming up. This is hand soap for the bathroom dispensers."

Aunt Clara had turned off the dishwasher by the time Maggie got back with the mop. Bubbles were still oozing from it. "Oh my stars, you're right. What was I thinking?"

The front door opened again, making a little chiming noise to let them know there were new customers.

"I'll clean this up," Aunt Clara said. "You tend to the customers. They're more important than this mess."

"Hi, Maggie." Angela Hightower smiled and greeted her when she came back out of the kitchen. "Am I the first one here for the book club?"

"It looks like it. I saved your tables in the corner. Would you like something to drink while you're waiting?"

"That'd be great. Maybe a little half and half—half sweet tea and half no-sugar tea." Angela laughed, tossing her dark blond, shoulder-length hair. "My son is getting married in six weeks and I'm trying to lose a few pounds."

"No pie today?"

"Don't be silly. Why do you think I'm drinking half and half? I'm going to wait for pie until the other girls get here.

We like to order different slices and share them around, you know?"

"I do." Maggie put her order pad in the pocket of her jeans. "I'll get your tea. What book did you read this month?"

"Something unusual for us—a murder mystery. Jean hardly had the stomach for it. But I thought it was good. Nice to read something besides family problems and books about women finding themselves. I don't understand why all those women feel so lost in the first place."

Maggie shook her head and hid her smile as she went to fetch the tea. She liked Angela, who was plainspoken and always ready to try something new. Aunt Clara told her Angela sold real estate and was on her fourth marriage, this time to a man almost half her age.

"The rest of the book club won't be far behind," Aunt Clara said as Maggie poured tea into an ice-packed glass. "I hope we have enough variety for them. I really need to teach you how to make piecrust. It's the hardest part."

"I could never make crust like you do." Maggie put a slice of lemon on the lip of the glass. "I think we should keep things the way they are. You know I have to find another job. Don't change things that have worked for years on my account."

There would have to be changes, Maggie knew. She'd been surprised by both her aunt's forgetfulness and the shabby condition of the pie shop. Aunt Clara wasn't getting any younger. She might not be able to continue with the shop.

"It's not that hard once you know the secret," Aunt Clara said. "The women of our family have passed it on for three generations now. If you don't learn, it dies with me. You're all I have, Maggie. We have to stick together."

Maggie smiled and kissed her aunt, a strong feeling of guilt clutching at her heart. She knew Aunt Clara needed her, but she couldn't stay here tending the pie shop the rest of her life. She had her own dreams and ambitions.

She'd been good at what she did for the bank, bringing in millions of dollars with new clients every year. If she got a second chance, she knew she could do it again. She could be that blazing star, living the high life and feeling the satisfaction that came with it.

By the time Maggie took the iced tea to Angela, Jean and Barb were there. They'd already pushed some tables together in the corner and pulled up more chairs.

Jean was a nursing instructor at the university. She was very thin and always wore scrubs. Barb, a counselor at the school, wore a perpetual frown, as though life had let her down. The three women had been friends since childhood. None of them had ever lived outside of North Carolina—or Durham, for that matter.

They were examples of the women Maggie *didn't* want to be.

"So that's another sweet tea and a coffee." Maggie wrote in her order book.

"Decaf," Jean said. "I've already got the jitters from my new class. It scares me sometimes to think the people I teach might take care of me someday. I hope I die on the side of the road with the level of health care I see coming up."

"Got it." Maggie joked with the women about Jean's new hair color and Betty's rubber mud boots. As she'd learned in college when she worked here, talking to her customers got her bigger tips.

"Let's wait for Liz and Sissy to order pie," Angela said, clearly the leader of the group. "Have you heard anything about Mann Development lately, Maggie? Any new offers on the shop?"

"Not as far as I know," Maggie replied. "I don't think they'll be back again with another offer after Aunt Clara ran them off with her pepper spray."

All the ladies from the book club laughed at that image, except Angela. "They'll be back. This piece of property is too important to that new medical office building. You know, your aunt should take advantage of the next offer. She could live in luxury the last few years of her life."

Maggie's generous mouth tightened a little at her words. "I think Aunt Clara is doing fine. She doesn't need Mann's money to live a good life."

Angela smiled in a slightly devious way that made Maggie feel like she would never trust the other woman to buy or sell a piece of property for her.

"You and I both know you won't be here forever, sweetie. You've had a few hard breaks, but you'll be gone again in no time, leaving Clara to sort this out alone. All I'm saying is, why not take advantage of a good thing? If you encourage her now, you won't have to feel guilty when you climb on that plane."

Maggie didn't know what to say. Angela's words hit too close to the truth not to lodge in her chest. She was saying all the things Maggie had been thinking—and feeling guilty for.

"I'll let Aunt Clara know that you're waiting for Liz and Sissy before you order pie. Thanks."

As Maggie walked away from the table in the corner, she heard Angela continue, "All I did was tell her the way it is. We all know Clara can't fight progress."

# Two

Her shoulders stiff with fury, Maggie ducked behind the counter and started a fresh pot of coffee. Angela was wrong about Aunt Clara having to cope with Mann Development. Let them have the old building. She could make a nice profit and go to New York with Maggie. Aunt Clara could live fine without it.

It was very quiet in the kitchen. Maggie glanced in back to see what her aunt was doing. “Making new piecrust?”

“We don’t need it yet.” Clara brought out the big sack of flour and a few measuring cups. “But I think now would be as good a time as any for you to learn the recipe.”

"We're pretty busy." Maggie tried to put her off. "Why don't you write it down and I can look over it later?"

"This recipe has never been written down, honey. It has passed from mouth to ear for three generations. I surely won't be the one to break that tradition."

"Well maybe later then, when we close up for the night. Or tomorrow. We could come in early and you could show me. I don't think I can make piecrust and wait on tables at the same time."

Aunt Clara laughed. "You sound so old, Maggie. You're barely in your thirties. When I was your age, I could make pie, wait on tables, and still have time for a quick cuddle in the kitchen with your Uncle Fred."

Maggie smiled at the picture her aunt painted. Her aunt and uncle had been very much in love. She'd seen it every day as she was growing up. They'd shared that love with her.

It was a much different time, a happier time. Maybe it was because she'd been a kid and hadn't known anything about the world.

Maggie smelled the coffee brewing. "I just think we should wait for the right time. I'm going to take the coffee and tea out to the book club ladies. I'll be right back."

Feeling like she had escaped an execution—her own—Maggie poured tea into a glass and coffee into a mug. She never thought it would come to this. Who knew there was a secret family recipe for piecrust? Aunt Clara had never mentioned it before. Why now?

How was she going to explain that the only food she'd ever made was something that came out of a microwave oven? Even popcorn was tricky for her sometimes. She obviously didn't get the family gene for cooking that her mother and aunt had.

She was good with numbers. She'd cleared up Aunt Clara's bad accounting in the first few days she'd been back. She was good with computers. She'd even understood the cash register that her aunt had declared impossible.

Wasn't that enough?

Maggie felt sure she would never make even an adequate piecrust much less the kind people raved over. Something had to happen that would get her out of this situation. Aunt Clara too, it seemed. She realized that she couldn't leave her alone for another ten years.

She thought about the offer for Pie in the Sky from Mann Development. She hadn't seen the numbers, but it might be worth exploring. All she needed was a good job. She could convince Aunt Clara to sell the pie shop and they could go away together.

Maybe they could go on a cruise to the Bahamas or something. There were plenty of exciting things to do when you had money.

Maggie was dropping off the tea and coffee and picking up another order for Diet Coke from Sissy, who'd arrived while she'd been in back, when two things happened.

She heard a *ping* from her email, telling her that a possible job offer was waiting for her.

At the same instant, the chime on the front door rang and Louis Goldberg, her ex-boss, walked into Pie in the Sky.

Maggie dropped the Diet Coke on the floor. "Lou!" she squealed.

Her mind ran amok with possibilities. He was here to ask her to come back. There had been a mistake of some sort that he'd just realized. The bank had found the real culprit.

He'd come because the bank had decided to prosecute her after all.

All of these ideas ran through her head. She didn't want to pick one. She just wanted it to be good news.

Lou stared back at her, then as suddenly as he'd shown up, he walked back out the door.

It only took an instant for Maggie to follow him. She didn't even stop to clean up the Diet Coke. "Lou? What's going on?"

"Maggie." He shook his balding head and his whole large body began to tremble. His red-rimmed blue eyes teared up. "Seeing you in that getup was too much for me. I can't believe I did this to you. I'm so sorry."

She glanced into the pie shop window to make sure Aunt Clara didn't need her. Excitement buzzed through her like an electric current. *Yes!*

"Why don't you come back inside and I'll get you some pie." She could afford to be generous. "It will make you feel better and we can talk."

He nodded, sniffing hard and wiping his nose with his handkerchief. He was wearing an expensive gray suit and a red, white, and blue tie with a little flag for a tie tack. Lou was nothing if not patriotic.

"That sounds good. Thanks."

Maggie put him at a table on the side of the shop by the windows, away from the sometimes noisy book club. She needed to concentrate and didn't want to be overheard. Her heart was beating double time in her chest. *This is it!*

She got Lou a piece of Dangerously Damson pie and a cup of coffee. As she crossed the floor from the counter to his table, Mark got up to ask for more coffee and they collided.

"I'm so sorry." He tried to wipe the spilled coffee from the table, floor, and Maggie's wrist.

"It's okay." Lou's pie seemed to be fine—a little coffee sloshed on the plate. She wiped that away with a napkin. Her wrist burned a little, but it was nothing compared to her burning curiosity to hear what Lou had to say.

"Are you sure?" Mark tried to help her with the pie and coffee she carried.

"I'm sure." She smiled at him. He was such a nice guy. "I'll get you some coffee."

Maggie gave Lou his pie and coffee, then poured coffee for Mark and checked with everyone (except the rude student) to see if they were okay for a few minutes.

Finally, she set her cell phone to record whatever Lou had to say. She'd learned her lesson from the whole experience and didn't want to take anything for granted.

But if it all worked out—*wow!*

Trying not to get too excited after her six weeks of hell, she sat down across from the man who'd mentored and encouraged her for the last ten years.

Of course he'd also been the one who'd accused her of embezzlement and fired her. She figured he had no choice in that matter.

"What do you mean you did this to me?" Her voice was suddenly raspy. She cleared her throat.

He ate a piece of pie, coughed, and gulped some coffee. He seemed to be having some difficulty swallowing. She chalked that up to anxiety.

"You were falsely accused," he finally explained. "I know now that you didn't embezzle that money. The person who accused you—let's just say he's higher up on the food chain—he's the one who took the money."

"Who is that, Lou?"

He ate more pie. "You know, this stuff is really good. You always said you couldn't boil water."

Maggie was through stalling. "I want to know who did this to me."

"Don't worry. Trust me. I'm gonna do right by you. I'm going to hold a press conference, right here in . . ."

"Durham," she supplied when he looked blank. "Can't you tell me now? What will that mean? Will the bank hire me back?"

"Oh, you'll get your job back," he promised, finishing his pie and coffee. "You and I stand together, there's no telling what we can do. There's no reason for you to suffer like *this* anymore. You were meant for better."

His voice had started getting louder as he'd finished. Maggie was sure everyone in the shop had heard that last bit. She knew grandstanding when she heard it. Lou wanted the credit for rooting out the real embezzler. That was fine with her.

She was a little embarrassed by what he'd said. Yes, she felt she was capable of more, but Pie in the Sky wasn't exactly the dregs of the earth and she certainly wasn't suffering—except at his hand.

Maggie excused herself and went to get more coffee for Lou and everyone else. Her rude student was packing up his charts and getting ready to leave. The members of the book club looked at her curiously. She ignored them.

Fortunately, Aunt Clara had been in the kitchen and hadn't heard any of it.

"More pie?" she asked Lou before she sat back down.

"No, thanks." He slurped the rest of his coffee, choked again, then smiled at her. He looked a little pale as he put a fifty-dollar bill on the table. "Be here tomorrow morning, ten a.m. sharp. We'll expose what really happened at the bank. Once the media has the information, we'll both be in the clear, Maggie. We'll both be safe."

Safe? She thought about his choice of words. It seemed an odd way to put it.

She watched him walk out of the pie shop, wishing he'd told her who'd framed her before he told the rest of the world.

What if he had a heart attack, God forbid, and the information was lost with him? Even though she had the recording of what he'd said in her hand, she wasn't sure if that was enough without the person's name to back it up.

Higher up on the food chain, huh?

Maggie tried to think which of Lou's bosses that could be. She couldn't imagine any of those people wanting to pin this on her—she barely knew them. She'd always supposed she was beneath their notice.

Apparently not.

*How could someone just randomly pick me to take the fall for this?* she wondered as she cleaned off tables and put plates, cups, and silverware into the now-compliant dishwasher. *Why me?*

It was going to be a long wait for the press conference.

She wasn't sure what to wear. All of her good clothes were gone. She only had a few pairs of jeans and some Pie in the Sky T-shirts. She hadn't had her nails or hair done since she got here. Her face was a mess—no facials.

Putting all of that aside, she mopped coffee from the tile floor in the empty pie shop. It was four, and they were open another two hours. This was going to be one of the slow days. Time was going to drag if she didn't find something to do.

She checked her last email. It was only spam. Nothing yet from Claudia.

Full of energy and excitement—*cautionary* excitement—she tackled cleaning everything she could reach in the front of the shop.

With Uncle Fred gone, Aunt Clara hadn't been able to keep up with all the dust and grime tracked in every day by hundreds of feet. Waitresses came and went like the pies consumed there. They didn't care about the pie shop.

The tables were cracked and scarred in many places, the blue chairs the same. The tile floor was chipped and dreary in a way that couldn't be cleaned. The counter needed replacing along with the pie stands and refrigerated glass cases.

Maggie scrubbed everything, from the ceiling fan that barely turned to the window ledges that needed painting. She even wiped down the old blue-and-white Hot Pie Now neon sign that flashed wearily in the window.

Exhausted, Maggie hauled the trash to the back door and put away the mop and bucket. She looked at the clock in the kitchen—it was barely five fifteen.

"You're full of energy today," Aunt Clara remarked. "Maybe now would be a good time for you to make your first piecrust."

Maggie accepted the inevitable. Aunt Clara wanted to pass on the family recipe. This might be the last chance she had to learn it. "Sure. Let me put this trash out in the Dumpster and we'll make some pie."

"You're going to be fabulous at it."

The back door to the shop was stuck. No matter how hard Maggie pushed, it wouldn't open. "I'm going outside to check this," she told her aunt. "I'll be right back."

All the little shops in the plaza kept their trash in the back for easy pickup on the same day. There was plenty of it built up already even though trash day was two days away.

Maggie threw her bag of trash into the Dumpster and rounded the corner to see if a bag of someone else's trash was blocking the back door. She stopped once she saw what the problem was.

Lou Goldberg was lying across the back step. His eyes were open as though he were staring at the blue sky.

Except Lou would never see another blue sky again.

# Three

Aunt Clara and Maggie sat inside the pie shop and talked quietly about what had happened while the police looked at the crime scene.

Maggie explained about Lou, who he was and why he was there. Aunt Clara sighed and shook her head, muttering about ill omens and other bad things. Her words filled Maggie with more dread than the idea of trying to make piecrust.

One of the first officers on the scene introduced them to a middle-aged, hard-faced man. Detective Frank Waters was wearing a cheap brown suit and never cracked a smile. He explained that Lou was dead—cause yet unknown.

"Mr. Goldberg's body will be taken to the Medical Examiner's Office at which time we will find out exactly what happened to him," he told Aunt Clara and Maggie.

"That's terrible," Aunt Clara said. "Poor man."

"Can you tell me why Mr. Goldberg was here?" He scrutinized them. "I'm sure he didn't come all this way for the pie."

Maggie wasn't sure exactly how forthcoming she should be with the detective. Maybe Lou had that heart attack she'd been worried about.

*Maybe it was something else.*

After all, Lou had been talking about ratting on another man for embezzlement. If Lou had mentioned his plans to that man—well—that could have created a situation.

"Ms. Grady?" Detective Waters snapped his fingers to get Maggie's attention. "Do you remember serving this man in the pie shop or not?"

"Yes," she carefully answered. "He was here. He ate Dangerously Damson pie and drank coffee."

"Dangerously Damson, huh?" He smirked as he wrote in his notebook. "Did he seem sick or anything? Anything unusual happen?"

"No," Maggie said. "Nothing unusual."

"You should tell him about why your friend was here, Maggie," Aunt Clara said with a sweet smile.

"Yes, Maggie," the detective mimicked. "Why don't you tell me about your friend?"

*Thanks, Aunt Clara.*

"He wasn't exactly my friend," she started to explain. "Well, he was until he fired me six weeks ago."

*No! That sounded bad.*

"Why were you fired, Ms. Grady?" the detective asked.

"It was all a big mistake." Aunt Clara wandered in to help. "The bank she worked for thought she'd stolen money from them, but of course, that wasn't true. Maggie isn't a thief. Are you, sweetheart?"

Maggie sighed. Heavily. "No, Aunt Clara."

Between the two of them, she'd probably be in jail by tonight.

"How much money?" the detective asked.

"About three million," Maggie admitted, feeling trapped.

He looked up from his notebook. "Dollars?"

"Yes. But Aunt Clara is right. It isn't true. In fact, that's why Lou was here, to tell me who really took the money."

"And that was?" Detective Waters prompted, his chewed-up pencil poised for her answer.

"He didn't say," Maggie replied. "He told me he'd arranged a press conference for tomorrow. He said the real thief is a big name at the bank."

"No clue who it was?" Detective Waters nodded as he wrote.

"No." Maggie bit her lip. This sounded terrible—possibly worse than the first time she'd heard it. "I recorded our conversation on my phone."

"Really?" His eyes narrowed. "Was that for your protection because you knew people would be asking questions later when he was found dead?"

"It was for *my* protection. But not for that reason." She

fumbled around in her pocket trying to get her cell phone out. Her thrift store jeans were about a half size too small. It made the pockets tight. On the other hand, the jeans made her look about five pounds smaller.

Maggie finally produced the phone with a flourish. Detective Waters took it from her, put it into a plastic bag, and sealed it.

"Hey! That's my phone."

"Not now. Now it's evidence." He got up from the table. "I'll check your story out and get back with you. In the meantime, don't take any long vacations. I might have a few more questions after I explore some other angles."

"Oh, you don't have to worry about that," Aunt Clara told him. "She used to go on wonderful vacations all around the world—Paris, London, Rome—but not now. The bank took everything. She was very angry. She's handled it well. Such a pity."

Detective Waters nodded. "Good thing. Look, I hate to do this, but your pie shop is going to have to be closed for a few days until crime scene has a chance to go over everything. Sorry for the inconvenience."

"Oh dear." Aunt Clara looked worried. "My piecrust will go bad."

"We'll get it done as soon as we can," he promised. "If there's nothing wrong, you should be back up and running pretty quickly."

"Thanks." Maggie held Aunt Clara's trembling hand. "I get the phone back too, right?"

Detective Waters didn't reply. The police officer who'd introduced him watched as they got their belongings together—

after he'd searched their purses. Maggie was able to take her laptop home with her. Aunt Clara had bought it for her, used, so she could look for work.

Before they knew it, Maggie and Aunt Clara were out on the sidewalk while the police were in the pie shop. The door was locked behind them and covered with crime scene tape. The police had even confiscated their shop keys.

Maggie put her arm around her aunt. "Don't worry. It'll be okay. Once the detective gives us the go-ahead, we'll come right back and open up again."

She wasn't feeling as optimistic as she sounded, but it wouldn't do any good for Aunt Clara to worry about it.

They walked away from Pie in the Sky past the Spin and Go Laundromat. Saul Weissman, the owner there, offered his condolences. He was a short, round man with gray hair and glasses.

Maggie was sure he had a crush on Aunt Clara from the way he acted—always protective and eager to please. But if her aunt had any feelings for him besides friendship, she'd never confessed them to her niece.

"This is awful," he said. "How can they come in and close you down this way? Of course, you didn't have anything to do with this tragedy, Clara. We can't choose our *family*."

"It's a misunderstanding, Mr. Weissman," Maggie explained, trying to keep her temper under control. "It will all be cleared up in a few days."

He didn't look convinced.

Raji Singh joined them from the Bombay Grill, one of the other shops in the plaza. "No, Saul is right." His dark face was stricken and worried above his bright red shirt. "It only makes a stronger case for Mann Development to come in and take our shops away."

"No one is taking anyone's shop away," Saul said in a decisive way. "Clara is just in the middle of this. Once it gets sorted out, we'll be fine."

"I hope so," Raji said. "I truly hope so. My wife and I are very happy here so close to the campus. We don't want to leave."

Aunt Clara looked up with tears in her eyes. "This is the first time Pie in the Sky has been closed for more than a holiday. I didn't even close for Fred's death."

Maggie ignored the two men and hugged her aunt. "Let's go home. Everything's going to be fine."

• • •

The house Maggie had grown up in was an older, two-story red brick a short walk away from the pie shop. The brick had mellowed in the hot Carolina sun to a pinkish color. The once white shutters and door had faded to gray with the years.

A huge old magnolia tree stood in the front yard with a few brick-outlined flowerbeds that held azaleas and boxwoods. Maggie remembered red and yellow tulips blooming here every spring from her childhood.

Everything about the house spoke of neglect, Maggie noticed as they walked up the cracked concrete stairs to the house. She supposed after Uncle Fred had died, it had been hard for Aunt Clara to get the larger things done. After straightening up her aunt's ledgers on the computer, Maggie was painfully aware that the pie shop barely made ends meet.

Inside the house were the same carpets and furniture that had been there for as long as Maggie could recall. She'd never seen a dust bunny on any of the hardwood floors, but the walls needed painting and the whole place needed some sprucing up.

There was no way she could help now—at least not until she found another job. She regretted the years she could have and didn't act. She hadn't even thought her aunt might need help.

It had taken a fall from privilege and grace to wake her up. Maggie was grateful to realize how blind she'd been and she was determined to make it up to her aunt in some way.

For now, she was going to have to focus on getting her job back. If Lou knew she was innocent, someone else must know too. She still had some contacts, people who could check into it for her. If nothing else, she could call the New York police and tell them what had happened.

The two women dropped into wood chairs with flower cushions in the kitchen. For a long time, they simply sat and stared, too upset to speak, as the evening waned into night.

"Well, this will never do." Aunt Clara finally got up and went to the refrigerator. "I've got this eggplant in here, Maggie. I'm going to fry it up and we'll eat it. Uncle Fred always loved eggplant, remember?"

"I remember." Maggie smiled. "He loved it with a ton of cheese and tomato sauce on it. I don't think he really liked the eggplant."

Aunt Clara laughed. "I think you're right. I'm not crazy about it either, still I don't want to see it go to waste. Mrs. Thompson gave me a bunch of it from her garden."

Maggie agreed and snapped some green beans, also from Mrs. Thompson.

Clara peeled and sliced then fried the breaded eggplant. "You know, we've got some curry in there that Raji gave us too."

"Sounds like a feast to me!"

After Maggie had made the sweet tea and poured it into tall ice-filled glasses, the two women were sitting down to eat when the doorbell rang.

"I'm Ryan Summerour," the man on the porch said when Maggie opened the door. "I'm with the *Durham Weekly*. I wanted to talk with Maggie Grady or Clara Lowder. Are they in?"

Maggie knew trouble when she saw it.

The reporter had slightly curly blond hair, big blue eyes, and a flirty smile Maggie didn't trust. He looked to be in his late thirties, maybe forty. He wore jeans and a Duke jacket that he looked good in. He probably knew it too.

Maggie didn't buy it. This was bad news for her and her aunt. It meant the local newspaper wanted to cover the story about Lou's death.

She'd had her fill of reporters when she left the bank. Their questions had been insulting and horrible.

Before she could say no thanks and slam the door in Ryan Summerour's face, Aunt Clara came from the kitchen and welcomed him into her home.

"I read your paper every week, cover to cover," she told the reporter. "I don't like the daily, you know. It's such a rag. Nothing but crime and traffic accidents."

"Thanks," he responded. "I appreciate that—?"

"Oh! I'm Clara Lowder and this is my niece, Maggie Grady."

"It's nice to meet you, Mrs. Lowder."

He was talking to Aunt Clara, Maggie noticed, though he was looking at her. She was sure he already knew what had happened. He'd come to torture them about it. She had to find a way to get rid of him, despite Aunt Clara's hero worship.

"We were sitting down for dinner." Maggie thought that might deter him until she could talk to her aunt and warn her about interviews.

"Maggie's right." Aunt Clara smiled and took his arm. "Lucky we have plenty. Maybe you could join us."

Ryan's gaze zeroed in on Maggie again. "I'd be delighted."

*Great.*

They walked back to the kitchen together where the eggplant, green beans, and curry were waiting. Aunt Clara asked him to sit down and had Maggie get him a glass of tea.

"I heard that you had some bad news at your shop today," Ryan began pleasantly. "I was wondering if you'd like to talk about it for the paper."

"Certainly!" Aunt Clara danced around the kitchen getting more napkins. "I think that would be fine."

Maggie smiled at the reporter. "Will you excuse us, Mr. Summerour?"

She grabbed Aunt Clara's hand and pulled her out of the kitchen, closing the door behind them. "We can't talk to him," she whispered.

"Why not?"

"Because he'll put it in the paper," Maggie said. "You don't want that."

"Of course I do!" Aunt Clara grinned impishly, her wrinkled face showing some of her youth. "Ryan Summerour is a trustworthy journalist, like his father before him. He'll do right by us. Now come and eat before everything gets cold."

"Aunt Clara—"

"Cheer up, Maggie," her aunt advised. "It's not like we killed someone!"

# Four

Ryan Summerour was witty, charming, and never pushed for the story they all knew he wanted. He raved about the eggplant and the green beans and even helped do the dishes when the meal was over.

Aunt Clara rambled on about everything under the sun—from the pie shop to Fred's death and Maggie coming home in disgrace.

It was a good thing Ryan seemed to have a big appetite, because Maggie couldn't eat a thing. It was bad enough that he was a reporter. Aunt Clara didn't seem to understand that he could print anything she told him. Trusting him to do the right thing was crazy.

Maggie was angry too. She knew the reporter was leading Aunt Clara on to get his story. No telling what kind of awful garbage he would end up saying about them in the paper. She had to find a way to end the evening with him.

They went into the living room when the kitchen was clean. Clara had barely sat down when she remembered that she had some Amazing Apple pie in the refrigerator and went to put on some coffee. She refused both their offers of help, and even winked at Maggie before she left.

*Oh no.*

Maggie knew what that meant. Aunt Clara had always been fond of matchmaking. It hadn't happened since Maggie had come back. The past, though, was another story. Her aunt had managed to set her up with her friends' sons and nephews a few times in college.

"Your aunt is quite a woman," Ryan said when they were alone.

"She is," Maggie replied in an irritable voice. She'd reached her limit with this tell-all. Now that they were alone, she could tell him to get out.

"You must be very proud of her."

"I am."

"I get the feeling you aren't as happy about me being here as your aunt."

"Really? I think you should leave now. I'd appreciate it if you'd keep Aunt Clara out of your story. She doesn't know anything about what happened. She doesn't deserve to be ridiculed for the benefit of your readers. She's an old lady who just sees the good in everyone. You shouldn't use her to sell papers. I don't care what you say about me."

Maggie got to her feet for good measure.

Ryan seemed unfazed by her rant. "That's fine. I appreciate your honesty. But if you don't want me to ask your aunt questions about what happened today at Pie in the Sky, I suggest you start giving me some information I can use. You're the involved party here, right?"

He was tougher than she'd thought, though not as mean spirited. The last thing she'd wanted was to come back home from ruining her own reputation just to ruin her aunt's.

"What does that mean?" she demanded. "Do you think I had something to do with Lou's death?"

"The only thing I know right now is that the police have you listed as a person of interest in the case. I've been involved with several murder cases. That usually means they think you were involved in some way. I won't be the only reporter on your doorstep once all of this gets out."

*That's just great.*

Maggie tried to think of a way to defuse this situation—she'd have to deal with the rest of it later. Obviously, Ryan was going to print something about what had happened. Maybe she could convince him to print her side of it.

"I'll tell you as much as I know," she said. "You'd better be as trustworthy as my aunt thinks you are."

Carefully, with halting words and long pauses, she poured out her whole story to him. She was angry, but she'd managed not to cry. It was a relief, in a way, to tell it from start to finish. The ending, for that moment at least, being Lou's death.

Ryan nodded as he quickly wrote down everything she said in a battered notebook. “So you think your ex-boss was killed to keep the real story about the bank theft quiet?”

Maggie got up and paced the room, across the worn Persian carpet, between the Windsor chairs, as the antique mantel clock chimed nine. “I don’t know. It seems far-fetched. He probably had a heart attack. He wasn’t in the best shape.”

“But you have suspicions?”

“The police made me think there might be something more. I guess that’s why you’re here too, Mr. Summerour.”

“Please, call me Ryan.”

“All right, Ryan. You can call me Maggie.” She paced again for a moment. “Lou said he’d called a press conference for tomorrow morning where he’d expose the real thief to the world. He was good at grand gestures. I’m sure that’s why he didn’t tell me who it was. He wanted me to be as surprised as everyone else. That was Lou—always looking for the drama.”

Ryan raised his eyebrows. “If he did announce a press conference, he didn’t tell my paper. Have you heard about it from any other news source?”

She could tell from the way he’d said it that it was an unforgivable slight. “Maybe he sent it to one of the other reporters at your paper.”

“I’m it,” he confessed. “Owner. Publisher. Reporter. Janitor. If I didn’t get word—”

“Maybe he meant TV news.”

He put his notebook away and studied her for a moment. “I’d like to give you the benefit of the doubt on this, Maggie.

My paper is a weekly, so it doesn't come out again until next Wednesday. Let's see what happens between now and then. The case could have broken wide open by then. It's the curse of publishing a weekly."

She was completely amazed by his attitude. Maybe Aunt Clara was right and he wasn't so bad. She didn't quite trust him. At this point, it would be hard to trust anyone. "Thanks. I really appreciate that."

"You have to be honest with me." He got to his feet. "I want to help you and your aunt. If anything else comes up that the police don't know about, you have to share it with me. Don't let me read some groundbreaking evidence on someone's blog."

"Okay. I can do that. You promise to leave Aunt Clara out of it?"

"I do."

Aunt Clara came in at that moment, pulling the tea cart laden with coffee, cups, and slices of apple pie. Her timing was perfect, of course, since she'd been listening to their conversation from around the corner. "Who wants dessert?"

• • •

Ryan stayed for another half hour. He regaled them with funny stories about the newspaper business that he'd grown up in. He made them laugh when he told them about helping his parents with everything from rolling papers to being hoisted up on his father's shoulders to take pictures. It seemed that he'd been destined to work as a newspaper reporter.

After he'd said good night, Aunt Clara saw him to the door and returned with a brilliant smile.

"Wasn't he a nice man? Did you find out if he was single? I didn't see a wedding band on his finger when he took his pie and coffee, did you?"

Maggie grimaced. "I *knew* that's what you were thinking. How could you even consider matchmaking at a time like this? I didn't ask him if he was single. I didn't even think about it."

"But he's very handsome too, don't you think?"

"I didn't notice," Maggie lied as she took the dirty plates and cups to the kitchen. She'd noticed that Ryan was good looking. She wasn't blind. It just wasn't the right time or place for romance.

Aunt Clara looked hurt. "I'm worried about you. I don't want you to be alone when something happens to me. You need someone to love you and share this house with you, when the time comes. Although, it would be nice if you'd have a few babies *before* the time came."

Maggie put her arm around her aunt and kissed her cheek. "I know I've been a rotten niece. I'm going to try and make that up to you. I don't know if I can find a husband and have children right away, but I'll do anything else I can to make your life better."

"I have a wonderful life already," her aunt protested.

As they turned out the lights in the front of the house, Maggie said, "I was thinking when I get my old job back, or another job, that we could sell the pie shop and the house. You could come and live with me in New York. What do you think about that?"

Aunt Clara looked around the kitchen. "I don't think I could do that. I appreciate the offer, but this is my home. You do what you have to do, honey. I'll be fine."

Neither one of them had much to say after that as they washed dishes and straightened up in the kitchen before they headed to bed.

• • •

Maggie thought about her aunt's response to moving to New York the rest of the night. She didn't even bother trying to sleep. Between Aunt Clara's declaration and what had happened with Lou, her eyes weren't going to close. She stayed up reading and watching news on her laptop.

It was strange seeing Lou's face on the 10:00 p.m. local news. The description of his death was sketchy, followed by the comment, "and the police are still investigating."

Maggie knew Ryan was right about what was coming up for her and Aunt Clara, at least until the next big story came along. She hoped she could shield her aunt from most of the unpleasantness.

Between Detective Waters's questions and Ryan's short interview, she felt cornered. She hoped she wasn't the only suspect, if it turned out that Lou's death wasn't a natural one. That would be an even worse scenario from the end of her exciting life of the last ten years.

Maggie'd thought nothing could be as bad as being fired from her job for stealing money and having to beg for a bus ticket home. She'd thought that was the bottom of the barrel.

She'd been wrong.

Coming home to Aunt Clara had showed her what a shallow, heartless person she'd been to the woman who'd raised her.

Now she might be a suspect in a murder case. How much more bad news could she take?

Maggie looked around her old bedroom, filled with china dolls and softball trophies from her childhood. Even the thick rope ladder she'd used to climb from the roof to the old oak tree outside her window was still there.

Uncle Fred had always understood her need for independence. He'd been ingenious at finding ways to help her.

She wouldn't trust the rope to accomplish that feat again, but it had been an important part of her life at one time—like Uncle Fred and Aunt Clara. She'd left all of that behind to try and make up for all the emotional baggage she still carried after the loss of her parents. She'd thought having a wildly successful career would fill that dark place.

It never had.

The end of her beloved career had shown her where her true allegiance was. Aunt Clara would always welcome her home with open arms, no matter what happened. Maggie had desperately needed her that rainy night, when a police officer had dropped her off at her aunt's front door after her parents had been killed. She'd only been four. Aunt Clara had been there then, and she was here now, when her life was in upheaval again.

She couldn't let her aunt down again, no matter what. Maybe it was a good thing that she'd been fired, Maggie mused. She was here for a reason right now. She couldn't leave Aunt Clara again and go back to that other life. Those days were behind her. No job could be more important than what she owed her aunt.

She was frightened about the future. She didn't know what she should do next.

Clearing her name of any wrongdoing—including embezzlement and possible murder—seemed to be her first priority. She couldn't be here for Aunt Clara if she went to prison.

Gray light was slipping through the curtains when Maggie looked at the old Cinderella alarm clock next to the bed. She'd been surprised to find that it still worked. It had been a gift for her tenth birthday.

It was 7:00 a.m. Maybe she could prove something to the police, herself, and Ryan Summerour by going to the press conference Lou said he'd set up. Maybe there would be some answers there.

# Five

Maggie put on her best jeans and a blue Pie in the Sky T-shirt. She'd been lucky to find a few T-shirts in her size from her aunt's stash. She'd also found one of Uncle Fred's old blue sport coats and wore it to dress up the outfit. Uncle Fred had always been thin so it fit her fine.

After she'd washed her hair, she pulled it back from her face. She needed to look tougher, less easily pushed around. She may have been down, but she wasn't out. Not by a long shot.

She put on her only pair of earrings, gold hoops Lou had

given her for her thirtieth birthday. She'd managed to bring them back with her because she was wearing them the day she lost her job. There was a lot of irony wrapped up in those earrings.

The effect in the mirror wasn't fantastic. She looked like she'd been up all night—her face was pale and there were dark circles under her eyes. She also looked smart and mature. She wasn't some kid just starting out.

With everything she would be dealing with that day, smart and mature was good. She needed people to believe her, despite her recent history.

Aunt Clara fretted through breakfast about what she would do with herself that day. With the pie shop closed, she couldn't imagine how to fill her time.

"I'm going to check out Lou's press conference." Maggie helped herself to cereal and milk. "Maybe you should stay in with a good book today. I don't know what's going to be waiting out there for us. Lou's death was all over the news last night."

"I don't want to see the shop all closed up like that. It always seems so sad and alone when it's closed." Aunt Clara sat down with her cup of tea. "You look wonderful. So much like your mother at your age. Maybe that nice reporter will be there too. I hope the police reopen the shop quickly. A person could go stir-crazy sitting around. I've never been good at that."

Maggie was glad her aunt didn't want to go to the pie shop. She felt sure Ryan would be there after their conversation the night before. "I wouldn't plan on the shop reopening so soon, but I'll ask if there's any timetable on that—if Detective Waters shows up."

Aunt Clara sighed again. "Maybe I'll go to the library. I've been meaning to look at some new pie recipes. Maybe I could get some new ideas for the mystery pie. I have some thoughts about it. Nothing carved in stone as yet."

Maggie was glad to hear her aunt had thought of something constructive to do that would take her mind off of the pie shop being closed, even if it still involved pie making.

"Maybe when we both get back we can get serious about that piecrust you wanted to show me," she said to her aunt.

Aunt Clara's eyes lit up. "Now that's a good idea. This would be the perfect opportunity for me to show you how it's done. You're a genius, Maggie."

*Might as well face it.*

If Maggie was going to stay and help Aunt Clara, she was going to have to learn to make piecrust. It might be bad at first, but surely she'd get better. It wasn't rocket science.

She'd never bothered with cooking before—Aunt Clara would find that out right away. She was willing to work hard at it though. Maybe that counted in the art of pie making. It had to be somewhere in her genetics, after all.

She opened the front door and a surge of reporters pushed toward her, yelling out questions. She closed the door quickly.

First, she needed to tackle getting out of the house unnoticed.

"I'm going out the back way," Maggie told her aunt.

"Give me a few minutes before you leave. The reporters should follow me."

"Were they TV reporters?" Aunt Clara asked with a gleam in her green eyes.

"I don't know. Maybe. Why?"

"Good publicity. I might have to bake some pies and give out slices with business cards." Aunt Clara smiled. "Don't worry about me, honey. You go on to your press conference."

Maggie couldn't think of anything else she could say that would keep Aunt Clara from confronting the reporters outside the house. She hoped her aunt knew what she was doing.

The backyard was small with only one large tree in it. There were fences around it on all three sides. Maggie hoped the Walkers, who lived next door, had never repaired the spot Maggie and their son, David, had loosened into a swinging gate between their yards.

It had come in handy through many adventures. Maggie wondered what had become of David. He'd wanted to be a geologist, though she wasn't sure if he even knew what it was when he decided.

It was a long time ago. They'd been good friends until high school. She couldn't remember why they stopped being friends.

The opening was still there. Maggie went through it with a little more difficulty than she remembered from her childhood. She went out across the Walkers' property, escaping from the press that was still waiting in front of her door.

She'd have to remember to ask Aunt Clara what had happened to David.

Maggie made good time walking to the pie shop. She saw Ryan talking to Detective Waters in front of Pie in the Sky as she approached. Saul from the Spin and Go was with them. They were all gesturing at the pie shop.

*Not a good sign.*

They saw her too quickly. She'd hoped to sneak up on them. No matter. She raised her chin and gave them a haughty look. None of them appeared openly hostile. No friendly hellos either.

Detective Waters glanced at his wristwatch. "It's almost ten and no media for the supposed press conference, Maggie. How do you account for that?"

"I wasn't the one who set it up," she responded. "I only told you what Lou said."

Saul humphed. "All these years I've been right beside the pie shop, no trouble. This one comes in"—he pointed his thumb at Maggie—"and right away, people start dying."

"I hate to tell you this, but I worked here through college before you were even living in Durham, Mr. Weissman," she fired back. "And people aren't dying. One man died. He happened to be my friend."

She was getting a little tired of being treated like a two-year-old. She ate people like this for breakfast at her bank job. Being accused of being a thief and running home with her tail between her legs was turning her into sponge cake. It was time she got over it.

"No one's accusing anyone of anything, at this point," Detective Waters said. "The police department is investigating. That's it."

"Have you got a report that says what killed Lou yet?" Maggie demanded, mindful of Ryan listening.

"We know it wasn't a heart attack." Detective Waters also seemed to watch his words with Ryan there. "The medical examiner isn't sure what it was yet. He thinks it might've been some kind of poison. We're waiting on the tox screen right now."

"Since other people ate and drank the same pie and coffee here that Lou did yesterday and there hasn't been a rash of poison deaths," Maggie pointed out, "I guess if he was poisoned, he got it somewhere else."

Frank shrugged his shoulders beneath his thin jacket. "Yeah. I thought of that. We have to finish up here anyway. As soon as we know what killed Mr. Goldberg, we'll let everyone know."

The police detective nodded to all of them then got in his late-model brown Toyota and drove away.

Saul shook his head and went back inside the Spin and Go.

Maggie stared defiantly into Ryan's blue eyes. She told herself she was ready for whatever he planned to say. She could handle herself. She was through with apologizing for things she hadn't done.

"Don't mind him," Ryan finally said. "Frank is okay for a cop. He's probably cranky. His wife went to the beach with friends for a week, leaving him alone with the kids. It happens every year."

Maggie had opened her mouth, prepared for a rebuttal of whatever he'd said. She closed it without speaking, surprised by his words. Was he really on her side?

"Are you all right?"

"No. Not really." She was having trouble formulating words. "You believe me about Lou?"

He took out his cell phone. "This came yesterday. It went into my spam filter so I didn't see it until this morning. I showed it to Frank too."

It was Lou's press release. It said exactly what he'd said it would. There was no new information for her from it, but it existed. It *really* existed.

"You got it." Tears fell down her cheeks in a rush of relief. Somebody besides Aunt Clara was on her side. She hugged Ryan and thanked him a few dozen times before she realized how crazy she sounded and backed off. "Sorry."

"That's okay." He put away his phone. "Let me buy you some coffee. I'm afraid the best coffee isn't available right now." He nodded at the pie shop. "We'll have to go to Biscuitland."

They started walking. "You've been in the pie shop before?"

"Sure. I went to Duke. I think we all came to Pie in the Sky at one time or another."

"Recently?"

"I was here a couple of weeks ago. There was this grumpy waitress, very pretty, but a little on the neglectful side. Maybe she was distracted. I had to ask twice for a coffee refill with my pie."

Maggie's heart fluttered a little. The grumpy part was bad. She didn't mean to be grumpy. It was nice of him to say she was pretty. She hadn't felt pretty, or even human, for the last few weeks.

"Sorry. It's been a rough time for me. Come in again after we reopen and I promise better service."

"Any word on when the shop will open again?"

"No. I was supposed to ask Frank. Have you heard anything?"

"Not a thing. Frank didn't seem to feel like sharing. But the press release makes your story more credible. That makes his job harder. I'm sure he would've liked it if you were a slam dunk."

Biscuitland was only a couple blocks up. It was a dingy little diner that served breakfast all day and night with their specialty, biscuits. The coffee was terrible, but sitting down for a few minutes while she drank it made Maggie feel a little better.

It didn't hurt that Ryan was across from her, drinking coffee and buttering a biscuit. It was good to know she could start to trust someone else.

"You were right about the press beating down our door this morning," she told him. "I tried to get Aunt Clara away from them. She wanted to give them pie to advertise the shop."

He laughed. "She's a character. How does she feel about all of this?"

"I'm not sure. I hope she believes that I didn't kill anyone or steal anything."

"I'm sure she does."

"Are you going to share that email with the other reporters?"

"No. I don't have to share information with them. I might be the only one who still has this piece of the puzzle next week. I'm sorry if that makes it harder for you."

Of course he had his own best interests at heart.

Still, the more Maggie looked at him, the more she could

appreciate that his eyes were very blue, like the afternoon sky rather than blueberries. He had a nice smile, and she liked the way his blond hair curled at the edges.

He looked very athletic too—more like a runner than a weight lifter. He was wearing a dark suit and blue tie this morning with a white dress shirt. The suit looked like it had been tailored for him, making his shoulders look broader and his waist narrower.

Aunt Clara would be delighted to know that he wasn't wearing a wedding band. There wasn't even a white line on his finger.

Maggie finally stopped staring at him when he looked up from his biscuit and smiled at her. She cleared her throat and took a sip of coffee to mask her embarrassment at being caught checking him out.

"Why do you think no one else showed up for the press conference? Do you think they just deleted their emails?"

"I'm not really sure. It would've been only local media anyway. That was yesterday's news. Today, your ex-boss is dead. Whatever he was going to say is gone with him. People lose interest quickly. It might come back up again if the police decide he was murdered. Nothing like a good murder to stir the pot."

"But you came."

"That's different. I met *you*." He offered her half of his biscuit.

Maggie didn't take it, but she took a big sip of coffee to mask her sudden nervousness. Ryan hadn't meant it in a romantic way. This was business, but her heart danced around some in her chest.

"Being a weekly paper is more like being a magazine than a newspaper," he explained. "We have to go deeper than the daily headlines and look at the whole story. People like that. They subscribe to the *Durham Weekly* because of it. I try to give my readers an intelligent view of what happened. Sometimes it takes more than one issue. That's okay."

Ryan had such passion and commitment to what he did that Maggie suddenly couldn't wait to get home and read a copy of the paper. Newspapers might be dying out, but she couldn't imagine his interest ever waning.

"Why did *you* come out this morning?" he asked. "You had to know the kind of reception you'd get, especially from Frank. You know, killers do that kind of thing, right? The police count on it. Arsonists come back too. They like to see the aftermath. It might not have been your best move. It made you look a little guilty."

She hadn't thought of that before she came.

"I don't know. I thought I might figure something out about what happened to Lou. I did, I guess. I know he didn't die from a heart attack, and that he was serious about telling the world the truth about me."

"You also found out that Frank isn't sure about you being a person of interest at all. He's looking in other directions. He's on shaky ground right now. With Lou being from out of town, Frank has to work twice as hard."

"I suppose that's true." She didn't know if that was good news for her or not, but hearing Ryan say it made her feel better.

It had been a long time since she'd had a personal, non-work-related experience with a man, even longer than the last six weeks. It made her feel a little giddy and flushed.

Her job for the bank was too hectic for a personal life. It wasn't only not visiting or calling Aunt Clara. She barely had time to think most of the time. That's why when Lou had first told her about the theft, she'd had to think twice to know if it was simply a careless mistake on her part. Once she'd realized how big the theft was, she'd known it wasn't her fault. It was too late then.

There was no one to turn to when she'd come home, except Aunt Clara. She hadn't kept up with her friends from Duke. They had no other relatives. It was nice talking to Ryan about everything.

Maggie forced herself to quit thinking about Ryan in *that* way. She had to concentrate on clearing her name. He could be a big help in that direction.

It didn't hurt that he looked so good too.

"Do people really poison each other anymore?" Maggie though out loud. "That sounds so Romeo and Juliet. Most people have guns. Why not just shoot Lou in the alley if you wanted to get rid of him?"

"Maybe whoever did it wanted to make it look like it happened at the pie shop—involving you once your background with Lou came out. It's a good cover. It might have given the killer time to get away. Lou could've been poisoned hours before and not died until he was leaving Pie in the Sky. Very effective."

"Glad you're a fan." She thought about it a little more. "But that would mean Lou had to tell his killer that he was going to see me. What if he'd told me who the person was who framed me? That seems to be a big risk for the killer. A bullet would've been faster, more thorough."

Ryan shrugged, washing down the last of his biscuit with coffee. "Maybe not if the killer knew about the press conference. You said Lou was a grandstander and that's why you thought he wouldn't tell you about what happened without all the fanfare. Maybe the killer felt confident that Lou wouldn't say anything until then."

"So someone who knew him fairly well?" Maggie thought again about the men and women who were Lou's bosses and coworkers. "There are hundreds of possibilities. Lou said the person who really took that money was higher up than him. I reported directly to Lou, but I met plenty of the bank's vice presidents, senior vice presidents, and so on at Christmas parties and other social functions. It could be any of them. I keep wondering why one of them would choose to frame me for this. Why not pick Lou?"

"Good question. Maybe the thief liked Lou and didn't want him to get into trouble. Or maybe he needed Lou to cover up future thefts. He didn't count on him caring about you so much that he'd tell everyone the truth when he found out." Ryan looked at his cell phone and handed her a business card. "I have to go to a groundbreaking ceremony. Call me if you hear anything new."

Maggie looked at his card. "Thanks for listening and strategizing with me. It helped."

"Not a problem." He looked into her eyes. "For what it's worth, I believe you, Maggie. It might be hard to figure out exactly what happened to Lou. If Frank finds out Lou was poisoned, you might be on his radar again. I'll talk to you later."

# Six

Maggie knew Ryan was right. If there was any way to avoid being a suspect in Lou's death, she would find it. She felt like she was in the middle, though, and there was no way out.

She reminded herself that the police had no real evidence linking her to Lou's death, even if it turned out to be a murder. But that gave her very little comfort. If Lou was right about evidence being manufactured to pin the embezzlement on her, anything was possible.

There had to be some way to prove she was innocent.

She walked back down to the pie shop. With a quick look

over her shoulder to make sure she was alone, she went into the alley behind the shops to examine the spot where she'd found Lou.

There was nothing unusual to see except some crime scene tape.

She let out a frustrated sigh. "Why didn't you tell me who framed me? Maybe we could have confronted him together and he'd have known there was no point in killing you. We'd both be happier this morning."

She was talking to the stairs and it wasn't doing her much good. She wished she'd said that to Lou yesterday. Who knew something like this would happen?

*You did. You thought about something happening that would prevent Lou from clearing your name and you didn't act on it.*

"Excuse me."

Maggie jumped. A big man in a black suit stood next to her. He was wearing a black fedora and looking at the empty stairs too.

"Sorry. Just talking to myself," she said with an embarrassed smile. "If you're looking for pie, the shop is closed."

The man in the black fedora smiled. "I'm actually looking for Clara Lowder. You wouldn't happen to be her niece, Maggie, would you?"

Maggie looked at him closer. Not many men in Durham wore a fedora or carried a gold-handled cane. He was also wearing an expensive gold watch. His whole demeanor was one of wealth and power, even though he was standing in the alley. She imagined he would be overpowering no matter where he stood.

"Who are you?"

"You *must* be Maggie. I see the resemblance. I've heard so much about you." He extended his gloved hand to her. "I'm Albert Mann. I own Mann Development. Clara was very excited about you coming back the last time I spoke with her. You two had been apart for a while."

Maggie doubted they'd had any kind of intimate chat. Aunt Clara loathed this man. "I don't think Aunt Clara shared anything with you."

"Please, call me Albert. I've sat in that pie shop plenty of times eating pie with your aunt before this whole negotiation turned ugly." He shook his head and pointed his finger at her. "I think you're the one to blame for that, young woman."

"Me? I think it's that Aunt Clara doesn't want to sell the pie shop. Maybe you should look for another piece of property."

"She wasn't so against it until you came back. Now she seems to think you're staying here with her so she doesn't need to sell."

"Cut the crap, Albert. I've been in the banking business for a long time. You've been pressuring my aunt to sell. Why don't you leave her alone? Maybe she'll sell when she's ready to retire."

"I haven't forced anyone to do anything. Careful what you say—you might be in court for slander as well as stealing money from your former employer." He smirked. "You're developing quite a rap sheet, aren't you? Now the police think you might have killed the man you found here yesterday."

"You can't bully me. I've known too many men like you.

You're not getting the pie shop until Aunt Clara is ready. Back off."

He took a deep breath, as though to steady himself. His gloved hands gave him away—they were clenched in fists. "I'm not trying to bully anyone, Maggie. I've tried to convince your aunt that it would benefit her to sell to me. That's a statement of fact. If Clara misinterpreted my words, I'm sorry."

Maggie hadn't been around during any encounters between this man and Aunt Clara. A few of his representatives had come into the pie shop in the last six weeks. They'd been obnoxious and arrogant. She supposed she couldn't necessarily blame him for that, but she remained cautious.

"You can stop sending in your goon squad lawyers trying to convince her otherwise too. No offer is going to be attractive to her. This place means something to her, something more than money. Maybe you can't understand that."

"Think about what's at stake here. Your aunt isn't getting any younger. You've been in the shop. The place reeks of benign neglect. She's barely scraping by and can't reinvest to keep it up. She can't run the place by herself. I'm sure you see that too."

"She won't be running it by herself anymore," Maggie said. "I'll be here helping her from now on."

He laughed. "For how long? You're back now but you'll be gone again soon. Think about your aunt's future and what's best for her. She could buy herself into a nice retirement spot where she wouldn't have to get up at five a.m. and walk down to this dingy shop and make piecrust. Surely you don't want her to end her days this way."

Maggie frowned. She knew he was playing on her guilt, but it was still working.

*He may be a scumbag, but what if he's right? What if it doesn't work out for me to stay here? How can the pie shop support both of us when it's barely supporting Aunt Clara? But if I leave again, Aunt Clara will be scraping by until everything falls in on her.*

"How much are we talking about?" she asked in a cold voice.

He named a price. "A generous sum, you'll agree."

Maggie bit her tongue to keep from reacting. Generous? It was amazing.

The property was older and hadn't been maintained. The amount of money he mentioned could probably pay for all five shops in the area *and* the land they were on. She admitted she didn't know anything about property values in Durham, but she could find out.

She glanced at Albert Mann, who stood close to her like a large black shadow, waiting for her answer.

She recalled the medical office building deal he was after. No doubt this was a lowball offer, even though it seemed great. He wanted to make as much profit as he could.

Not that it mattered.

She was sure she wouldn't be able to talk Aunt Clara into selling the pie shop unless she physically couldn't get there every day. It was her life. Albert Mann would go on to something else. Her aunt wouldn't. That made the property priceless.

Still, it was a lot of money. The house could be repaired and maintained for many years, if it was properly invested.

Aunt Clara wouldn't have to worry about anything again. She could make pies for the library bake sale. Maggie's banking mind was already creating a portfolio for her aunt that would double the money in no time.

Despite all of that commonsense theory, she said no. "We're not interested. My aunt loves this place. You can't put a price on how much it means to her. It's a good offer, but not to give up something that's important to her."

He looked at her shrewdly. "You drive a hard bargain. I mean to have this land. Let me see what I can do to sweeten the pot." He gave her his card. "I'll let you know."

Maggie watched him walk away. He carefully avoided any of the trash and potholes in the old alley.

That he might be willing to pay more for the pie shop didn't surprise her. She'd thought he was probably holding back. How valuable could the property be? Even though the shop was run down, it didn't mean the land wasn't worth millions.

She needed to have a look at the real estate market. No doubt the land closest to the university was worth more. Just the fact that Albert Mann wanted to build a medical office here made the price go up.

Two women in crime scene coveralls walked past her into the pie shop. The police were still going over everything. She could see them inside taking samples of pie and everything else that had been for sale. Cans of soda were emptied and discarded. Bags of flour samples were taken and the rest thrown away.

She hoped it didn't take weeks to figure out what had killed Lou—and that whatever it was, wasn't in the pie shop.

Aunt Clara might not have any choice but to take Mann's offer. Between being shut down and all of her food investment being destroyed, it might be bad enough to keep Pie in the Sky closed forever.

Maggie thought about Lou again on her way back to the house. It was too late to save him. She had to think how she could save herself and Aunt Clara. She had to find some answers for both the bank theft and Lou's death. She couldn't wait until the police showed up at her door with an arrest warrant.

She hadn't brought much information with her. There was a flash drive of bank policy that had escaped from New York. It had been on her key chain. She was going to have to rely mostly on her memory and what she could find about the bank and its senior staff on the Internet.

Someone far up on the ladder would've handled this differently. That sort of person wouldn't even know her name. This had to be someone only a rung or two above Lou. Probably someone he'd reported to, or had been involved with on a project.

Maggie got home and called Aunt Clara's name. The reporters were gone from the front stairs. Her aunt was gone too. Maybe she was still looking up pie recipes at the library.

Exhausted from her lack of sleep the night before but determined to begin the quest to clear her name, Maggie got out her laptop. She was still working on it when she heard her aunt come home. Maggie didn't look up as she continued looking through the bank information on her flash drive.

Aunt Clara watched her for a few minutes, standing

close beside her. She sighed heavily several times to get her attention.

Maggie looked up from the bank files after saving a few likely suspects in a list she could give to the police. She wasn't sure if the Durham police could check these out. They might have to give the names to the police in New York.

Aunt Clara sighed heavily again.

"Find any good recipes at the library?" she finally asked her aunt.

"Yes. And I also saw that obnoxious Lenora Rhyne. She was there with her daughter. It seems they're going into business together, opening one of those consignment places. She likes to rub it in that I don't have a daughter. It's annoying."

"I'm sure it is," Maggie said absently, her mind still on her suspect list.

"There was also a very nice man there who was interested in pies."

"Mmm-hmm."

"Now that we're going to run the pie shop together, it changes everything. I'd like to make you half owner of Pie in the Sky."

That got Maggie's full attention. She closed her laptop. "Why? It's okay the way it is, isn't it?"

Her aunt sat on one of the damask occasional chairs. "I'd feel better about it. That way, you get half of the profits and make half of the decisions. It would be nice to know someone else is helping shoulder that burden. Like it was when your uncle was alive."

Maggie took her aunt's cool, soft hand in hers. "You don't have to do that to have me work with you, Aunt Clara. I don't think I deserve a partnership yet."

"Well, I agree, at least not until I show you the piecrust recipe. But that won't take long. I've already contacted my lawyer. He'll have the papers drawn up right away." Aunt Clara smiled and hugged her. "I have a very good feeling about this."

Maggie wished she could say the same. She hated to think that her aunt felt like she had to resort to this to make her more responsible. "All right. If it makes you feel better, that's fine. Maybe we could meet Lenora Rhyne and her daughter for lunch one day and you could rub our partnership in her face."

Aunt Clara giggled. "Not a bad idea. What do you say to lunch and some piecrust making?"

Maggie groaned slightly. She knew she had to do this. It was a small thing, but it was important to her aunt. Surely she could figure it out. She'd watched Aunt Clara make pie hundreds of times. Her aunt always paid more attention to their conversations than to her crust making, her fingers knowing exactly what to do.

Maybe she wasn't the world's greatest cook, Maggie thought, but she could learn this for Aunt Clara.

They had a light lunch of salad and some chicken. After cleaning off the table, Aunt Clara got out all her crust-making utensils.

"All of these things belonged to my mother," she explained to Maggie. "Your mother and I learned to make piecrust when we were children. I'm sorry I didn't carry on that tradition. You should have known how to do this a long time ago."

"Maybe that would've helped." Maggie picked up the brown ceramic bowl. "I'm afraid I'm not much of a cook. I hope you're not too disappointed. I've been putting this off because I didn't want you to know."

"Don't be silly," Aunt Clara scolded in a voice Maggie remembered from her childhood when she'd lied or stayed out too late. "Of course you can cook. You haven't really tried is all."

Maggie smiled nervously and listened to what her aunt had to say.

"Now, the biggest secret of making the perfect piecrust every time is to make sure that everything is ice cold. That makes the crust flaky instead of chewy. You chill your bowl as well."

Clara put on her apron and measured two cups of flour into the bowl she took out of the refrigerator. "After you get the flour in the bowl, you add one cup of chilled shortening to it. Then add your one and a half teaspoons of salt in there too."

Maggie put on an apron and made mental notes, knowing there was sure to be a test later when Aunt Clara wanted her to make her own piecrust.

"Now you want to work in the shortening quickly, with a light hand. Our family has always prided itself on not using a pastry blender or any other implement to cut in the shortening. Nothing can take the place of the human hand, you see."

It looked easy enough, Maggie thought. Maybe she could do it.

"Most people work the shortening in until the particles are about the size of peas." Aunt Clara continued rubbing the flour and shortening lightly using her fingertips. "But the secret to really good piecrust is that the particles are even smaller than peas. Just be patient and keep working your dough. Not too much, keep it light."

"What size would you say those particles should be?" Maggie asked her so she'd know later.

"You remember that time you got in trouble for accidentally shooting little David Walker next door with his BB gun?"

Maggie smiled at that memory despite the amount of trouble she'd been in at the time. Aunt Clara and Uncle Fred had told her not to spend time with David when he had the gun. He'd threatened to use it on her and Maggie had taken it from him. It had fired accidentally during that transfer. David had to have a BB taken out of his arm.

"Sure. So, BB size?"

"Exactly." Aunt Clara tipped the bowl toward Maggie to make sure she saw the size. "This part is very important."

"Whatever happened to David?" Maggie asked, thinking about the boy next door again.

"I think he went into the navy. He might be out now. Maybe he's not married."

Maggie smiled. "I thought you liked Ryan."

"I do. He seems like a very nice man. There's no reason you can't shop around, right?"

That almost made Maggie burst out laughing.

Next, Aunt Clara took some cold water out of the refrigerator. "It has to be as cold as it can be to get the proper consistency."

She began sprinkling the cold water, only one tablespoon at a time, mixing it with her fingers. When the particles were moistened enough, they began to stick together.

"Don't use any more water than you have to and mix quickly so the crust bakes up flaky instead of tough. Cover the dough. I always use a clean tea towel, even at the shop. Then we have to let it chill for at least thirty minutes before we roll it out."

"That doesn't seem too bad," Maggie said. "I thought it would be harder."

"It's not hard at all." Aunt Clara put the bowl back into the refrigerator. "You have to remember the measurements and keep everything cold. Then mix with your fingers and you've got it."

"Okay."

"Of course, there's the rolling part, and baking is important too," Aunt Clara said. "You'll get it. The women in our family always do."

"So what's your favorite kind of pie?"

Aunt Clara thought a minute. "It was always coconut custard."

Maggie thought about the pie menu at the shop, which she'd memorized. "There's no coconut custard on the menu. Why don't you make that kind?"

Tears welled in her aunt's eyes. "Because I can't make it like your mother could. No one ever has. I gave up trying a long time ago. Some foods are better because of the people who make them. It's more than a recipe. It's love."

Maggie hugged her aunt. She'd barely been four when her parents had been killed. "I wish I could remember her. What was her favorite kind?"

"It was my deep-dish cherry pie. Delia loved cherry pie. That was her favorite. I stopped making it when she died. I couldn't do it anymore. It was too painful to think about her."

The two women stood in their tight embrace for a few minutes. There was still so much they didn't know or understand about each other.

Aunt Clara sniffed and pulled a hankie from the pocket in her spring-green apron. "While we're waiting, I was thinking about looking upstairs in the attic for some of your mother's old clothes. I think the two of you were about the same size. It would be better than you borrowing Fred's old things. Let's take a look, shall we?"

They went up the long stairs that led from the kitchen into the attic. The peculiar smell of old house and musty clothes permeated the area. Aunt Clara switched on the light as they went up.

Maggie hadn't been in the attic since she'd left home to go to New York. She'd spent many hours up here dreaming when she was a kid. It seemed like all of her dreams had to do with getting away from this place. She'd always felt there was something better waiting for her, something for her to find.

Now that she'd found it—for better or worse—she wasn't

sure what she was thinking so many years ago. She wished in many ways that she'd never left Durham. She used to make fun of people who stayed home and never longed for anything else. Not anymore.

They spent the next hour looking through chests of clothes, some Aunt Clara's and Uncle Fred's, others belonging to her mother. There were plenty of hats too—some outrageous ones that Aunt Clara said had belonged to Maggie's grandmother. Others were more conservative.

Maggie ended up taking boxes full of her mother's clothes and some hats down the long stairs from the attic. She wasn't sure if she'd wear all of them or not, but it would be interesting looking at them.

Most of them were classic and could be worn as easily now as thirty years ago. It was fun thinking about her mother and her wearing the same size. Her mother had only been a few years older than Maggie when she'd died.

"That was an excellent shopping trip, don't you think?" Aunt Clara asked with a smile. She was the first one down. When she opened the door into the kitchen, she gasped. "Oh dear. Maggie, I think someone was here while we were in the attic."

# Seven

Maggie looked around the kitchen, wondering how anyone could have been in the house without them knowing.

There was no doubt that they had been.

Silverware and other utensils were scattered in the kitchen on the floor and table. Cabinets were emptied. Even the trashcan was on its side, obviously having been ransacked by someone.

In the living room, pillows were tossed and sofa cushions removed. Aunt Clara's big rolltop desk had drawers left open. Pens and paper were tossed everywhere.

"My laptop," Maggie mourned. "They took my laptop."

At least she'd thought to remove the flash drive. It was still in her pocket.

Upstairs, the bedrooms were the same. The beds were torn apart, drawers left open and contents dumped on the floor. The bathroom cabinets had been emptied too. Even the dirty towels and clothes in the hampers were taken out.

Nothing was broken. Furniture wasn't tipped over. Whoever searched the house—Maggie felt sure that's what they'd been doing—had been very careful and very quiet. She believed that meant they knew she and Aunt Clara were upstairs in the attic the whole time.

That was even scarier. What if they'd come down sooner?

"They could have killed us." Maggie filled in the answer to her own question.

She dialed 911 despite her aunt's wish not to have her do so. Aunt Clara didn't want to make a big deal out of it.

Maggie wasn't sure if her aunt didn't want the police to see the house trashed or just didn't want everyone to know. "We have to report this. I'm sorry, Aunt Clara. It could be involved with what happened to Lou. We have to tell the police. It could be important."

Aunt Clara shushed her. "Don't be silly. This kind of thing happens sometimes, I understand. Let's not panic, honey. It's not that bad. We can clean it up in no time. No real harm done. I feel foolish calling the police over something so small. They have murders to solve and drunk drivers to keep off the road."

Nothing she could say would keep Maggie from reporting the crime. Maggie explained that it had to be done to use Aunt Clara's insurance to replace her laptop. "They won't take our word for it. This is something we have to do."

It only took five minutes for two patrol cars to appear in front of the house. It took a few extra minutes for the officers to get inside. They had to maneuver through the crowd of reporters on the doorstep again.

No doubt they had police scanners and this was part of the bigger story, Maggie guessed. Now she and Aunt Clara were targeted again since the house had been broken into. How much more dramatic and newsworthy could a suspected killer/bank embezzler be?

It took another ten minutes for Frank Waters to join them there.

The police officers asked dozens of questions about the incident, looking a little skeptical when Aunt Clara and Maggie said they hadn't heard anything, even though they'd been in the attic.

The police asked if anything of value had been taken. Maggie was quick to say that her laptop was gone. She showed the officer where it had been. She even had the evidence to prove she owned it—thanks to the receipt she'd saved.

She'd decided after coming home that she was never going to own anything without a receipt again. It had made it too easy for the bank to confiscate what she owned after she'd been fired.

Frank listened and watched the proceedings with a jaundiced eye. He didn't say anything to the officers who were investigating. Aunt Clara brought him a cup of coffee, as she did the rest of the officers. She apologized for not having slices of pie for each of them.

Maggie could tell it was unusual for Frank to be there after a robbery. The police officers kept looking at him and one or two asked why he was there. They were obviously surprised to see him.

Frank shrugged and kept his motives to himself. It seemed to make the officers a little nervous and self-conscious. Maybe they were worried that he was watching to see if they were doing something wrong.

She hoped seeing the house this way might prove to Frank that something else was going on, underlying Lou's death. The story wasn't finished because Lou had died. There was still something very wrong. Maybe something that could jeopardize her and Aunt Clara's lives.

The only thing that appeared to be missing was her laptop containing the information that could clear her name. Surely that meant something important. The thieves were somehow involved in Maggie's being accused of embezzlement, which made them part of Lou's death.

At least that's what she got from it.

Frank crouched by the front door that had been forcibly opened in the foyer. "It doesn't look like it took much effort to get in here. You ladies need a dead bolt."

"Is that it?" Maggie asked out of panic, desperation, and fear. "Our home is broken into after my friend is killed and all you can say is that we need a dead bolt?"

"What did you expect? Were you looking for a marching band? Maybe you thought we'd take you into protective custody to make sure you were safe?"

"Even you should be able to see this was something more. Someone was searching our home, and took my laptop. It had all the information I've been gathering about possible suspects in Lou's death and my embezzlement charge."

"You must be one of those conspiracy nuts. Houses get broken into every day."

"Then why are you here, hmm?" Aunt Clara put her hands on her hips and impatiently tapped her foot. "I think you're here, Detective Waters, because you *know* something else is happening."

Frank scowled. "Look, I admit that something seems wrong here. That's why I came out when I heard the call. It's like when a store gets robbed, and then the store owner's home gets robbed the next day. I don't like it."

"So you think there may be a link between Lou's death and this break-in." Maggie felt as relieved as if he'd said she had won a million dollars.

"Maybe." He scratched his head. "I don't like to make assumptions with no proof. It's as likely that whoever broke in here saw your address on TV and thought they'd clean you out. They broke in, took the easy valuable to carry—the laptop. That makes sense too."

"I'm glad you think so." Maggie was quivering with fear and rage. "That doesn't make us feel any safer."

"Look. I think you're in some kind of trouble. I don't mean to sound like I don't want to help. I need proof to move on anything. So far, I have your past issues with your ex-boss, a press release that says you didn't steal any money, and a break-in with a missing laptop. That's not much to go on."

Maggie was fuming. "If I were a killer and a thief, I'd want to make sure no one had evidence that could prove it. I'd come and search this house and take my laptop so I could see what was on it. Then I could decide if I needed to be killed too."

Frank nodded. "That is one possible explanation. We have no real proof of that, Maggie. That's what I run on. Right now, I can only investigate what I have and hope something else comes up that leads me to the next place."

She sank back into a chair, suddenly running out of steam. "By the time you get that proof, we could be the next victims."

He sat down beside her. "The boys are gonna take fingerprints. We'll see if any of those match the ones we've found in the pie shop. We'll keep our ears open for your laptop being found somewhere. That's the best I can do for now. How about you?"

"Me?"

"Yes, you. What kind of information were you looking at? You should've been sharing that with me, not storing it up for someone to steal. I want you to write down anything you think could be useful and bring it to me."

She stared at him mutinously.

He smiled at Aunt Clara. "Mrs. Lowder, I'm sorry this has happened to you. Is there anything you can think of that might make some sense of this matter?"

"Only what Maggie has already said, Detective. I stand beside my niece. She didn't steal anything or kill anyone."

"Okay then." He shrugged into his coat. "I'm heading out. It was good to see you both. Take care. Better get dead bolts for the front and back doors. Maybe even consider a security system."

• • •

Maggie and Aunt Clara stood with their arms around each other after seeing the last of the police officers to the door. They were both scared to death.

The officers warned them to get new locks as quickly as possible. The last officer even put a piece of duct tape on the front door to make sure it would stay closed.

Reporters snapped pictures as the police were leaving, calling out Maggie's name and asking for an interview. They came right up to the door and tried to get pictures of the inside of the house before the door was taped closed.

"Where were they when the thieves broke into the house?" Maggie asked. "They should've gotten pictures of the real criminals."

"Let's get this cleaned up and watch some TV," Aunt Clara suggested. "Everything will look better in the morning."

While they put everything away, Maggie called a locksmith. They were going to have a dead bolt on the outside doors before they went to sleep that night. It was going to be hard enough not to jump at every noise they heard as they were going to sleep, even with the doors locked up tight.

Maggie believed Lou's death, the break-in, and losing her job were connected, proof or no proof. She didn't know how or why, but she felt it inside. She had to think of a way to prove it to Frank.

For now, the killer/thief knew there was no proof to

worry about. He'd probably already looked through her laptop and not found anything of substance. There was so little there, he'd probably sleep well that night while she and Aunt Clara were shivering in their beds.

She'd felt so fortunate when the bank had decided not to press charges. She'd thought if she could only get home again, everything would be fine. That hadn't worked out quite as she'd planned.

It suddenly hit her that the bank might not have pressed charges because the person who'd made that decision was the one guilty of embezzlement. Maggie felt as if a cartoon lightbulb lit up on top of her head.

After all, a police investigation might have uncovered her innocence, and the other person's guilt. Of course, she had no idea who that was. Only Lou would have known that information. He'd carried it with him to the grave.

Now all she had to do was convince someone else to see it that way and find enough information to give Frank something to investigate. Any way she looked at it was maddening.

Neither of the women wanted to finish the piecrust that night. When everything was back where it belonged, they huddled over the kitchen table, whispering, until the locksmith got there. It was as though they were too scared to raise their voices for fear of being overheard.

The locksmith was a jolly man with a booming voice. He commiserated with them over the break-in and told them terrible stories about other break-ins he'd worked before. The stories were so fantastic that Aunt Clara and Maggie actually began to feel a little better. At least they were still alive.

He put in two new locks and dead bolts in each door and even did a temporary repair on the front door so they could close it without the duct tape.

The reporters almost mauled him for information as he worked on the front door. Aunt Clara paid him when he was finished and Maggie let him out through the back door.

It was expensive—Maggie hoped Aunt Clara could afford it. She vowed to pay her back as soon as she had some money of her own. This was her responsibility. She felt bad that Aunt Clara was not only dragged into it, but had to finance it too.

When the press finally went away, Aunt Clara and Maggie tested the new locks. The doors were secure. Each of them put their new keys away in safe places, although neither of them felt a lot safer.

"Now what?" Aunt Clara jumped as the doorbell rang. They both crept to the front door together and Maggie peered through the peephole.

It was Ryan. He'd heard about the break-in on the police scanner that he monitored for the paper. "Are you two okay?"

Maggie stepped back and let him in the house.

He studied their pale, frightened faces. "You both look a little shaken."

"We're fine," Maggie said raggedly. She realized she was holding both her hands in tight fists and forced herself to relax.

"Fine might not be the best word," Aunt Clara said. "We've survived so far. It's been a long day."

She offered to make coffee for him. Ryan suggested they

all go out for dinner. "It's after eight and I haven't eaten. I don't think you have either. It would do you both good to get out of the house. My treat."

Maggie and Aunt Clara went with him reluctantly.

Aunt Clara had offered to stay home so she could make sure everything was safe. "Plus I don't know if I can eat anything tonight. I think you two should go without me."

Maggie finally convinced her to go—and locked both doors twice, checking them inside and out—before they left.

It seemed ironic to her as she performed this task that she'd lived all those years in the city and never had a break-in.

The circumstances were different, she grimly reminded herself as they got into Ryan's late-model Honda. People weren't calling her a thief, liar, and killer. Her life had been normal then.

It was a pity party, no doubt. She knew that and decided to stop feeling sorry for herself. She had to concentrate on what she was doing—working on her plan to clear her name.

Ryan took them to a nice little Italian place with red-and-white checkered tablecloths and candles in Chianti bottles with wax dripping down the sides. It was very charming and intimate—a good choice for their frazzled nerves.

Between glasses of wine and courses of salad, soup, and pasta—of which Aunt Clara managed to eat a fair share—Maggie told Ryan all her suspicions. She even laid out her new theory about why the bank hadn't prosecuted her.

It was good to say it out loud, even if it was only in a whisper.

Ryan took it all in calmly. He asked questions when she

paused for breath and made a few remarks about Frank's attitude.

"He has to keep his distance and observe this situation as it unfolds around you. It's likely the answers will involve you, but there's no proof yet. It's his job to be objective, Maggie."

"Were you a cop or something?" Maggie asked. He sounded too aware of how a detective would feel. She didn't really want to hear Frank's point of view.

"No." He smiled and picked up another bread stick. "I trained to be one but—"

"That's when your father had the heart attack and he would've had to close the paper if you hadn't stepped in," Aunt Clara added. "I remember. Your father was a very good writer, although he used to get my husband, Fred, all riled up with his editorials."

"You were planning to be a cop?" Maggie was amazed. "It must be a lot different working for a newspaper instead."

"It's different. I guess it was always in my blood anyway. I didn't plan on doing this—never wanted to step into my father's shoes—but it's okay now. I enjoy it."

"How's your father doing these days?" Aunt Clara asked as she bit into a cannoli. "Is he enjoying his retirement?"

"He's fine. Thanks for asking. He spends most of his time on the golf course. Once in a while, he comes into the office and I have to remind him that the doctor said he can't do the job anymore. It's hard for him. He's not that old and he misses his former life. He likes to keep up with what's going on."

Maggie suspected from his tone that Ryan's father

might like to be more involved with the paper than Ryan wanted.

"Poor man," Aunt Clara said. "Remind me to send him a pie."

"That's sweet of you. I'm sure he'd appreciate it, Clara. We don't get very much home cooking since neither one of us cooks."

They didn't really talk any more about Lou's death or Frank's investigation. Ryan talked about things that were going on in the community. Aunt Clara talked about the pie shop being closed.

Maggie thought about whoever had broken into the house and why they'd taken the laptop. It seemed a good bet that the guilty person, who'd really embezzled from the bank, had started this chain of events. This person knew Lou was about to clear her name and had acted violently to prevent that. Afterward, they were worried about Maggie figuring it out. They wanted to know what she knew.

It was a chilling thought that she and Aunt Clara could've been asleep when the thieves had come. The event could have been so much worse. Yet, even though nothing had happened to them, Maggie was nervous about going home again.

As they were getting ready to leave the restaurant, Maggie and Aunt Clara thanked Ryan for the delicious dinner.

"You're very welcome." He held the door for them. "Maggie, you're also welcome to come and use the computers at the newspaper whenever you like until you get your laptop replaced. If there's anything else I can do, please let me know."

Stuffed full of good food, Maggie thanked him profusely, almost ready to weep at his kindness and generosity. He was a good man. Aunt Clara had been right to point out his qualities to her earlier.

In the car, on the way back to the house, her aunt pushed it one step further. "You know, Ryan, I was surprised that your *wife* didn't come with you this evening."

*How can she think of matchmaking at a time like this?* Maggie shook her head. She was almost too tired to care. Besides, she was already pretty sure he was single.

"I've come close to getting married a few times, Clara," he said. "But I've never made it to the finish line. There was a girl in college. That was a long time ago. My mom and dad had been married fifty-two years when she passed. He keeps wondering when I'm going to settle down. I always tell him I'm looking for the right woman who'll put up with me."

Aunt Clara giggled. She had the answer she wanted.

Maggie knew what Aunt Clara was after. She'd seen her aunt staring at Ryan's hands all evening. Not all married men wore wedding rings. She was making sure that he was marriage material.

That had been one aspect of living without family that she hadn't minded. No one constantly pushed people into her path thinking she should get married. In fact, very few of her friends in New York were married. Some had moved in together. That was the extent of their commitment.

She didn't feel like she had ever even come close, as Ryan had said. She had plenty of friends and acquaintances to visit museums, go to bars, and watch Broadway plays with. There had been a few men who were special.

Never anyone she was serious about. She was happy being single.

She still was, for that matter.

Ryan dropped them off at the house—after coming inside and making sure they were alone. Aunt Clara immediately went up to bed—with a wink at Maggie.

"I hope she'll be okay." Ryan watched her go. "Sometimes it's hard to get over things like this."

"I know. She's very resilient. I think it might be from running the pie shop, first with my uncle, then alone."

"I know what you mean. My mother and father started the newspaper together forty-six years ago. When you grow up as part of a working family business, it makes you more independent than most people. You have to be ready for anything."

Maggie smiled and tentatively reached her hand toward him. "Thank you for a nice evening, Ryan. I really appreciate your help in all this. I feel kind of lost right now. I don't really know what I'm doing. Maybe I should've worked more at the pie shop when I was growing up. Nothing I've ever done has prepared me for this."

"I think you're holding up pretty well, considering the circumstances. You'll get through it. I can see you come from tough stock."

They stood there looking at each other for a few seconds. She wasn't exactly sure how it happened, but in the next instant, they were in each other's arms, kissing.

# Eight

Maggie opened her green eyes and looked into Ryan's blue ones, their faces close together.

"Wow," he said. "That was something."

"Yeah," she muttered. "Something."

"Something good, right? I thought it was good."

"Oh! Yes. Something good." She grinned at him like a crazy person. Later she could blame her lack of cool on the fact that it had been a while. Now she wanted to make sure he understood that she'd liked it. "I wasn't expecting you . . . it."

"Me either. I've thought about it since I met you, though."

"It was probably Aunt Clara throwing me at you."

"I don't think so. I think it was all you. I didn't need any prompting."

"Really?" She was pleased, but embarrassed that she couldn't say the same thing. "I'm sorry. I was so caught up in Lou's death and everything . . ." She trailed off, not sure what else to say.

"It's okay." He touched his finger to the side of her face. "Now that it's happened, how about lunch tomorrow?"

"Since I'm on hiatus from the pie shop, that sounds great. Thanks again for offering to let me use one of your computers. It'll save me a trip to the library."

"Sure. You could come in tomorrow morning and then we could go out to lunch."

"That sounds great. Thanks."

"Well, I guess I should go." There was a regretful tone to his voice. "Dinner was fun. I'll see you tomorrow."

"Okay. Good night, Ryan."

Maggie watched him walk to his car and get in before she closed the front door. She turned around with a big smile on her face then almost jumped out of her skin when she saw Aunt Clara standing there with pink cream smeared on her face.

"Well?" Aunt Clara smiled. "Was I right about the two of you?"

"It looks like it. Of course, it was only a kiss."

*A really nice kiss!*

"He kissed you? Rats! I missed it. Come in the living room and tell me all about it."

After making hot chocolate with little marshmallows,

they sat in the living room and talked about Ryan, his father, and the newspaper.

"I think he's exactly what you need right now, Maggie," Aunt Clara said. "Someone who can help out. Someone you can believe in."

Maggie agreed. "He does seem really nice, and he's a pretty good kisser too."

Aunt Clara giggled. "Your Uncle Fred was the best kisser in Durham when we were dating. I dated a lot of boys—you should in order to know the right one when he comes along. I could never convince you of that. You were always so serious and intent on getting away from home by yourself. You weren't interested in any of the boys who wanted to date you."

"Like who?" Maggie couldn't think of anyone who even seemed to like her when she was growing up.

"Like David Walker next door. The two of you were fine until you hit high school. Then you were all SATs and getting ready for college. He was right there and you never noticed. It was kind of pathetic, really. Puppy love, your Uncle Fred used to call it."

"I don't remember it that way. I never thought of David as boyfriend material." Maggie sighed, thinking about those unhappy times. "I used to think it didn't matter. I was alone, and the only way I could ever be happy was to get away and live another life. I was stupid back then."

"Not stupid," Aunt Clara said. "You experienced a terrible tragedy when you lost your parents. Uncle Fred and I tried to fill in for them. We could only do what you would let us do. And you made it. You escaped. I'm sorry it didn't have the happy ending you were looking for."

Maggie got up and hugged her, then picked up their empty cups. "I was stupid and I love you for not agreeing with me, but I know better. I hope I'm smarter now. You and Uncle Fred were great. I'm sorry I didn't appreciate you when I was younger. Your face cream is cracking. I think that means we should go to bed."

Aunt Clara reached up and touched the pink cream that had been her nightly beauty ritual for at least fifty years. "You're absolutely right. Good night, Maggie. Sweet dreams."

Maggie went to bed that night thinking about Ryan instead of people breaking into the house.

His kiss had been so unexpected. It was like one minute, they were friends, and the next, they were kissing like lovers.

It was a great kiss too. She smiled as she put on her shorts and tank top to go to bed. It was just right—not too pushy, like some she'd had—not too wimpy either.

She was thrilled and excited. It felt like a light at the end of a very long, dark tunnel that she'd been moving through. She didn't know him well enough to guess if they had a future together. She didn't care. It was a good start in a new and promising direction.

Around midnight, Maggie got up again. She turned on the bedside lamp, careful not to make any noise. She didn't want to frighten Aunt Clara. She'd heard an unusual noise downstairs, but when she looked she couldn't find anything wrong. Probably the neighbor's cats outside. Sometimes they got a little loud.

Her mother's clothes and personal items beckoned to her when she got back to her bedroom. Without hesitation, she put the boxes and suitcases on the bed and sat, cross-legged, looking through them.

They were a treasure trove of dresses, shirts and pants, books, jewelry, and other intimate objects that people collect in their lives. It was hard to believe there was so much here that she'd never seen.

She'd heard stories about her parents from Aunt Clara and Uncle Fred her whole life. For a while, she'd resented her parents for dying and leaving her. She'd grown out of that phase pretty quickly. Uncle Fred had told her to change her attitude or she'd lose privileges she valued. Of the two of them, her uncle had been much stricter.

Still, she wondered why she'd never looked through her mother's possessions before. She realized she'd never asked about them. Maybe Aunt Clara was worried that she wouldn't appreciate them until now.

Some of the clothes were too old-fashioned to even think of wearing—a blue polyester jumpsuit and red sequined sunglasses—those weren't things she'd ever wear. There were also disco outfits that looked like something out of a 1970s movie. Her mother had probably loved John Travolta.

Other clothes were timeless, very nice, and in good condition. Some of them would need to be dry-cleaned. Others needed washing. Between them, she could have a whole new wardrobe.

Everything there was from the time before her mother was married. She wondered why her mother hadn't taken the items with her when she'd moved out. Maybe she always meant to get them and never got around to it. As far as Maggie knew, Clara and her sister, Delia, had been very close.

Delia had moved away with her husband, Maggie's father, John. Their family home had become the repository for all the things the sisters had grown up with. Maggie's family had lived in this house for more than a hundred years.

There were no pictures of Maggie's father or baby things from Maggie. Aunt Clara had given her those items as she'd grown up.

There were drawings of horses and the magnolia tree out front with her mother's name scrawled across the back or the bottom. There were notes with boys' phone numbers and school information, including some really bad algebra grades on tests.

There were also some pictures of her mother when she'd been in high school. There was even one at the pie shop where her mother was smiling and serving pie to her friends with Aunt Clara and Uncle Fred looking on.

Maggie hadn't realized how alike she and her mother were. She had plenty of older pictures of her mother and father after they were married, and with her as a baby.

These pictures were very different. It could've been Maggie in some of them. As teenagers, she and her mother had been remarkably similar.

Maggie was up until 2:00 a.m. before exhaustion claimed her and she switched off the light, falling asleep in the midst of her mother's clothes. She hadn't made it to the journal her mother had kept through high school and college. That would have to wait for another time.

Aunt Clara was up at five, her usual time, even though they didn't have to go and make pies. There was one particularly loud crash that brought Maggie to her feet. She ran down the stairs to the kitchen and stared at her aunt with red-rimmed eyes.

"Everything okay?" she asked in a sleep-slurred voice.

"Sorry. I accidentally dropped the frying pan." Aunt Clara studied her niece with a knowing eye. "Go back to bed. You were up too late to be up again now. You don't want to meet Ryan for lunch with those circles under your eyes. Scoot."

She agreed and went back upstairs. Aunt Clara started frying bacon and that was it. Maggie got up and showered then put on her jeans and a T-shirt before going back downstairs. If she had some dark circles, Ryan would have to understand.

Over breakfast, the two women discussed financial matters. Aunt Clara had a nice annuity that had been set up years before. It would be tight for her to live without money from the pie shop, but it could be done. Maggie hated to think what kind of condition the house would fall into if that happened.

At least she knew they could survive for a while, until the police were done investigating Lou's death there. Maggie thought about going out to get another job. It would be difficult without a work history for the past ten years of her life. The bank had made it clear that they wouldn't give her references.

Even worse, everyone in the area knew about Lou's death and her connection to him, including the embezzlement, thanks to the local media. Her chances of finding any work were doubtful until all of this was cleared up.

Still, she felt like a useless slug, living off of her aunt. She couldn't remember when she hadn't worked.

Maybe she could use a different name.

When Maggie suggested this idea, Aunt Clara was quick to shoot it down. "No reason to panic yet, honey. The police will be done soon and I'll need you at the pie shop. In the meantime, let's finish that piecrust, shall we?"

• • •

They brought out the bowl with the chilled dough in it. Maggie poked it. It didn't look like much—a white lump that could have been clay.

Aunt Clara brought out her pastry board, which was made from black-and-white-speckled marble. She put it on the counter. "I've had this since goodness knows when. I've tried everything else and I like the marble board best. That's why you see the larger one at the pie shop. You might like a different kind better once you get started."

Aunt Clara took the dough out of the bowl after dusting the board lightly with flour. "Don't use too much flour on this. It will make your crust dry. Keeping the dough cold enough should keep it from sticking."

She showed Maggie how to flatten the dough to start rolling it. The wood rolling pin she took out was ancient. It looked like it had rolled out thousands of piecrusts.

"You have a marble rolling pin at the pie shop," Maggie observed. "Which do you like better?"

"I like the marble better when I need to get things done.

I like the feel of the wood better at home when I can take my time."

Maggie shrugged. "Why not buy some of those frozen crusts Mr. Gino is always trying to get you to use?" Mr. Gino was the supplier for everything except piecrust at Pie in the Sky.

Aunt Clara's face was a mask of horror. "Why not put plastic grass in the front yard? Why not eat canned peaches when fresh ones are in season? Have you ever eaten a frozen piecrust?"

Maggie was sorry she'd asked. "Not here. Maybe in New York. The pie was cooked so I couldn't tell."

"Believe me, there's no comparison between my piecrust and those frozen ones. Now pay attention."

Aunt Clara began rolling the crust with smooth, even strokes after lightly flouring the rolling pin so the crust wouldn't stick to it. "You'll roll this until it's about one-eighth inch to one-quarter inch thick. Use short strokes with the rolling pin, from the center of the dough to the edge."

Maggie kept her mouth shut after the disastrous comment about frozen piecrust. She reminded herself that she was there to learn, not to suggest newfangled ways of doing things. Aunt Clara obviously knew what was best. She'd been making the most delicious pies in Durham for more than forty years and had won many awards.

"Turn the dough frequently to keep it round." Aunt Clara nodded to the cabinet by the refrigerator. "Would you get me a pie pan, honey?"

Maggie opened the door. There were dozens of different sizes and types of pie pans. "Which one do you want?"

"We'll need the eight inch. The larger ones are nine inch. The others are used for tarts."

"Why are some of them metal?" Maggie took a few out. "Do you want a metal or ceramic pie pan?"

"I like the metal for the flaky pastry. I rarely use the ceramic. They were gifts from friends and family down through the years. I don't have the heart to throw them away."

Maggie felt better educated about piecrust now and chose the eight-inch metal pie pan since she knew they were making flaky crust.

"Thanks, honey. Now don't turn the crust over when you're ready to put it in the pan. That's a mistake many cooks make. The crust is better with the rolled side up."

Maggie watched as her aunt put the crust into the pan. "Don't you need to butter the pan or something, like when you make cake mixes? And what about those little splits in the dough?"

"There's no reason to put anything between the crust and the pan," Aunt Clara told her. "Because the crust is floured and dry, not wet, like cake mix, it shouldn't stick. As for those pesky splits at the edges, use your fingers to press them back together. See? They're fine now."

Aunt Clara hunted around for something to go into her piecrust. "I think I have some leftover filling from that apple pie we ate the other night. We'll have to make a crumb topping for it. I think I have everything else we need."

While she talked, Aunt Clara got out the apple filling, which was in a closed plastic bowl in the fridge. She walked back to the counter. "Remember never to stretch your crust, Maggie. Kind of ease it into place. It will get all out of shape when you cook it if you don't. I like to trim the edge and flute the rim, to make it look pretty. Prick the shell a few times with a fork to keep it from puffing up when you bake it."

She pricked the shell a few times. "Some people use pie weights. I don't think that's necessary. It's your choice when you're on your own. And that's it. We'll bake this in the oven at about three hundred and fifty degrees for ten minutes. Then all we have to do is let it cool and fill it."

"And make crumb crust for the topping," Maggie said. "I love crumb crust. I don't know how to make it."

Aunt Clara smiled. "You will." She went to the oven to turn it on when the doorbell rang.

"I'll get it," Maggie offered.

She opened the door carefully to a familiar face, surprised to find the reporters missing from the front lawn. "Mr. Isleb." She was stunned to see one of the bank's executive vice presidents there. "Won't you come in?"

# Nine

Stan Isleb had been Lou's boss. He was a short, fragile-looking man with dainty features. His full head of obviously dyed black hair didn't make his wrinkled face look any younger. His suit and shoes were expensive looking. Maggie once heard that he never bought less than the best and that his wife was the same way. He'd been at the bank forever. Maggie had only met him once and been acknowledged by him—that had been the day she'd started at the bank.

"Thank you, Ms. Grady." He gestured to the young man

beside him. "This is my assistant, Ron. I hope we're not catching you at a bad time."

"Not at all." She led the way into the sunny living room, aware at once of its shabbiness compared to his Manhattan office. She'd also heard stories about his fabulous apartment. "Please, sit down. Would you like some coffee?"

"Who is it, Maggie?" Aunt Clara was wiping flour from her hands as she walked into the room. "Not those annoying police officers again, I hope."

Maggie introduced her aunt to Stan and her aunt's face turned red. "I'm so sorry," Aunt Clara said. "Let me make some coffee."

"Thank you, Mrs. Lowder," Stan said. "I appreciate the hospitality. I've never been this far south. I've heard a lot about the friendliness of southern people. It certainly seems to be true for you, and it runs in the family."

Ron, who was perched on the end of a chair, jumped up to run into the kitchen with Aunt Clara. "Let me help you, Mrs. Lowder. I know exactly how Mr. Isleb likes his coffee."

That left Maggie alone with Stan. He was sure to be there for an explanation of what had happened to Lou. She hoped he didn't blame her too.

"I'm so sorry about Lou's death," she started. "He was a very good friend to me while I worked at the bank."

"Lou was a fine man. He was my brother-in-law, you know. My wife is devastated."

Maggie was stunned. She'd worked with Lou all those years and never knew that he was related to Stan.

"I'm sure she is. It's a terrible tragedy."

"Is there any further news about how he died?" Stan

pointedly asked her. "The police have told me they don't believe it was natural causes, but they have no real theories yet. I can't imagine anyone who would want to hurt Lou, can you?"

"No. I can't imagine it." Maggie was beginning to feel uncomfortable. After all, Stan was exactly the suspect she thought she was looking for. He was higher up than Lou at the bank. He could have a reason to blame her for the embezzlement while protecting Lou.

And here he was—sitting in her home the night after the burglary. She couldn't imagine Stan actually breaking in to steal her laptop, but he could have hired someone else to do it.

He raised one dark brow. "Really? Even though he fired you at the bank for your crimes? I must confess that you were the first person I thought of when I heard the news from my wife. Sometimes the best friends make the worst enemies."

Maggie felt her face flush with anger and embarrassment. "I assure you, Mr. Isleb, I didn't hurt Lou. I don't appreciate you coming here and accusing me of it either. Lou came here to tell me that he knew who the real thief was. I had nothing to gain and everything to lose by his death."

Isleb nodded. "I *see*."

Maggie wondered what was going on behind his cold, calculating eyes. Had he come all the way here to try and make her look guiltier? Was he trying to throw off any possible suspicion from himself to her?

She realized Stan could cause her a lot of grief if he thought she was to blame for Lou's death. That was all

Frank needed to hear—someone else, someone with money and power, not to mention a dead family member—thought she'd played a part in this.

"You know, Lou told me that someone higher up the ladder at the bank was behind this." She stared right back at him. "He didn't say who that was, Mr. Isleb. Any ideas?"

If it was possible, his face got even harder. She'd expected as much. He hadn't attained his place at the bank without being a tough, aggressive man.

"I received an email from Lou about this unfortunate issue, Ms. Grady. He was never good at letting sleeping dogs lie. He told me that he planned to exonerate you. He didn't say why it was so important to him. But then, he always had *special* feelings for you, didn't he?"

*What?* "What are you trying to say?"

He sniffed and looked away from her as though what he had to say was distasteful to him. "We all know Lou and his wife were experiencing difficulties in their relationship. They broke up after you left the city. Many have speculated that he was having an affair with *you*."

She caught her breath. "The only special relationship we had was that he was my mentor. I don't know why he was trying to clear my name. Maybe he had a guilty conscience."

"Perhaps."

Aunt Clara and Ron picked that moment to appear with the coffee. His assistant walked the tea cart in so quickly that the china cups rattled together. Stan glanced at him and he slowed down, muttering an apology.

Aunt Clara followed him, sans her flour-covered apron, and poured coffee for her and Maggie. Ron rushed to pour

Stan's coffee and add the barest hint of cream to it, no sugar. He handed the cup to his employer as though it were a priceless treasure.

Of course, Aunt Clara had included a few pieces of pie with the coffee. Stan and Ron refused. Maggie took a slice of the apple pie so her aunt's feelings wouldn't be hurt.

Despite the other two people in the room, Maggie wanted to be sure that Stan understood she wasn't having an affair with Lou. She took a bite of pie and washed it down with a gulp of coffee.

"I didn't know about Lou and his wife having problems. I hadn't seen or heard from him in the last six weeks since he fired me. He appeared out of nowhere at the pie shop to tell me that he knew I was innocent and that he knew who was guilty of stealing that money. He left right after he told me. A whole shop full of people can testify to that, if necessary."

Stan sipped his coffee, made a face, and replaced the cup on the saucer. "I wish he'd confided his plans to me before impetuously jumping on a plane and coming here. He told me about the press conference. I don't know what he hoped to gain by it. The matter was closed, as far as the bank was concerned."

"Maybe he was looking for justice," she suggested. "Maybe the culprit was someone close to him, someone he was afraid of. Do you have any idea who Lou was talking about, Mr. Isleb?" Her tone implied what her words didn't come right out and say.

"Not at all," Isleb said. "I'm not convinced Lou knew what he was talking about, Ms. Grady. It's possible his findings were flawed because he was so eager to prove you were innocent. Anyone could have been blamed to take your place."

"Or I could've been blamed to take anyone else's place." She smiled at him. "Even yours, Mr. Isleb."

There was an awkward silence between them as they were all seated in the living room with their cups.

Maggie understood now why Stan had come to visit. No doubt he'd say something to the police about his belief that she was having an affair with Lou. That news outweighed the good news about the email that added to the evidence that she was innocent. It potentially gave her two reasons to have killed Lou.

Thinking about it made Maggie uneasy. She kept her mouth shut, worried that the old phrase the police used on TV shows could apply—whatever she said could be used against her.

Aunt Clara had no problem talking to Stan. She rattled on about the pie shop and teaching Maggie how to make piecrust. She asked about Stan's children and grandchildren and took an interest in Ron's dating problems. If she felt awkward at all with them, Maggie couldn't tell.

Usually, Maggie was like her aunt. She could talk to anyone about anything. It was something that had made her good at her job. She'd met and spoken to thousands of people in her dealings for the bank. It seemed she'd left that skill behind, at least for the moment.

"What do you think happened to my brother-in-law, Mrs. Lowder?" Stan asked. "Were you at the pie shop the day he came to call on your niece?"

Aunt Clara shrugged her thin shoulders. "I don't know.

It looked like he'd passed out on the back stairs at the pie shop. I thought at first he'd had a heart attack or something. Someone mentioned poison. I hope that isn't true."

"So you were there? You saw your niece with Lou?" Stan persisted.

"Yes, I was there that day. Maggie was very excited to see him," Aunt Clara added. "It's ridiculous for anyone to think she could be involved in this. The police have shut down my pie shop to check everything. It's very disturbing. Not at all good for my reputation."

Stan sipped his coffee again before abruptly getting to his feet. "I appreciate you speaking with me, Ms. Grady, Mrs. Lowder. I'll be here until this matter is settled. Needless to say, my wife is very determined to find out what happened to her brother. We'll be deeply involved with the investigation and may even offer a reward for information. Ron will give you our numbers in case something else occurs. Good day."

The younger man hurriedly gave Maggie and Aunt Clara business cards from their hotel. He'd neatly printed Stan's contact info on them.

Maggie showed the two men to the front door and watched as they walked out to the silver Lexus. Ron held the back door open for Stan then climbed into the driver's seat and slowly moved away from the curb.

It was probably as close as Stan could get to a limo—his usual mode of transportation—on the spur of the moment.

"You know, I don't really think that man cared that his brother-in-law is dead," Aunt Clara said. "His wife might be grief stricken, but he isn't."

"What makes you say that?" Maggie was surprised by her condemnation.

"I don't know. Gut instinct, I guess. I've got a nose for people. That's what your uncle always said."

"I didn't even realize Lou had a sister or that she was married to Stan. I didn't even think about Lou's family and how this affects them. I guess I've been so busy feeling sorry for myself, I didn't have time to think about anyone else." Maggie closed the front door.

"Come away, honey," Aunt Clara said. "You've been through a lot yourself at the hands of these people. Let's bake that crust and make the crumb topping before you go put on something pretty and meet Ryan."

While the piecrust baked, Aunt Clara showed Maggie how to mix flour, butter, sugar, and cinnamon to make a crumb topping for the pie. They sprinkled it over the apples after putting them into the pie shell.

"Now, you go up and change while I put this in for a few minutes. Then you can take it with you to the newspaper office. Nothing impresses a man like knowing a woman is a good cook."

Maggie smiled. "I think there may be a few other things that impress men more."

"Those things might catch a man's eye," Aunt Clara said knowingly. "They don't stay with him. Although, I'd say you've got what it takes to catch a man's eye too."

"Maybe I should put off this lunch with Ryan." Maggie suddenly had cold feet. "Just until I can wash some of my mother's old things. He's going to think I only have jeans and T-shirts. And he'd be mostly right."

"About that, I knew you'd have to sort through those old things. They'll have to be cleaned and such. I went out yesterday when you were wearing Uncle Fred's old sports coat and picked up a little something for you. I hung it on the bathroom door this morning."

"Aunt Clara, you shouldn't have done that. Money is tight and I don't know when I can pay you back."

"Never mind. Go and change. We'll work on your mother's clothes later."

Maggie kissed and hugged her. "You're the best."

Aunt Clara had excellent taste in clothes. Maggie loved the classic longer skirt and tailored shirt she'd found. It had tiny blue flowers in it with green leaves almost exactly the color of her eyes. She'd also bought a pair of matching green pumps that completed the outfit.

Maggie spun around in the full-length mirror that had been mounted on the back of her bedroom door when she was about fifteen. She felt a little more lighthearted and pretty, as Aunt Clara had said. Maybe she was up to having lunch with Ryan after all.

After going downstairs and twirling around for Aunt Clara, she took the warm packaged pie and left the house with a sense of confidence for the first time in weeks. Maybe the pie wouldn't win Ryan over, but it smelled delicious. On the other hand, with the suddenly cheerful mood she was in, anything was possible.

Maggie had noticed the address of the newspaper office in the masthead last night, after reading two or three *Durham Weekly* newspapers between looking at her mother's clothes.

Ryan was a good writer. He seemed to have a knack for getting to the heart of the story. He didn't only skim the edges, as he'd said. He looked for all the nuances that electronic media didn't have time for. It seemed to be paying off for him—his paper was still around even though many others had folded.

The newspaper office was located a few blocks from the pie shop. It was housed in an older building that was clean and well kept even though it showed its age. The green vinyl siding was something not seen much anymore on newer buildings.

Always looking at the financial side, Maggie imagined the newspaper had been here for decades. The building was probably paid for, like the pie shop. And like the pie shop, there probably wasn't much money left over after expenses to do much in the way of upgrades.

Ryan's Honda was out in front. She smiled as a little zing of excitement shot through her. It was wonderful to finally look forward to something. It was a balm for her heart after everything that had happened.

She took a deep breath, straightened her shoulders, and smiled as she walked through the door.

"You know as well as I do that you shouldn't be dating the woman." An older man wearing a tweed coat with brown patches on the elbows was shouting at Ryan.

Maggie saw the family resemblance at once. This had to be Ryan's father.

"There's no law against going to lunch with someone because she's a person of interest in a murder investigation," Ryan yelled back.

The two men were facing each other in a large outer office filled with bundles of newspapers, computers, and a few old typewriters. The last seemed to be gathering dust in the corners. There were also awards posted liberally on all the walls.

The whole space looked like Maggie would have expected. There was even the strong smell of ink in the air. She didn't see any printing machines. She supposed those were in the back.

"In my day, only second-rate reporters dated women to chat them up for information," Ryan's father continued. "I never wrote about someone I was dating."

"You never dated anyone after you and Mom started the paper," his son reminded him.

"It can lead to all manner of difficulties," his father continued as though he hadn't spoken. "Surely you can see that?"

"Dad—"

"I'm telling you, son, you should dump her now before you drag down the reputation your mother and I built up for forty years."

"Just back off, Dad. You don't know what you're talking about and you're getting too upset over a simple lunch. Maggie Grady is an interesting woman, whether she murdered someone or not."

Maggie realized she must have gasped or made some other sound that gave her away. What did they say about eavesdroppers never hearing anything good about themselves?

Both men turned and stared at her.

Before either of them could speak, Maggie fled back out the door and into the blinding sunshine. She ran right into someone standing on the sidewalk and dropped the warm apple pie.

"Good to see you again." Frank caught her by the arm, ignoring the white pie box on the ground. "I'd like you to take a little ride to the station with me."

# Ten

Frank brought two Styrofoam cups of coffee into the small, drab room where Maggie waited. The table and two chairs barely fit into the tiny space.

She'd had to maneuver between the wall and the side of the table to get into the seat that faced the door. She wanted to be able to see what was coming at her. She was tired of being blindsided by so many recent events.

Frank really hadn't said anything useful on the drive to the police station. It was all about the weather and the Duke Blue Devil basketball team's winning streak. Maggie knew the big questions were waiting for her at the station.

She had said no when Frank asked her if she wanted to have an attorney present. He'd assured her that she wasn't being arrested, or even accused of anything. He had some questions he wanted her to answer about new evidence that had come to him.

She was innocent. She didn't need an attorney and she trusted Frank, mostly because Ryan had said he was a good man. She knew she could convince Frank that she wasn't part of Lou's death.

Something else must have happened, as Ryan had predicted, so Frank felt justified bringing her in for questioning. If Maggie had to make an educated guess, she'd say it was Stan Isleb. No doubt he'd come to convince Frank that she was guilty because people thought she and Lou were having an affair.

*Just wait until Frank hears what I have to say about you, Stan!*

Maggie thought about what she'd witnessed at the newspaper office. Obviously Ryan's father didn't like the idea of them being together. She didn't think Ryan had kissed her, or wanted to spend time with her, just for a story. She'd already poured her heart out to him.

Maybe this was why Ryan and his father didn't get along very well. She'd sensed it last night when Ryan was talking about him.

Her reaction to overhearing the conversation had been a stupid, knee-jerk one. She was on edge right now, that's all. Of course Ryan wasn't having lunch with her to get his story. She'd wasted a perfectly good pie on the sidewalk because she felt stupid for a minute.

Her mind kept wandering. Where was Frank? This interview was starting to seem like something from a bad spy movie.

At least Aunt Clara had expected her to be out for a while. She couldn't call and tell her this had happened—Frank still had her cell phone. It was probably just as well. She didn't want to worry her.

Frank finally came back into the room. "It's not as good as the coffee at the pie shop." He put a cup in front of her. "But it's what we've got and it's free."

"You've been to the pie shop?"

"Sure. I grew up here and went to Duke. Who hasn't been to Pie in the Sky?"

She smiled. "That's nice. Have you been there since I got back?"

He cleared his throat and opened a folder he'd had tucked under his arm when he'd come back into the room. "If you don't mind, I'll ask the questions."

She took a sip of the coffee. It was bad. Very bad. Worse than the coffee at Biscuitland. Her face probably looked like Stan's when he'd tasted Aunt Clara's coffee. "Let's get it over with."

"I like that attitude." He read some of the file, his lips moving even though he didn't say anything out loud. "It says here you served Lou pie and coffee while you talked to him. What did you talk about?"

"I already explained this to you."

"Humor me, Maggie."

She told him again what Lou had said. "It hasn't changed."

"I can see that." He looked at the file again. "Why do

you think Lou gave you a heads-up on this? Why not hold his little press conference and you'd find out then?"

"I don't know. He acted like he was sorry for firing me. I thought he wanted to make things right between us."

"And why do you think he came all the way down here to Durham instead of taking care of it in New York?"

"I have no idea. I didn't expect him to show up. It was a complete surprise."

He nodded. "You didn't talk to him after you were fired, did you? I mean, there wasn't a regular email kind of thing going on, right?"

"No. We weren't exactly friendly after that."

"What about your other relationship with the deceased? We've heard there were rumors at the bank that you and Mr. Goldberg were lovers."

*He'd definitely talked with Stan already.*

"Lou and I were never lovers. I don't even know where that came from. When I left the city, I never expected to see him again."

"And that's why you were upset when you saw him here. It was a reminder of everything you'd lost at his hands. There was a small part of you that wanted revenge, wasn't there?"

"No. There wasn't any part of me that wanted revenge. That doesn't even make any sense. My best bet to get back into the bank and the life I loved died on the stairs behind the pie shop. What would I gain by killing Lou?"

Frank blinked a few times and sat back in his chair. "The autopsy shows that Louis Goldberg died only a few hours after you claim to have given him pie to eat. He must've realized something was wrong and tried to get into Pie in the Sky from the back. Maybe he realized he'd been poisoned. Maybe he thought you did it."

"Seriously? I thought we were past this, Frank! Because I have a new theory to tell you that could mean Stan Isleb is the killer."

"Have you ever heard of arsenic?"

"Arsenic?" Maggie thought about it. "That's a poison, right? Is that what killed Lou?"

"You tell me."

"I don't even know where to get arsenic."

"It's readily available. Anyone could get enough to kill someone. It doesn't take much."

"I don't believe this." She looked around the room. "It's stupid to think I killed Lou. The whole time you're focused on me, the real killer is getting away."

"We don't know where the arsenic came from—yet. But we'll figure it out." He sounded very sure of himself. "Forensics being what it is today, we can say exactly where it came from. When we know, it will be easy to guess the rest."

"I hope so, because I didn't do it. It would be nice if you'd find out what happened quickly." Maggie was getting tired of being browbeaten. "I don't have much of a reputation to ruin. I'd like to keep what I have."

"Do you have any idea where we should start looking? I can tell you we didn't find any trace of arsenic at your pie shop. Could it have come from your home?"

"What?"

"We'll know very soon now anyway. You could make it easier on yourself and tell us before we find it. The DA likes that kind of cooperation. He sees it as an act of contrition."

"Are you searching my aunt's house?"

He didn't answer the question. "It's easier with you out of the way, don't you think? I haven't heard anything back yet. You still have time to tell us all about it."

*So much for Aunt Clara not knowing about what happened.*

"That's terrible. I can't believe you can just go in and search people's houses."

"I know. I feel real bad about it."

"My aunt hasn't done anything to anyone. She shouldn't have to go through this."

He pushed a piece of paper toward her. "This is your last chance to confess, Maggie. Write it all down now before we have the real evidence."

Rebelliously, she wrote on the paper. *I didn't kill Lou Goldberg. Check out Stan Isleb.*

"Okay. That's fine." He looked at the paper then crumpled it up. "Have it your way. Don't say I didn't give you a chance."

Frank left her alone in the small room again. Now she wished she could call Aunt Clara. She wasn't sure what she'd say. Maybe she could at least commiserate with her about her house being torn apart—again.

She stared at the walls, imagining how scared and upset her aunt had to be feeling as the police searched the house. She had no doubt they would say terrible things to her too, as Frank had to Maggie. By now, Aunt Clara must also be wondering if Maggie had killed Lou.

At that moment, she was genuinely sorry she'd come back to Durham. She hadn't known where else to go. She'd never envisioned anything like this happening.

Frank finally returned. "Looks like you're free to go. There was nothing at the house. Nothing at the pie shop either."

"What about Stan Isleb? I know he was here. He visited me this morning with that crap about me having an affair with Lou. I know that's where you got that idea. Have you checked into him at all? Maybe you should haul him in here for questioning."

Frank's mouth tightened. "Go home, Maggie."

She'd been sitting in the uncomfortable wood chair for hours. It was painful to stand. She gathered her things and walked as fast as she could toward the door. She didn't want to be there even a moment longer than she had to.

"Just one thing, Frank. How are you going to question Stan after he goes back to New York? Once he's gone, you're stuck with me. And I didn't do it."

Maggie could feel the other officers eyeing her as she walked through the station. She didn't breathe until she was outside.

It was only after she'd stepped out on the stairs that she realized it was dark. The day was completely gone. She'd lost the whole thing sitting in a police station, accused of a crime she didn't commit.

There was no time to feel sorry for herself. She had to get home as quickly as possible and talk to Aunt Clara.

"Maggie!" Ryan was leaning against the brick wall inside the shelter of the front overhang.

She was stunned to see him there. “How did you know where I was?”

“I followed you over here from the office. They wouldn’t let me in to talk to you so I waited. Are you all right? What happened?”

“I can’t explain now. I have to get home. The police searched my aunt’s house. I don’t want to think about what she’s been through because of me.”

“Let me take you.”

“I don’t need your help. I need a bus.”

“My car would be faster, especially at this time of night.”

She didn’t say yes or no, yet suddenly she was in his car. He pulled out of the police parking lot and into traffic.

“What did Frank say to you?” he asked. “Do you need a lawyer?”

His questioning made her realize where she was and what she was doing. “Is your father okay with you being here?”

He pulled the Honda to the side of the busy street. “I know you heard what my father said, Maggie. It doesn’t mean anything. He doesn’t understand.”

She looked into his face, illuminated by the dash light. “Why would he think such a thing?”

“It’s the way he is. He wants to run the paper but he can’t anymore. It’s made him bitter. I think he’s afraid I’m going to leave and let the paper die. His idea for my life is that I run the paper twenty-four/seven and not have a life outside of it.”

“That’s crazy. He can’t expect that from you, Ryan.”

“I know. He’s my personal cross to bear right now.” He

looked closely into her face. "But you know I won't write anything except the facts of the case, right? I won't even write that, if you don't want me to."

"Thank you."

"He's probably right about me not being objective. I don't care. The newspaper can't be my whole life."

"I didn't think you kissed me and wanted to have lunch with me because you were writing about Lou's death. I didn't know what was going on, Ryan, but I trust you not to put something bad about me into the paper."

He put his arms around her, awkwardly because of the steering wheel. "I know we've just met. It's probably not much to go on—"

Maggie kissed him before he could finish. "I like you too, Ryan. I'm so glad you're here right now."

"Good. That's very good." Ryan sounded bemused. "It's great, in fact."

There was a rap at the driver's-side window as they kissed again. Ryan rolled down the glass and a police officer stuck his head in the car.

"Maybe you two could take this home for the night," he suggested in an irritated voice.

"Sorry, Officer," Ryan said. "We're leaving now."

"Good. I'd expect this from teenagers—you two oughta know better."

When the cranky officer had moved his head, Ryan rolled up the window. He looked at Maggie and the two of them burst out laughing.

It was a stress breaker after all the tension of the day.

Maggie was thankful for the officer's intervention, although at first she'd wondered if the police were starting to follow her.

Ryan cleared his throat and pulled the Honda back out into traffic. "Anyway, I'm glad you feel the same. I know this is a bad time for you and your aunt. I hope you'll let me help."

"I don't know what to say," she said. "I mean, what can we do?"

"We can help the police figure out who killed Lou. We can clear your name. I've always wanted to solve a murder."

"That sounds great. Where do we start?"

"Tell me everything that Frank said to you while you were in the police station. You probably don't realize it yet, but you learned some things we can use."

# Eleven

Maggie thought about it. Maybe he was right. It wasn't easy to keep track of all the information in her head since it was spinning with the events of the last few weeks. She didn't know what she could have missed, but she was willing to trust Ryan with the information.

She blurted out everything that had happened that morning—from the police searching her purse to Frank telling her the house and pie shop were clean and which poison had killed Lou.

"Arsenic?" Ryan said. "Are you sure?"

"That's what he said. Why?"

"That's old school. I didn't know anyone even used arsenic anymore. There are so many more sophisticated ways of poisoning someone. Some of those would be difficult for the medical examiner to spot. There are tests for arsenic poisoning."

Maggie stared at him. "How do you know all that?"

"I like to read about true crime." He shrugged. "I guess it's left over from my first love. Some part of me still wishes I was with the police instead of writing about them."

"So what does that mean? Is arsenic bad to use?"

"No, not really. Usually killers want to disguise the poison they use. In this case, since they were setting you up, they probably didn't care. Arsenic is easy to come by. That's why it's one of the oldest poisons. It's simple to use and very effective. It only takes one tenth of a gram to kill someone. It's tasteless and a white powder, like sugar."

"It's kind of creepy that you know that," she said.

"Yeah, well, it's just a hobby."

"How long does it take this stuff to work?" she asked him.

"Maybe three hours. Give or take. It would all depend on Lou and how it affected him."

"So he could have ingested the poison before he came to the pie shop and still seemed okay?"

"Maybe not okay exactly, but you'd have to know what you were looking for to diagnose him. It was hours later that you found him. Without seeing the medical examiner's report, it's just as possible he was poisoned at the pie shop or at someplace after he left you."

"I guess the only way we're going to find out who killed him is to find out who the real thief was. Lou probably went to see him before he came to see me. He seems to have told everyone else that he planned to reveal the thief."

Ryan parked the car in front of Aunt Clara's house. "Now we're talking. It should be a small list of people who knew what was going on."

"Maybe." She told him about her visit from Stan. "He looks really guilty to me. He fits all the criteria I was creating my list from, before my laptop was stolen."

"I know a man who knows a man who can get access to cell phone numbers." Ryan picked up the white pie box from the backseat. He smiled when he saw the surprised look on Maggie's face. "What? I looked inside when I found it. It's a little messed up, but it tastes great. Thanks for bringing it."

He locked the car after they got out then followed Maggie up the sidewalk to the house.

Maggie put the quest to find out who killed Lou behind her for a while. She dreaded the condition she'd find Aunt Clara in when she went inside.

She unlocked the door and looked around. Everything seemed okay. They certainly were neat in their search, unlike the people who broke in and took her laptop. "Aunt Clara?"

"Maggie?" Aunt Clara called back from the kitchen. "Thank goodness. I was beginning to get worried about you. I mean, Ryan seems like a nice young man. Who can tell these days? You could've been dead in a ditch somewhere."

Maggie ran back to the kitchen and hugged her aunt, leaving Ryan standing at the door. "Are you okay? I was so worried. They didn't badger you about Lou's death, did they?"

Aunt Clara stopped pouring hot milk from a pan into a cup with chocolate in it. "What are you talking about? Who could have badgered me about Lou's death? The only other person I've seen was that very respectful police officer who gave me a formal notice that the pie shop can open again tomorrow. Isn't that good news?"

Maggie stared at her, not understanding. "Detective Waters said they were searching the house for arsenic while he questioned me at the police station."

Aunt Clara stared back. "He was questioning you about arsenic? Why in the world would he do such a thing?"

"I might be able to explain this." Ryan came into the room. "It was Frank's way of stressing you, Maggie, getting you to admit to something. You can't say that he completely lied since he probably sent that officer over here with the notice. He didn't have enough evidence to get a search warrant. It's an old trick of the trade. You'd be surprised how often it works. Of course, you have to be guilty of something first."

Both women stared at him as though he was a stranger. Two red spots came up on his cheeks. He sniffed the air appreciatively. "Is that hot chocolate? That sounds like it would be good with the rest of this pie."

Aunt Clara and Maggie laughed and hugged each other.

They all sat around the kitchen table a few minutes later, Maggie and Aunt Clara eating fresh ginger snaps and Ryan eating a large portion of the apple crumb pie. The house was quiet around them in a good way. It was nice for things to be normal.

"So if the pie shop is in the clear and they don't have enough evidence to search the house, I'm okay, right?" Maggie asked Ryan.

"For now. You're the only one they know of with motive and opportunity. If that's the best they can do, the DA won't prosecute. Everything else is circumstantial. Unless he finds some hard evidence to back it up, Frank can't proceed. If they don't find anything else, Lou's death will become another cold case."

"But we're not going to let that happen." Maggie chewed on a ginger snap and drank the last of her hot chocolate. "What do we have to do to get those cell phone records from your friend of a friend?"

"Give him a hundred dollars." Ryan cut another piece from his pie. "He can have it back to us within twenty-four hours. I think my friend's friend might work for the cell phone company. Don't quote me on that."

"A hundred dollars." Maggie sighed. There was a time when that had meant very little to her. Not now. She didn't know how she could come up with that much money right away.

"I have that much in my egg money," Aunt Clara volunteered. "Let's use it and catch the bad guy."

"Egg money?" Maggie laughed. "What does that mean?"

"You're too young to remember. A man used to come around and bring eggs when I was a little girl. You never knew when he was coming, so you kept a little spare cash somewhere to give him. Otherwise, who knew when he'd be back?"

As Aunt Clara explained, she went to a small white ceramic jar by the refrigerator and took out a hundred dollars. "What can I say? Old habits die hard."

Ryan took the money from her. "I'll get this to him right away."

Maggie had a change of heart and put her hand on his that held the money. "Maybe we should just leave this alone. Pie in the Sky can open again tomorrow. Maybe I should keep my head down and wait for this to all blow over."

Ryan shrugged. "It's your choice."

But Aunt Clara wouldn't hear of it. "You know, I always taught you to fight for what you want, honey. You can't let people like that man who came to visit us besmirch your good name and get away with it. I'd pay a lot more than this to see your name cleared."

Maggie frowned. "Aunt Clara, the money—"

"Not another word about the money. Let's just let Ryan get on with it."

Ryan still looked at Maggie. She finally nodded and he put the money away. "That's right. You said Lou's brother-in-law came to visit," he said. "You felt like he could have killed Lou. What made him seem guilty to you?"

• • •

Maggie rolled over and slammed her hand down on her old princess alarm clock when it went off at 5:00 a.m. the next day. She and Ryan had been up talking until past midnight. It had taken her at least an hour after that to get to sleep. She was still exhausted.

Aunt Clara was wide awake, dressed, and ready to go. She looked in on Maggie at 5:15. "You're still not up? We have to work today. There are no pies made. Hurry, lazy-bones. You won't have time to shower if you're not up soon."

Her voice permeated Maggie's dream and made her get sluggishly out of bed. A tepid shower woke her up enough to put on her jeans and Pie in the Sky T-shirt. She brushed her hair and smiled at herself in the foggy bathroom mirror. For once, since she'd been back home, she was looking forward to the new day.

Maggie made piecrust right beside Aunt Clara before the pie shop opened that day. She eyed her crust critically. It wasn't quite as neat as her aunt's crust, but it was coming along. She hoped it tasted as good. She was doing everything she should be. Aunt Clara told her not to be such a worry wart.

They filled dozens of pies. Bountiful Blueberry, Popular Peach, and Chocoholic Cream pie were always favorites. Aunt Clara declared the pie special of the day to be Lotsa Lemon Meringue. That meant a ton of lemons to squeeze and egg whites to beat. Maggie thought it might be the hardest pie to make. Aunt Clara liked everything to be fresh and from scratch.

The front counter was clean, as were the floors and all the tables and chairs. Maggie filled the glass counter display cases and made coffee at 7:30 for the 8:00 a.m. rush that usually hit them during the week.

There had been nothing left out after the police had finished searching for clues to find Lou's killer. The shop wasn't trashed, though, as they sometimes showed on TV police programs. She was glad they were neat about their job. She hadn't looked forward to cleaning up an extra mess.

Everything looked just like they'd left it the day Lou was killed.

The shop smelled heavenly after all the frantic baking. Usually there were one or two pies to start with, but the police search had left them empty-handed. The three pies that had been there were destroyed.

Maggie made a sign on neon poster board for the front window that said Pie in the Sky was open for business. It replaced the Closed by Order of Durham PD sign that had been there. She hoped the investigation and ensuing publicity from the newspapers and TV stations wouldn't close the shop down permanently.

She didn't know what to expect. What if none of the customers came back again?

At seven forty-five right before they were going to open, Donna Davis, the blond, petite, always-tan owner of Triple Tan and Tattoo, knocked on the door. She had a basket almost as big as herself filled with flowers and fruit.

"Just wanted to let you know we were worried about you all and we're glad to have you back." The pink and purple tattoo butterfly on her cheek appeared to move its wings as she spoke. It had a riveting effect of making people stare at the tattoo during conversations with her.

Donna and Aunt Clara hugged each other tightly. They'd been friends since Triple Tan had opened a few years ago.

"You're such a sweetheart," Aunt Clara said. "I'm so glad to be back. I really missed this place."

A few moments later, the owners of X-Press It, the UPS and mailbox store, came in to see how things were going. Artie Morgan and Rick Russell were fresh out of Duke. Aunt

Clara couldn't tell them apart and always called them the twins.

Maggie had to admit they were about the same height and weight, short brown hair and brown eyes. They at least looked like brothers.

"Just wanted you to know we're behind you, Clara. Glad you're back again."

"Thanks so much. That means a lot to me," Aunt Clara said.

"I hope this doesn't mean you're going to sell the shop," one of them—Maggie couldn't tell them apart either—asked.

"Heavens no! This shop is my home away from home. It is certainly not for sale."

They left with a lemon pie and a quart of coffee. Aunt Clara appreciated them buying the pie and coffee more than the big basket of flowers and fruit, since they were the first customers of the day.

"I have a good feeling about today," she said as she had Maggie ring up the sale. "We're going to be all right."

By eight fifteen, the pie shop was packed. Saul Weissman from the Laundromat and Raji Singh from the grill had come by for pie and coffee during the rush. Raji gave Aunt Clara a statue of Ganesha. "He's the Hindu god of overcoming obstacles. He'll get you through this."

Aunt Clara and Maggie thanked them as they rushed around serving pie with coffee and tea. It seemed as though all their customers who normally came on different days were there that morning to wish them well and ask questions about what had happened.

"I guess you were right," Maggie told her aunt when they were still packed at nine thirty. "There must not be any bad publicity. Most of the people coming in now aren't even regulars."

"It helps to have friends too." Aunt Clara quickly set four new pies in the oven. "Some of these people have been coming here since we first opened."

"I hope we get some new regulars from these other people," Maggie replied. "And that we don't run out of coffee."

"Thanks for reminding me." Aunt Clara picked up the phone in the kitchen. "We missed our regular delivery day with Mr. Gino while we were closed. I'll give him a call and see if he can swing by today sometime. He's usually good about that kind of thing, although he charges a small service fee when it's not his usual day."

Frank came into the shop and looked around at all the people. He was lucky to find a chair and table where he sat down for a few minutes and had a cup of coffee. He didn't say much to Maggie, just that he was glad people were back eating pie again.

She hated to admit it—she was glad when he left.

Angela from the book club came in, even though it wasn't book club day. She brought Aunt Clara a new pie plate she'd made in her ceramics class. The top of it was covered in ceramic strawberries and lifted up to show the pie inside.

"I'm so happy for you." She gave Aunt Clara a big hug. "I'm glad you've come out on top of this."

But when Aunt Clara had gone back into the kitchen, Angela pulled Maggie aside and said, "Wouldn't this have been the smartest time to sell to Mann Development? I mean, the place was closed down. How well will it do from now on after the police investigation?"

Maggie definitely didn't like Angela when she talked like this. "You can see we're plenty busy right now. I think everything will be fine."

Angela shrugged, her long blond hair falling across her shoulders. "I hope you're right. If you change your mind, I'll be happy to sit in on any agreement you come to with Mann Development. Just as a friend. I've worked with the company before."

Maggie thanked her again. It was getting to be a little more difficult to thank Angela for help they clearly didn't want or need. She wondered if Angela thought she could make some profit from this. Or if she might even be working with Mann Development.

Either way, Maggie was happy Aunt Clara wasn't going to use the ceramic pie plate Angela gave her. It did make her think about displaying all those decorative pie plates Aunt Clara had saved but never used.

Albert Mann himself paid them a visit a little later in the day. He was wearing his usual black fedora and expensive black coat, even though it was barely cool enough for a light jacket.

He looked around the crowded pie shop as though he'd expected not to see anyone there. Then he turned around and walked back out without a word. He was probably disappointed. An empty pie shop might have meant a quick sale. Maggie was glad to see him go.

Mark Beck came in too. There was no place for him to

sit but he had pie and coffee anyway, leaning against the wall by the counter.

"I'm so sorry for your troubles," he said. "I couldn't believe they closed you down."

"I know." Maggie refilled his cup. "But we're going to be okay."

"Are you going to get your job back at the bank?" He took a bite of lemon meringue pie.

She stared at him, bright spots of color in her cheeks. Seriously, was she never going to get over being embarrassed about it?

"Sorry." He chewed and swallowed his pie. "I read about you getting fired from the bank for embezzlement. Those newspaper people really go into a lot of detail, don't they? I didn't mean to embarrass you, Maggie."

"That's okay." She wiped the counter with a rag. "I'm sure I could get my job with the bank back, but I don't want it now. I'm going to help Aunt Clara make the pie shop profitable again."

He grinned. "Brava! I know you have other marketable skills, but I like you here."

"Thanks." So everyone knew all about her past right now. It would be yesterday's news within a week or two. In a year, no one would even remember it.

"I've got to be going." He looked around the crowded room. "I heard this place—all the shops—are up for sale. Any truth in that?"

"It's not true exactly. Mann Development wants to buy them and build a medical office complex. None of them are actually for sale, as far as I know. I know Pie in the Sky isn't."

"Who are the owners? Is each shop owned by someone different?"

"I don't really know," she admitted. "Excuse me, Mark. I have to check on everyone else. Thanks for stopping by."

Maggie was still too rushed after that to even think about Mark's question. When Pie in the Sky finally quieted down, around twelve thirty, Ryan came in with lunch for her and Aunt Clara.

"I thought you might be tired of looking at pie. I stopped by around nine on my way to the paper and took a few pictures. You were swamped."

"I guess we were," Maggie said. "I didn't even see you."

"Albert Mann was here." Ryan gave her a container of Chinese noodles. "I'll bet he was disappointed. He could've come in and gotten this place for a song if none of the customers came back."

"That man was here?" Aunt Clara demanded. "I wish I'd known. I would've given him a piece of my mind."

Maggie handed her the first box of noodles Ryan had given her and kept the next one for herself. "He was only here for a minute. Probably scoping out the place, like Ryan said. I don't think he was very happy to see us so busy."

While they ate, Ryan told them he'd checked in with an old friend who worked at the medical examiner's office. "He said we weren't dealing with regular arsenic in Lou's death."

Maggie glanced at her noodles, not sure she wanted to talk about this while they were eating. It didn't seem to bother Aunt Clara or Ryan, so she ignored her squeamishness. "What does that mean?"

"It means that the average person who wants to kill someone with arsenic would just turn to their handy bag of rat poison. That would do the trick."

"What a terrible way to rid oneself of pests," Aunt Clara said.

Maggie put down her chopsticks. "What kind of arsenic is it?"

"It's synthetic arsenic." Ryan's enthusiasm for his subject was apparent. "Arsenic pentoxide. Not rare. They use it for various manufacturing purposes. It's a lot stronger than the kind in rat poison."

"That sounds great," Maggie said, lacking his enthusiasm. "Will that make it harder to figure out where it came from?"

"No. That's the good part. It should be easier. My friend said he hasn't heard anything about the police locating the arsenic. He said several investigators are looking into it. It's going to take some time to research. That's partly why they don't have anything yet. It's not something everyone could get their hands on."

"Have either of you considered that Mr. Goldberg's death might not have anything to do with what happened to Maggie?" Aunt Clara slurped her last noodle and looked up at them.

# Twelve

What do you mean?" Maggie asked.

"I mean just what you and Ryan were saying before. What if Albert Mann did this to close the pie shop so he could buy it for less money?"

Ryan nodded. "That could be a possibility."

"It seems a little coincidental," Maggie added. "Just as Lou is about to spill the beans on someone higher up at the bank, he's murdered."

"Sometimes things seem coincidental but they aren't at all," Aunt Clara quipped. "And one could say someone dying after eating my pie would be coincidental. Something like this could have ruined my name and reputation. I would have no choice but to sell to that brute."

"She makes a good point." Ryan shrugged. "Are you going to eat the rest of your noodles, Maggie?"

"No." She slid the box toward him. "Sorry. My stomach isn't as strong as yours and Aunt Clara's, I guess."

"Thanks." He took the box of noodles from her. "I suppose it could go either way. The question for either scenario would be how do we figure out who's to blame?"

"There has to be a middle person in either option," Maggie said. "Albert Mann probably didn't even know Lou. He would have paid someone to pick a person at random."

Ryan agreed. "On the other hand, if Lou was killed by someone who wanted to stop him from having his press conference, like Stan Isleb, there would still have to be another person to do the dirty work. Like Mann, it sounds like Isleb wouldn't have been anywhere around when it happened. "

"I hope it wasn't a regular," Aunt Clara added. "I'd hate to think someone we see every day could do such a thing."

"We'll have to look in both directions," Ryan said. "And I have something to help you do that."

He brought out an older laptop in a black case and gave it to her. "I'm not using this one right now. You may as well have it. It may not be as fast as you're used to, but it still works."

"Thanks." She smiled at him and touched the bag. "I appreciate it."

They decided that Maggie would try to look up what she could about Stan Isleb.

"He might have gambling debts or some other reason for needing that money," Ryan said. "We need to know everything we can about him, especially if he has an alibi for when Lou was killed. That could get Frank's attention right away."

Aunt Clara was going to make a list of all the people who normally visited the pie shop that could be involved with Mann Development.

"I don't want to say anything bad about Angela," Maggie said, "but she's always talking to me about getting Aunt Clara to sell the shop. She's in real estate. Maybe Mann hired her to hang around and see what's going on."

"Angela?" Aunt Clara's green eyes widened. "She's been coming here for years, by herself, and with the book club. I can't believe she'd have anything to do with it."

"Was she here the day Lou died?" Ryan asked.

"Yes," Maggie said. "Maybe we should check her out."

Ryan looked up Angela Hightower on his cell phone. "She owns her own real estate business, Hightower Real Estate. Nice logo." He showed Maggie and her aunt.

"I guess that's as good a place to start as any," Maggie said.

Ryan glanced at his watch. "That's about all the help I can be right now. I'm sorry. I have to get the paper ready to go to press. Once I get that done, we'll see what else we can figure out."

Maggie thanked him for lunch. She wanted to kiss him good-bye but wasn't sure if they were at that point yet.

"I'm going back in the kitchen so you two can share a proper kiss before Ryan goes to work." Aunt Clara giggled as she turned her back on them. "Don't mind me. I would never stand in the way of romance."

Ryan smiled as she disappeared into the kitchen. "I like your aunt a lot."

"That's because what she's saying isn't embarrassing you."

"Let's put it this way—I'd trade her for my father any day." He put his arms around her. "And what's to be embarrassed about anyway? I like you. You like me. We're two consenting adults. We can legally kiss each other good-bye. Or hello, if the mood strikes us."

Maggie smiled and kissed him. "I guess you're right. It's been a while for me. In the city, I was too busy, and since I got home, I've been too depressed."

"Don't worry about it. We'll figure it out." He kissed her again. "Talk to you later. Call me if you think of anything else."

Maggie thanked him again for the use of the laptop and promised to call him. He waved when he got to his car. She sighed. It might be a bad time in her life right now, but Ryan was certainly a bright spot.

She tidied up the pie shop when he was gone. She'd had no opportunity to wipe down any of the tables during the long morning rush. Everything was a mess. There were thousands of fingerprints on the glass pie cases and coffee stains everywhere. She mopped the floor and made fresh tea in case there was an afternoon rush too.

Still, it was a good thing. Maybe the next few days might be slow after so many people came in on the same day. She wouldn't complain either way. It was nice to see so many people who wanted to express their well-wishes. Aunt Clara was right. It was good to have loyal friends.

"Maggie?" Aunt Clara called from the kitchen. "I think the refrigerator might be on the fritz. It's not keeping anything cold."

Maggie walked into the back. She was pretty sure this was the same refrigerator Aunt Clara had put in when she'd worked here in college. The poor old thing just couldn't handle it anymore. Definitely not a good time with Lotsa Lemon Meringue pies that needed to stay cold.

There was a knock at the back door. It was Mr. Gino, their supplier. He was a short Italian man, very muscular. He had a large black mustache that covered his mouth. He was always in a good mood, singing or smiling the whole time he made his deliveries.

"I brought what I could for you, Mrs. Clara," he said. "There are a few things I was out of on the truck. I'll get those to you tomorrow."

"I don't have anyplace to put them if they need refrigeration," Aunt Clara told him. "I'm sorry to waste your time. Our refrigerator just died."

"No problems. My son runs an appliance store. He'll get you a good deal on a new one and have it here this afternoon. Not to worry."

Aunt Clara agreed to Mr. Gino's proposal. Maggie pulled her to the side. "Can we afford it?"

"We can't have lemon meringue pie without it," her aunt reminded her. "Or chocolate cream pie, or whipped cream."

"I suppose that's true."

"Thank you, Mr. Gino." Aunt Clara turned back to him. "We'll take it."

"Good! Good! I'll give him a call. I have another delivery to make. I'll be back after the refrigerator is here to make sure it gets installed properly." He smiled, more a movement of his face than anything. Maggie couldn't see his lips under the heavy mustache.

"It's good to have you back and making the pies. You are my favorite customer." Mr. Gino hugged Maggie and Aunt Clara before he left, whistling an old Dean Martin tune: *When the moon hits your eye like a big pizza pie, that's amore.*

Maggie had a sinking feeling that Aunt Clara's bank account was dwindling away. At least the pie shop was open again. It would bring in money instead of everything going the other way.

The two women moved the pies that were already made and the whipped cream into the refrigerated pie case in the front of the shop. It was a tight fit, and wasn't as decorative as usual, but it worked. Now they just had to get the refrigerator installed before they needed to make more pie or fresh iced tea.

To keep her mind occupied during the slow time in the afternoon, Maggie looked up Stan Isleb on the Internet.

She couldn't imagine him poisoning someone, but on the other hand, she couldn't imagine *anyone* poisoning anyone.

Yet if Stan was the one who had stolen the money and had Lou blame it on her, it made sense. Because they were related, she could understand why Lou would do as he was told. He'd be afraid for his job, for one thing, yet not want to expose his brother-in-law and cause hardship to his sister.

Anything was possible. She'd certainly heard and seen it all when she worked for the bank. It didn't matter how much money a person made either. They could lose everything due to all kinds of circumstances.

Of course, there was nothing on the Internet that was so blatant. Stan had been awarded many honors by the bank in his years there. He'd risen from an entry-level position to be a powerful man.

He wasn't Lou's direct supervisor. They worked in different areas of the banking business. Stan was involved in bond trading.

Stan also gave to charities, helped orphans and firefighters. He seemed to be a model citizen. There were hundreds of smiling pictures of him in various locations around the country as he cut ribbons, ran races for breast cancer awareness, and held orphaned children in his lap.

Maggie sighed. This wasn't going to be easy.

While she was online, she looked up Angela Hightower too. Angela seemed to be doing very well. She was Real Estate Marketer of the Year last year in Durham. Her sales figures were impressive. She was on several boards around the city and was involved in various charities. She seemed to be a model citizen too.

Maybe she was looking in the wrong direction and needed to focus further *down* the food chain.

A few regular afternoon customers straggled in. One of them was the surly college student who'd been there the day Lou was killed.

Maybe he was involved in what had happened to Lou, she theorized. He didn't appear to be a model citizen and he made her life miserable. It was easy to think he could be guilty. It didn't make any sense, but it made it more fun serving him.

He barked out his order—tea and peach pie—then buried his nose in his books.

A group of students came in and took up a couple of tables, ordering one piece of pie and one large Coke for all of them to share. Maggie remembered doing the same thing many times when she was at Duke. Everyone chipped in so they could afford something.

There were a few restaurants that ran them out if they didn't each purchase food individually, but Aunt Clara had never operated Pie in the Sky that way. It was one reason the shop had become a haven for students. She also discounted older pies just before closing. Students took them home and ate them the next day or two for practically nothing. Maggie realized Aunt Clara's focus on her customers' needs was part of the success of the business.

When everyone was settled in front, Maggie checked on Aunt Clara in the kitchen. She was humming as she made piecrust. Her aunt was the most positive person she had ever known. Uncle Fred had been that way too. Every cloud had a silver lining for them. There was always a good way of looking at everything.

"Aunt Clara, who owns the land the shops are on here?"

"Your Uncle Fred and I bought it years ago, before you were born. We thought it would be a good investment."

Maggie could hardly believe her ears. "So you collect rent from the other shops?"

"Well, we started out that way. Saul pays regularly and

Raji does too. Donna is just getting started and those nice twins can't really afford rent yet. I'm sure in time they'll be able to pay something."

"So you have money coming in from that too? Why didn't I see that on your accounts?"

"I don't know, Maggie. I guess because you were straightening out the accounts for the pie shop. You didn't mention the other accounts."

Maggie fluted the edges of the two piecrusts Aunt Clara had made and set to the side for baking. "That's why Albert Mann is after *you* to sell. It doesn't matter if Raji or Saul want to do it. All that matters is you."

"I suppose so. You know I'll never sell. Saul and Raji are safe with me."

"Where does the rent money go?"

"Into the bank, of course. I haven't even looked at that account since your uncle died. He always took care of that side of the business. I'll check into that, Maggie."

"What about paying taxes on the land?"

Aunt Clara looked at her blankly. "You know, I've wondered about that. I guess I kind of assumed that the land was paid for so I didn't have to pay taxes on it like I do the house."

Maggie was horrified. "We have to look this up right away. I'm amazed the city hasn't already taken the property. Mann Development could find an easy way in by capitalizing on your unpaid taxes. And what bank has the rental funds?"

Uncle Fred had been dead for ten years. When Maggie went to the City of Durham's website, she found that it had been five years since taxes had been paid on the shop property. The amount, plus interest, was astonishing. They could lose everything just trying to catch it up.

There had to have been letters from the city that Aunt Clara must have ignored. She was surprised they hadn't already foreclosed.

Maggie wasn't sure what to do. Could she make a deal with the city to pay those back taxes in installments? She really needed a lawyer to give her some advice.

When she told Aunt Clara that they might have to talk to a lawyer, her aunt wasn't upset at all. "Maggie, you should call Ralph Heinz. He's a lawyer. I have his card here somewhere—maybe on the fridge. He'll do what he can to help."

Maggie looked at his business card, full of stains, edges curling, and went to call him. It couldn't hurt to ask.

Mr. Heinz's secretary said he wasn't in but would call back later. Maggie put the phone down and wondered what else she could do. She could feel Albert Mann breathing down her neck, finding out at the same time that Aunt Clara owed a fortune in back taxes with no way to repay it.

She waited on a few more college students who were studying for an exam. The phone still didn't ring. When it finally did, it was an order for three Popular Peach pies to go.

She was scrubbing the tables again when Ralph Heinz called back. Maggie explained the situation to him. Because he'd been her aunt and uncle's attorney, as well as their friend for so many years, he said he'd check into it and get back with her.

By that time, the pie shop was busy again. Almost every table was full. Maggie was rushing again from table to counter as Mr. Gino's nephew delivered and installed the new refrigerator. He even took away the old one.

Aunt Clara exclaimed excitedly over the new appliance, running her hands over the larger shelves and double doors. Maggie helped her switch everything over then had to go back out and see to the customers.

An older man she'd seen here before was waiting at the register. He was a little on the plump side with graying hair and thick glasses. He introduced himself as Ralph Heinz. "Could we talk in private for a moment? I hope Clara is here too."

Maggie led him into the kitchen, knowing this wasn't good news. He was holding a large envelope that he opened when she went to get Aunt Clara from the alley where she was dropping off some trash.

"Ralph!" Aunt Clara washed her hands and dried them quickly. "It's so good to see you!"

"You too, Clara." He smiled and his face turned a little pink. "I'm sorry I'm always in and out so quickly. Let's have lunch one day soon."

"Ralph was a good friend of Fred's," Aunt Clara explained.

"I have some bad news for you, I'm afraid," Ralph said. "The city won't take less for the taxes than the amount owed. The taxes are so late, you understand. They get a little peeved when they've been caught with their pants down, so to speak. Someone should have seen this years ago."

"What can we do?" Maggie asked.

"I've taken the liberty of having some papers drawn up." He showed them the documents. "Clara's house is up to date on its taxes and she owns it. The city is willing to put a lien on that property to pay for the taxes on this one. Normally, a lien on the pie shop property would be enough. In this case, they won't work with us on that."

"We can't do that," Maggie whispered. "If you can't pay it off, you'll lose everything."

Aunt Clara didn't hesitate. She signed the documents and thanked Ralph Heinz. "No reason to get so dramatic. Something will come up. It always does."

Ralph agreed with Maggie. "Are you sure about this, Clara? I can't take it back once the paperwork is filed. It might be better to retire and keep your house."

"Please, Aunt Clara—"

"File the papers, Ralph. Thank you for coming." Clara went briskly back to work. "Maggie? I think you have a customer at the counter."

A well-dressed woman was standing patiently at the counter as Maggie rushed out of the kitchen, her mind still whirling from this latest turn of events.

"Maggie Grady?" she inquired.

"Yes." Maggie grabbed the coffeepot in one hand and the pitcher of sweet tea in the other. "I'm sorry there aren't any chairs or tables right now. I'll clean one for you as soon as someone leaves."

"I'm not here for pie," the other woman said. "I'm Lou Goldberg's sister. I'm here to discuss what happened to him."

# Thirteen

"The police say you may have been the last person to see my brother alive." Jane Isleb started talking as soon as Maggie found a chair for her and they sat down behind the counter. She occasionally dabbed her tears with a delicate pink handkerchief.

Maggie felt sure she must have met her at some event or other, even though she didn't remember her. Jane wasn't a remarkable woman. It was surprising considering Stan's position at the bank. Most upper-level male management had gorgeous wives on their arms dripping in diamonds and wearing designer clothes. They always stood out at bank events.

Jane dressed simply, though Maggie knew her clothes were probably expensive. She wore her brown hair pulled back from her face. Her voice was cultured and wispy with just a hint of an accent from her hometown of Boston. She didn't even stand out in the pie shop.

"I'm not really sure if I was the last one to see your brother alive. I'm sorry." Maggie didn't want to give her any false hope. "It was hours after I spoke with him that he ended up in back of the shop. He could have met with anyone during that time. I wish I could be more help."

"I'd like you to be honest with me." Jane stared hard into Maggie's face. Maggie thought she saw a resemblance to Stan rather than Lou in her expression. "I'd like you to tell me exactly what Lou told you."

Maggie excused herself to take coffee and tea refills to a few customers. One man ordered a Bountiful Blueberry pie to go. She boxed that up and took it to him. The woman who'd called earlier came in for the three Popular Peach pies she'd ordered.

She hated having to leave such a delicate conversation. Still, she had to work. It would've been better if Jane had set something up for later after the pie shop had closed. Running back and forth, talking about Lou's final day on earth was a little awkward. Maggie could see Jane was suffering over the loss of her brother.

"Basically Lou told me that he knew who the real thief was at the bank," Maggie told her guest when she sat down again. "He told me he'd get my job back for me and that he was sorry it had happened."

Jane frowned. "No names? He didn't tell you who was guilty?"

"I don't want to speak ill of the dead," Maggie said. "You know Lou loved a show. He said he was scheduling a press conference so everyone would know at the same time. I wish he'd told me. It would've made everything a lot easier. Maybe he wouldn't have been killed."

Jane smiled. "That's Lou. He was a drama queen. I can almost hear him saying it. He loved the theater. I think he always imagined himself as just a player on a stage."

She carefully wiped tears from the corners of her red-rimmed eyes again.

Maggie was uncomfortable with this conversation in a way that she hadn't been with Stan. Jane had none of her husband's arrogance. She'd made it clear that she wanted to talk about it, but it felt like it was from a sense of profound grief. "Did he mention any of this to you, Jane?"

"He talked about it nonstop almost from the first moment after he'd fired you. He never believed you took the money. He drove his wife crazy with it—she left him two weeks after you were gone. We both thought he was having an affair with you."

"Stan told me that." Maggie was even more uncomfortable. How could anyone think there was something going on between her and Lou? "Honestly, I never thought of him that way. I don't think he had those feelings for me either."

"He called me right before he came here and told me he was going to set things right."

Maggie sighed. "Lou was a good man who wanted to

right a wrong. I wish he would have told me more while he was here. Instead, the police think I could have killed him. Crazy, huh?"

Jane immediately offered to help. "I'd be glad to tell the police what Lou told me about the theft, if that would help."

"I don't know if that would make any difference. Right now, I'm kind of in the clear on that. If that changes, I may need you. Thank you for offering."

"It's the least I can do."

"Do you have any idea who Lou was talking about, the person who took the money?"

"I really don't. I'm sorry. He called me on his way to the airport and said he'd figured it out. He said he was coming here to talk to you and he'd call back later. I never heard from him again. I guess he died with the secret."

"I'm sorry I had to ask. It's driving me crazy trying to figure it out."

"What do you mean?"

"I'd like to know who framed me. I'd like to clear my name. Right now, everyone in Durham thinks I embezzled money and may have committed murder. I'm sure you can understand how I feel."

"I do." Jane bit her lip. "Lou had access to a lot of personal information about the people he worked with. I don't know if you can find a way to duplicate that."

"I know. I'm doing what I can with what I have. I also think knowing who framed me could tell us who killed Lou."

"You mean that you think the thief from the bank killed Lou to keep him quiet?" Jane said it as though the idea hadn't occurred to her.

"That's exactly what I think. The killer followed Lou down here. He knew Lou was going to tell everyone the truth. He didn't want that to happen because it would ruin his life. Makes sense, doesn't it?"

Jane looked dazed. Maggie wondered if it crossed the other woman's mind that her husband could be the person they were talking about. It would be difficult for Jane if she suspected her husband murdered her brother.

Maggie was called away again to check on her customers. It was getting close to closing time, which meant cleanup. She hated to push Jane out of the shop, but she had a hundred things to do and it was obvious Jane didn't have any information she needed.

Jane must have felt the same way. When Maggie went back to tell her she would be in touch if she found out anything else, Jane was ready to go.

She gave Maggie a card with a cell phone number on it. "This is my number. Don't call Stan. I don't know what he'd think if he knew we were talking. He thinks you could have killed Lou too. Do you have a number where I could reach you?"

Maggie wrote the house number down on a napkin. "Do you think Stan might know who is behind all of this?"

Jane shrugged. "I don't really know. I do know he doesn't like the bank's name involved in all of this. I think he's more worried about the bank's shareholders than what happened to my brother. I want this to be over so I can take Lou back home to be buried with our parents."

Maggie watched Jane leave in the same car Stan had been in when he'd visited her house. She wondered if there was something more about Stan that Jane didn't want to say. The way she'd told her not to call him sounded more like a warning than just that he'd be upset with her. Was Jane suspicious of her husband at all?

Or was Maggie just reading more into it?

Seeing the last customer out the door, Maggie put Jane's card in the back pocket of her jeans then put out the Closed sign and locked the door.

Aunt Clara was exhausted after the long, difficult day. Maggie had her aunt sit down with a cup of tea as she began cleaning up.

"It was a good day," Aunt Clara said. "And I hope we never have another one like it. I love my customers. I just don't want to see all of them again at one time."

Maggie laughed as she wiped down all the tables and chairs with disinfectant cleaner. "At least there were customers to see. I'm really glad about that. I'm so sorry about the house. We'll have to think of some way to pay off that lien."

"Don't be silly. It's good for people to realize that they have something to lose. You could see that today. If Pie in the Sky had closed permanently, people would have to go to Biscuitland for coffee."

"Very true." She told her aunt about her recent visit to Biscuitland. "It helped that I was there with Ryan. He makes everything seem better. I know that sounds silly."

"I'm very happy about it. I think you and Ryan are just perfect together. I'd like to see our little family expand. That means nieces and nephews. They're the closest thing I'll have to grandchildren in this lifetime."

"That's a little further down the road. Maybe. Right now, Ryan's father doesn't think we should be together at all." Maggie told her about seeing the father and son arguing.

"That will pass with the rest of this awful stuff you've been going through. Did you have any time to research on the computer like you wanted to?"

"Not much. Jane Isleb, Stan's wife, came to see me. I'm not sure exactly why. I couldn't tell if she was worried about what her brother might have said to me before he died or if she just wanted someone to talk to about it. Or she might not know what to think."

"Maybe she thinks her husband took the money from the bank and killed her brother," Aunt Clara said. "Maybe he sent her here to pump you for information."

"I thought your favorite suspect was Albert Mann?"

"I don't really have a favorite right now. I'd settle for any of them coming forth to clear their conscience. Wouldn't that be nice? I'll bet Detective Waters would like that."

They both agreed on that—and that it wasn't going to happen.

Aunt Clara put away the pies that were left for tomorrow. She admired the new refrigerator again for a while. Maggie gasped at the price Mr. Gino's nephew had charged to take care of the problem.

The shop was clean and the trash ready to go out before the two of them turned off the lights and locked up.

Maggie stared at the closed door for a few minutes, trash in hand. The last time she'd taken the trash out after closing, Lou's poor, lifeless body had been there. Finally

Aunt Clara came over and wrestled it open for her with a quick, "Don't dwell on it, honey."

Even so, they'd both looked out carefully before Maggie stowed away the trash and quickly closed and locked the back door.

On the sidewalk, going toward Aunt Clara's house, Frank caught up with them. "Evening, ladies. Busy day, huh? Glad to see business wasn't hurt by the unfortunate circumstances."

Maggie noticed a police car following slowly along the curb beside them as they walked. "Are you following us?"

"If I was, you wouldn't know it. I'm good at my job."

"I would have brought you a slice of pie if I'd known you were going to be out here, Detective," Aunt Clara said with a smile.

"Thanks, Mrs. Lowder." He glanced at Maggie. "You know, you could learn a thing or two from your aunt here."

Maggie wasn't impressed. "If you're not following us, why are you here?"

"I was wondering why Louis Goldberg's sister visited you today."

Maggie wasn't sure she wanted to share information with him. They weren't exactly friendly. Of course, he was probably her best bet for actually finding Lou's killer.

"She wanted to know if her brother had any last words." It wasn't exactly a lie, Maggie decided. It was more a condensation.

"Really?" He sounded skeptical. "It seems odd to me that a man's sister would want to talk to a person who might have killed him."

"Detective Waters!" Aunt Clara said. "What a thing to say."

He had the grace to shrug. "I'm sorry, Mrs. Lowder. It's my job. Drives my wife crazy."

"I guess she doesn't think I killed her brother." Maggie clenched and unclenched her teeth. This was really getting annoying. "She was more interested in how he died and why the police haven't made any progress looking for Lou's killer."

"Come on now. That one hurt my feelings," Frank quipped. "After all, we're doing all we can. We don't have enough money to send me to the Big Apple. Besides, I have a feeling the person we're looking for is still right here in Durham. Not necessarily you, Maggie. Any ideas?"

"I don't know," she said. "If I did, I'd tell you so you could take the credit for it."

"Thanks. I think we can figure it out."

Despite the traffic on the road beside them, it was a pleasant night. It was quiet with no parties or sirens to take away from the peaceful, older neighborhood. The Laundromat next door was still open even though there were only a few people inside, and delicious scents from the Bombay Grill wafted toward them as they walked.

Maggie felt like they were an odd threesome with Frank walking between her and Aunt Clara. She kept her mouth closed and let Aunt Clara ramble on with Frank about various happenings around the city. She wasn't in the mood to talk. Her brain was working overtime on things she could do to save Aunt Clara's house and find Lou's killer.

They walked across the street just before Aunt Clara's

block. Once on the sidewalk, Frank said, "Just wondering what your boyfriend plans to put in his newspaper about the case tomorrow. Aren't you a little curious about that? The other papers weren't too kind to you, Maggie."

"You should probably ask him," she said.

He whistled then laughed. "You wouldn't have believed the stink he put up yesterday when you and I were trying to have a conversation. He did everything but call in the National Guard. That Ryan's got it bad for you."

"You mean when you unlawfully detained her," Aunt Clara said.

"Mrs. Lowder, I don't know what your niece told you—our conversation was perfectly legal. We weren't keeping her at the station against her will..We were just talking."

Maggie was happy and excited that Ryan had stood up for her. It had been a long time since someone had fought for her like that. Probably since she'd left home the first time.

"Anyway," Maggie said. "I don't know what Ryan plans to say. It's his newspaper. Why do you care?"

"I'll tell you why I care. Sometimes the media gets information from privileged sources," he replied a little heatedly. "Like you and your aunt here. It makes the police look bad and our captain doesn't like it. So if there are any surprises coming my way, I'd like to know about it. You could do yourself a favor by giving me a heads-up."

"I wouldn't tell you if I knew," Maggie replied with a grin. "Let's just leave it that I don't know. We'll both find out tomorrow."

"But aren't you a little curious?"

They'd reached the house by then. Maggie was looking forward to leaving Frank on the sidewalk as they went inside. She'd had enough of everyone for the day.

Just as she was about to bid him a good night and good riddance, a man stepped out of the shadows and opened the back door to a shiny black car.

For a moment, a light came on, illuminating the interior of the car. Maggie distinctly saw Mark Beck's anxious face inside the car as Albert Mann stepped out.

# Fourteen

It was all Maggie could do not to reach into the car and wring Mark's handsome, charming neck. He'd been flirting and lying to her for weeks.

Not to mention spying on them the whole time for Albert Mann. All the sweet smiles and extra tips were nothing more than his way of insinuating himself into her good graces. She was angry about every time she'd brought him more coffee or looked for the freshest piece of pie. She'd bought into his act and now she felt like a fool.

Much as she'd have liked to assault him right there and

then, Maggie realized she was in enough trouble without attacking him with Frank looking over her shoulder. Anger built up inside of her anyway. She looked away. She'd have to find another way of dealing with it.

She wouldn't make a scene in front of everyone. Let him hang himself. Now that she knew who and what he was, she'd be ready for him. She was pretty sure he hadn't seen her looking at him through the car window. What a surprise that was going to be.

The closing of the car door broke her chain of thought.

"Mrs. Lowder . . . Clara." Mann smiled and walked right up to Aunt Clara as though they were bosom buddies. "I'm so happy nothing terrible happened after you were forced to close the pie shop by the police. Especially after the sanctity of your home was destroyed with that horrendous break-in. What a tragic turn of events for you."

Maggie stood beside Frank, choosing him over Mann anytime. At least the police only wanted to solve their case. Albert Mann wanted to put her aunt out of business.

"What are you doing here?" Aunt Clara demanded. "I've told you before to stop harassing me. You shouldn't be at my home. I'm not selling the property to you. Go away."

"I have a good offer for you, a better offer, in light of your recent difficulties," Mann continued. "I spoke with your niece about this the first day the pie shop was closed. I assume she told you I was ready to increase the new sum I'm prepared to pay for the property."

Aunt Clara didn't even glance at Maggie to confirm or deny his statement. If he'd been trying to drive a wedge between them with that remark, it wasn't working. "I don't care, Albert. I'm tired and I'm going inside. Leave me alone."

"I'll be glad to come inside with you and we can discuss it." Mann smiled and took off his fedora.

"How many times do I have to say no?"

"At least hear me out, Clara." Mann put his hand on Aunt Clara's arm.

"I don't think you're listening to the lady." Frank stepped into the fray. "I think you should leave now. She's obviously not interested in hearing your offer."

Albert Mann looked down his rather large nose at the police detective. It was a lot like looking at a scruffy brown dog attacking a large black bear.

"I think you should mind your own business. Are you the little paperboy? I've heard about you. You're Maggie's new boyfriend. So sweet. You'll find there's not much that goes on where my interests lie that I'm not aware of."

Frank took out his badge and held it so the streetlight above them gleamed on it. "No. I'm the man who's going to arrest you if you keep harassing Mrs. Lowder and her niece. It's illegal to solicit on the streets of Durham without a permit. Do you have such a permit, sir?"

"Do you know who you're talking to?" Mann demanded, shaking his cane. "I could take your badge. Get out of here before I notice your name."

"It's Frank Waters. Detective Frank Waters." He almost stood chest-to-chest with the other man. They were both of equal height, but Albert Mann's girth was much greater. "And my offer to run you in still stands. Go home, sir."

Albert Mann glared at him then put his fedora back on his head. His driver opened the back door for him again.

"This won't be the last of it, Detective. Count on hearing from my lawyers about this harassment. I am a legitimate businessman with standing in this community. I am also a personal friend of the mayor."

Frank snarled at him. "I don't care who you're friends with. Get out of my face and off the street before I load your carcass into that police car right over there. You hear me?"

Mann got into the car and continued threatening Frank out of the side window as the driver pulled away from the curb.

Maggie was surprised at his childish behavior. He must want the property even more than she thought. She hadn't realized the lengths he'd be willing to go to get her aunt to sign on the dotted line.

Too bad for him that Mark wasn't smart enough to look up the unpaid taxes on the land. He could have had the property for cheap. She smiled, thinking about Mann's wrath if he ever found out. Maybe she'd have to be the one to mention it to him the next time they saw each other. She was sure there would be a next time.

She wasn't happy about how it had been done, but at least the pie shop was protected for now. Mann couldn't touch it.

"How long has this been going on?" Frank muttered to Maggie.

"For a while. He'd been pressuring her to sell before I got back. He comes into the shop and skulks around all the time. Aunt Clara pepper sprayed one of his flunkies because he was so obnoxious."

“Have you considered a restraining order? His behavior isn’t allowed by law. Your aunt could prevent it.”

“I don’t think she expected it to get this bad,” Maggie explained. “He’s stepped up his game a lot in the last few weeks. I think he might be getting a little desperate. He wasn’t very happy about the pie shop opening back up to such a crowd.”

“Has anyone considered that Lou Goldberg could have been collateral damage in the property fight?” Frank stared thoughtfully after the black car’s taillights.

“I did.” Aunt Clara perked right up when Mann was gone. “Would you like to come in and have some dinner so we can talk? I can hear quite well, Detective. No reason to mutter at Maggie.”

Frank took Aunt Clara up on her invitation to eat with them. He sent the patrol car away and even made polite conversation through their dinner of franks and beans.

Maggie was on edge the whole time. Even though he’d done them a favor by getting rid of Albert Mann, she was still wary of Frank.

He hadn’t been overly nasty to her when he’d questioned her at the police station, but he’d still lied to try and get her to confess. That didn’t make for pleasant conversation on her part.

She waited through the entire meal for him to bring up something about the murder investigation. He never mentioned it—not even in a witty way. His manner was calm and pleasant with no surprises.

Maggie wasn’t quite ready to accept him as a friend. She still had the feeling he was waiting for her to make a mistake or say the wrong thing.

He was only doing his job, she supposed. Some of his tactics struck her as underhanded, even though Ryan had assured her that all police officers did the same thing. They were single-minded, interested in solving the case.

Instead of talking about crime, they talked about Durham and their individual memories of growing up there and attending Duke University. The old school had changed a great deal between when Aunt Clara had gone there and when Maggie and Frank had. Maggie guessed he must be in his midforties.

She thought about telling him she'd seen Mark in the car with Mann. She wasn't sure he'd understand the connection. She could have explained, but she wasn't prepared to bring up the case, not when the conversation was so nice without it.

Instead, she waited impatiently for him to leave so she could tell Aunt Clara about Mark. She wanted to call Ryan and let him know too. Her anger and sense of betrayal needed to be vented. Polite conversation with Frank wasn't doing it.

Was the paper finished yet? She looked at the wall clock. It was after eight. She wasn't sure when it was safe to call Ryan. He didn't sound like he wanted to be disturbed until the paper was done. How long did it take to put out a newspaper? Would he call her when he was ready to go home?

After dinner Aunt Clara offered them coffee and pie. They ate Popular Peach pie in the living room and listened to music. Aunt Clara enjoyed classical music—especially piano concertos.

Frank told them that he enjoyed jazz and tried to get

down to the Outer Banks of North Carolina for the Duck Jazz Festival in October every year.

Maggie reluctantly admitted to a love of old rock and roll. Frank leaned that way too. They found that they both liked a few of the same bands—the Byrds, the Turtles, and the Monkees. Frank had seen the Monkees in concert once. They ended up with plenty to talk about.

At nine, Frank finally said he should be going. He'd already explained that he still had to pick up his two children from his mother-in-law's house that night. His wife was out of town with friends, just as Ryan had said.

Aunt Clara thanked him for a lovely evening, gave him a slice of peach pie, and told Maggie to walk him to the door. She winked at Maggie then began cleaning up.

Her aunt obviously hadn't understood that Frank was married. The wink had always been their signal that her aunt thought there was a marriageable man with her. Maggie understood it with Ryan, but Frank was off the market!

Maggie walked with him to the front door and opened it, glad Frank was leaving so she could relax. While the evening hadn't ended up being as bad as she'd imagined it would be, she was exhausted and wanted to go to bed. She glanced outside. The reporters hadn't returned.

"I didn't want to distress your aunt," Frank said on his way out, "but something could be up with this Mann person. I'll check into it tomorrow. You two watch your backs. And call me if anything out of the ordinary happens."

"What about his friend the mayor? You don't think he'll give you a hard time for what you said to him tonight?"

"If I had a dollar for everyone who said they were personal friends with the mayor or the governor, I'd be rich. The law is the law, in my book anyway. I don't care how rich or well connected a person is. I can lock them up the same." Frank shrugged. "The money part comes in after that. I can lock them up. That doesn't mean they stay there."

Maggie smiled and nodded. "Thanks."

"Thanks for a nice, adult evening. It's hard when my wife is out of town. I'm not as good with the kids as I'd like to be. The pie was fantastic, as always. I don't have anything against the two of you, you know. Don't hold it against me that the pie shop was closed. I was doing my job."

"Of course you were."

He studied her face in the dim foyer light. "Look, I know you've been through a rough time and I'm sorry about that. A man you knew was killed. We have to explore all avenues. I'm sure you want us to do our best to find your friend's killer."

"I understand." She wasn't sure she did understand, but she didn't want to debate it anymore with him that night. She no longer felt like he was serious about pursuing her for Lou's murder. That was enough for her. "Good night, Frank."

"Good night, Maggie."

She closed the door firmly behind him and locked up. She went back to the kitchen and helped Aunt Clara wash and dry the dishes then locked the back door. She'd never leave either door unlocked again, even to go upstairs.

"I think Frank is a very nice man and a good policeman," Aunt Clara said. "He's been doing his job, trying to find out who killed your friend."

"At my expense sometimes," Maggie muttered.

"It's nothing personal. He has to cross everyone who could be involved off of his suspect list. You need to watch more crime shows on TV. I understand the process perfectly."

Maggie laughed at that. "Maybe you're right. He didn't mention looking for the person who broke in here and stole my laptop. I should've asked him about that."

"I'm sure he's looking into that too. There are only so many hours in the day." Aunt Clara folded a clean tea towel. "Let's not talk about that anymore tonight. I like my murder mysteries to stay on television. This one is hitting a little too close to home."

"Okay." Maggie held her tongue about Mark being with Albert Mann. It was bad enough her aunt was involved in all of this. She didn't want to give her nightmares about not being able to trust her customers.

"You did very well today making piecrust," Aunt Clara said. "I was so proud. Did you have a piece of one of the pies you made?"

"No. I didn't really have time to. Was it terrible?"

Aunt Clara smiled and hugged her niece. "Not at all. It was very good."

"I know it's not up to your standards."

"I've been making piecrust for a long time. You'll get better as you continue making crust. It takes practice, like anything else."

"Thanks." Maggie put her hands into the pockets of her jeans. "It's something new for me. I'm really good with the microwave."

"I think you're going to be as good with the oven. Your mother would've been very proud of you today too."

"I appreciate that, Aunt Clara. Good night. I'll see you in the morning."

They both went upstairs, turning off lights as they went. Maggie was tired, but not sleepy. She stayed up with her lamp on looking at her mother's possessions again.

Tomorrow she'd take the clothes to the dry cleaners a block up from the pie shop in the afternoon when it got slow. The other clothes she'd wash. It was exciting to think about having something different to wear again. She thought about wearing those clothes the next time she and Ryan went out.

She'd tried calling Ryan's cell phone. It went to voice mail. She didn't leave him a message. He'd get back with her when he was ready. Getting the paper finished for press was obviously a big job. It probably didn't help that it was only him.

One thing that Frank had said still nagged at her. She was curious how Ryan would handle the newspaper article about what had happened at the pie shop—about her. She was willing to make some allowances. She couldn't see any way to tell the story without making her look a little bad. It was a question of exactly how bad she looked.

Some of the other newspapers and TV reporters had made her sound like some kind of manipulative, lying, thief/killer who probably shouldn't be out on the streets. One editorial had already questioned why the police hadn't arrested her.

She hoped Ryan hadn't painted her that way. She'd

trusted him to say what was right without being mean. She expected him to include the part about her being fired for stealing money—*allegedly* stealing money anyway. That was the basis for everything that had happened afterward.

He couldn't leave out the part about her finding Lou's body or being questioned by the police either. In short, reading whatever he wrote was going to make her wince.

She supposed she should be thicker skinned by now. Everyone in Durham already seemed to know what had happened. People had asked politely about it at the pie shop that day. She could tell they'd read and heard plenty about it.

Maggie thought about what Frank had said about Ryan having inside information about the case because he knew her and Aunt Clara. She didn't see how that could help or hurt her.

Still, she admitted, at least to herself, that she was nervous about it.

• • •

Not sleeping had its benefits. Maggie was up and dressed before Aunt Clara for a change. She made coffee and pancakes for them for breakfast and they were out the door earlier than usual.

The *Durham Weekly* was waiting on the front porch in a plastic bag to protect it from the rain.

Maggie picked it up as they started walking to the pie shop in the early morning darkness. She was anxious to read the article, but it was too dark. She had to wait until they got to the shop.

Aunt Clara was talking about making Amazing Apple with crumb topping her pie of the day as they walked by quiet houses. Lights went on as people started waking up.

As soon as they got to the pie shop, Maggie looked at the article. The story was on the front page of the paper, along with an unflattering photo of her.

As Ryan had promised, it went into much greater detail than the dailies had. Maggie did more than cringe as she read what he'd written. He'd not only used information he'd gotten from her and Aunt Clara, he'd said everything in a hurtful way that made her want to cry.

She couldn't believe he'd taken advantage of their new relationship. What a fool she'd been to trust him. She was so glad she hadn't gotten in touch with him last night or he probably would have used what she told him about Mark against her too.

Aunt Clara saw her stricken face as she put on her apron. "What is it? Are you sick?"

Maggie sat down in the first chair nearest the door. "No. I'm stupid." She gave the paper to Aunt Clara. "He said terrible things about us. I can't believe I trusted him, even after I asked about what his father had said to him. He lied to me. He used me to boost the sales of his paper."

Aunt Clara glanced at the paper, her lips moving as she read some of the hurtful article. "Good heavens! I am so sorry, Maggie. It was my fault for trying to push the two of you together. He seemed like such a nice man. I've always admired his writing."

Maggie wiped the tears from her eyes. Really, what was

one more betrayal? She'd thought things were getting better. She was wrong.

"It's okay. I'm sorry he was mean to you too. Obviously, he's a jerk." Maggie looked around the empty pie shop. "Never mind him. Let's get ready for the rush."

It was good to have something to do with her hands. Maggie matched Aunt Clara's pie shells and fillings. She made six Amazing Apple pies with crumb topping, and four Popular Peach before the shop opened.

Coffee was brewing and sweet tea was already cooling before the first customer stepped through the door. Unfortunately for Maggie, the first customer was Ryan.

Her smile left her face when she saw him. "What are you doing here?"

Ryan continued smiling. "Coming by for the first piece of pie of the day, I suppose." He tried to put his arm around her. She moved away. "Is something wrong?"

"Wrong? You are the worst of all the media people who've made fun of me and accused me of stealing and killing Lou. I didn't *know* any of them. I thought I *knew* you. I guess I was wrong."

His handsome face grew serious. "I'm sorry, Maggie. You knew how it was going to be. It was a hard story for me to write because of our relationship. I stuck to the facts. I didn't mean to hurt your feelings."

"Well, you don't have to worry about our relationship affecting your writing anymore." She went behind the counter and brought out the laptop he'd let her borrow. "Take this with you too. Sorry there isn't anything on there you can use.

Maybe you can find some other murder suspect who'll be as gullible as I have been and exploit her."

Ryan took the laptop and shook his head. "I really tried to keep it simple. I didn't want this to happen."

"Simple?" She picked up her copy of the paper. "And I quote, 'Maggie Grady couldn't find a company that would have her after she was charged with embezzlement by the bank she'd worked for in New York. She had to be content working at her aunt's pie shop close to the Duke campus where she spends her time praying she can find better work.' What do you call that?"

"What?" Ryan put the laptop down on a table and took the newspaper from her. "I didn't write that."

He read through the front-page story, a puzzled expression on his face at first, then he looked angry. Without another word, he threw down the paper and stormed out of the pie shop, leaving the laptop on the table.

"Well I never!" Aunt Clara said from the window between the kitchen and the eating area. "That's an unusual reaction. I thought you were the wronged party."

Maggie shrugged, still angry about his betrayal. Why had he acted like he didn't know what he'd written in his own paper? Just how stupid and gullible did he think she was?

She went to wipe off tables and mop invisible coffee stains on the floor. Anything to keep herself busy.

The pace picked up shortly after that, not giving her much time to think about what Ryan had done. She was at one of the small tables by the windows, pen and order pad in hand, when she saw her next customer—Mark Beck.

"I got a table today," he proclaimed proudly with a big smile.

"The better to spy on us?"

He looked as puzzled as Ryan had. She sighed. Was she never going to meet another person who didn't have some kind of personal agenda against her?

"What?" He fumbled with his tie, so apparent in his guilt it was comical. "Spy on you? I don't know what you mean."

She looked him in the eye. She was obviously a bad judge of character. She used to think she was good at seeing through people. Not anymore.

Not only had she thought he was attractive, she'd trusted him too. "I saw you in the back of Albert Mann's car last night at my aunt's house. You're working for him, aren't you?"

"He's a client at my firm, yes. I don't know what you're thinking, Maggie. I wouldn't do anything to hurt you or your aunt."

"This place has been my aunt's livelihood for more than forty years. Closing it down would hurt her and me. How do you explain your part in that?"

"That's relative, isn't it? Mr. Mann is offering a very nice price for this place." He glanced around the crowded pie shop. "Especially considering it's a little worn and in need of repair. He only wants the property. She could never get what he's offering if she sold the pie shop as is. She's fortunate to have this offer. You must realize that."

"I agreed with what you're saying for a while. Now I know that Aunt Clara doesn't want to sell. What part of that don't you and your boss get?"

He leaned closer to her and whispered, "Help me get this set up for Mr. Mann and I'll give you a piece of the pie, as it were." He grinned at his own joke.

"How does coming in here almost every day fit into Mann buying this place?"

"I'm like an advance scout. I estimate price and policy for him. I help him make deals."

"Then you need to go back to him and tell him we aren't selling—not for the price he's offering or any other price. That's it. You don't have to eat any more pie or bother coming in here again."

Mark stumbled to his feet and picked up his briefcase. "There's no reason to be hostile. I've tried to keep this on a friendly level. Mr. Mann doesn't like to leave any bad feelings behind when he closes a deal. I'm telling you right now, Maggie, that he's going to get this property. It's worth a lot of money to him since it's so close to the hospital. You might as well face it and help your aunt accept the inevitable."

"You are the most—" She huffed in frustration. "Just get out."

"Maggie, you're not seeing the whole picture."

"As a matter of fact, I do see the whole picture. Get out or I'll call the police. They like to hang around me too right now. I'm sure I could get someone here quickly."

He shrugged his shoulders in his expensive blue suit and left the pie shop.

Maggie had to take a moment to calm herself in the kitchen.

Aunt Clara was busy taking pies out of the oven and

didn't notice her standing there taking deep breaths for a few minutes. "Is something wrong? Angry customer?"

Maggie finally explained about Mark. "I asked him to leave. He didn't even try to deny it. I can't believe he could be right under our noses and we didn't see it."

"How could we? Albert Mann is such a snake. I guess he hires snakes to work for him. You can't tell by looking at people what they're like, honey. Sometimes we find things out the hard way."

Maggie agreed and hugged her aunt. "At least we know. I guess that will have to do for now, until the next spy shows up."

Aunt Clara agreed and returned to her baking. After a few minutes, Maggie went back out front and refilled everyone's coffee and tea. Two people ordered whole pies to go. She boxed up the two Bountiful Blueberry pies and rang them up with the rest of the customers' orders.

She'd just finished when the power went off. The whole pie shop went dark around her.

What now?

# Fifteen

Business had to come first.

The customers finished their pies and Maggie took cash or IOUs from them because the cash register wouldn't work without power. Aunt Clara still had several pies left. Once those were gone, they would have to close—the oven ran on electricity too.

The food in the refrigerator would be all right for a while. Maggie called the electric company and told them the pie shop had an outage. They promised to come as soon as possible.

She went next door to Spin and Go. Everything there was fine. Saul said they hadn't even had a flicker in their power. He went outside with Maggie behind the shops to look at the individual power meters.

"Here's your problem." He pointed to some wires going to the meter. "They've been cut. This has to be vandalism. No other way it could happen. I was an electrician for a while in my life. Nothing wears out like this."

Maggie agreed with him as she looked at the sliced wires. Saul took a picture of the damage with his cell phone camera and said he'd send her a copy for her, the police, and the insurance company.

The power company employee who came to assess the situation agreed that it was vandalism. "You people have had a lot of problems over here, dead bodies and all. No wonder something like this happens."

He was kind of grumpy about being there. There was a lot of heavy breathing and melodramatic rolling of his eyes. He must have moved the ball cap on his head a dozen times while he spoke.

If someone had purposefully cut the wires to the pie shop, she wasn't surprised. Her guess would be Mark. He was probably angry that she'd recognized him from the car last night. He was no doubt still trying to accomplish his mission—shutting down the pie shop.

It was hard to imagine him in his expensive suit standing in water puddles around garbage cans, but it was too much of a coincidence. If she could get her hands on him right now, she wouldn't be as polite as she had been earlier.

The pie shop was empty when she went back inside. She

consoled herself by thinking they would have been slow by this time of day anyway. It would've been much worse to have lost power first thing in the morning while they were baking and setting up for the rest of the day.

Mark wasn't as observant a scout for Albert Mann as he might think. Maggie was glad of it. She hoped he'd lose his job with Mann Development. It would serve him right.

"I've been working on this list of customers." Aunt Clara was sitting at one of the tables in front, ignoring the lack of light. "It's very difficult. I don't think any of these people would have wanted to kill your friend. I've known most of them for years. This has to be a mistake. Maybe I'm wrong about your friend's death being anything but a way to silence him."

"I know it's hard." Maggie sat down with her. "And it may not have been anyone here who gave Lou that poison. I hope not. After what happened with Ryan, and now Mark, I don't think we can really trust anyone."

"I suppose you're right." She sighed. "I remember seeing Mark here for a long time. I can't believe he's working for Albert Mann, trying to shut me down. What is the world coming to?"

"I don't know, Aunt Clara. I'm sorry this happened."

Aunt Clara patted her hand. "It's nothing to do with you, Maggie. Even if your friend's death is all about the theft from the bank, you're a victim of that too. You did nothing wrong. Sometimes we simply become targets for another person's greed, as I am with the pie shop."

Maggie wanted to agree with her. She felt like the wronged party in all of this. Still, she couldn't deny she'd brought all her baggage to Aunt Clara. She was grateful her aunt didn't see it that way. She wished she could see the brighter side that kept her aunt so positive.

"Look, Maggie." Aunt Clara pointed toward the door. "There's Ryan. I think that may be his father with him. He's a very distinguished-looking gentleman, isn't he?"

Maggie jumped to her feet and ran for the pie shop door. She'd left it open in case there were any cash-paying customers who might not mind eating in the dark.

Before she could get there and lock it, Ryan was already walking in.

"Is something wrong with the shop?" he asked.

"Yes." Maggie kept her hand on the door. "We're closed. You can leave now."

"We think that nasty so-in-so cut our power lines," Aunt Clara blurted out. "Maggie thinks it was that lawyer, Mark Beck, who was in the car with Albert Mann last night when they came to our house. That man will do anything to get this property."

"Why didn't you tell me he came to see you?" Ryan asked Maggie.

"I tried to call you last night and tell you. Frank walked us home from the pie shop. He took care of the problem. You were too busy libeling me in your newspaper to answer your phone. Please leave."

Ryan grabbed his father's arm and dragged him into the pie shop beside him. "Tell her the truth, Dad."

Garrett Summerour bowed his head. "I admit that I touched up Ryan's story without consulting him. He was emotionally involved and couldn't do his job. Reporters can't be objective if they have feelings for their subject. What he wrote was soft on you. I'm sorry."

Aunt Clara marched up to him. "Shame on you! The *Durham Weekly* is the only paper I read anymore because I trust what you tell me. How can I ever trust you again after this?"

Garrett stared at her. "I didn't lie about anything. I didn't say what happened in that weak voice that Ryan had adopted writing about your niece. I'm sorry if that distresses you. That's what we're supposed to do."

"Distresses us?" Maggie demanded. "Your article was worse than any other paper, and that's saying a lot. You went overboard trying to take away the humanity behind the story. I gave Ryan certain information he wouldn't have had if he hadn't said I could trust him not to do exactly what you did."

"Sometimes a reporter's job is difficult. We're responsible for saying things other people might not want to say," Garrett replied. "People get hurt once in a while. That's not our problem. I was telling the story in an objective way. I used your notes on the story in the best way possible."

"That was beyond objective," Ryan added. "If you don't print a retraction and my original piece, *tomorrow,* I'm gone. Do you understand? I'll find a job somewhere else."

"You know I can't keep the paper running, son. Not anymore," Garrett said. "The *Weekly* would fold. All the work your mother and I put into the paper would be lost. You promised you'd keep it going. You can't let us down because we disagree about this piece."

"You promised not to do something like this, even if we

disagreed. You said the paper was mine to run as I saw fit. This isn't the first time you've run roughshod over my articles, but it's the most important time. So here's my ultimatum—either you stop looking over my shoulder and swear never to rewrite what goes to the printer, or the paper is dead."

"This isn't easy for me," Garrett said. "I have strong opinions."

"I don't care, Dad. This is it. You and I have had squabbles about this kind of thing before, but not to this extent."

"All right." Garrett glared at his son. "It won't happen again. I'll pay for a retraction and a new paper to come out tomorrow, even though it will cost me a fortune. Does that satisfy everyone?"

Maggie's heart was suddenly feeling very light again knowing that Ryan hadn't fed her story to the wild beasts after all. Not light enough to let Garrett go without an apology from him, though.

Aunt Clara beat her to it. "I think my niece deserves an apology. Come to think of it, so does Pie in the Sky. You're lucky I have good customers. The way you make the shop sound in the paper, people shouldn't eat here because it's in such bad condition."

"I'm sorry, Mrs. Lowder," Garrett said. "And I'm sorry, Maggie. I misunderstood the situation. Murder sells papers, you know. I was only trying to help Ryan out."

Both women accepted his apology, and as if the pie shop did too, the lights suddenly came back on.

They were cheering when the grumpy electric technician came in through the back door. "I just got done talking to my boss. You all are gonna have to pay to have the lines repaired. Sorry. It's our new policy when it comes to vandalism."

He presented Aunt Clara with a bill. "You don't have to pay it right now. It will be on your next electric bill. Have a nice day."

Aunt Clara's eyes opened wide when she saw the amount due. "Highway robbery! If you want to write about something that will get people's attention, write about this." She showed the bill to Garrett, who agreed it was ridiculous.

"We can at least publish a letter to the editor," Ryan said. "The electric company shouldn't get away with this. They had a big rate increase earlier this year."

Aunt Clara promised to write the letter. She offered Garrett pie and coffee. He smiled and took a seat.

Now that Ryan wasn't the enemy, Maggie told him about their walk home with Frank, their surprise visit from Albert Mann, and seeing Mark Beck in the backseat of the car.

"The lawyer had enough nerve to come in this morning like it was nothing?" Ryan asked.

"He didn't know I'd seen him in the car," Maggie said. "He didn't think he'd done anything wrong anyway. He made it clear this morning that Mann is going to get this property, one way or another. To him, it's only another business deal."

"So you think he could be involved in what happened to Lou?" Ryan was eager to get to the heart of the story again. "People like that can go to extremes to get what they want."

"I don't know. I thought about it again when I saw the

wires out back. They were definitely cut." She showed him the picture she'd taken with her cell phone.

"You still think Lou was killed to cover up what he planned to announce?"

"I think so—although murder still seems a far cry from sending in spies and cutting electric wires," Maggie said.

"Your insurance should cover what the electric company wants for repairing that," Garrett said.

Aunt Clara brought out Popular Peach pie for both men and Maggie got them a cup of coffee.

Sheepishly, Aunt Clara said, "That might not be possible."

"What might not be possible?" Maggie asked.

"I don't think I remembered to renew the insurance for the shop," Aunt Clara said. "I'm pretty sure I renewed the insurance on the house. I'm not so sure about the pie shop."

Maggie frowned. "Don't worry about it. I'll take a look at it later."

Aunt Clara sat down with them. "I'm sorry. I remember thinking that nothing ever happens here, so why pay so much money to protect the shop? I guess I should have realized that's why your uncle always carried insurance on Pie in the Sky."

Ryan changed the subject. "The question is, can we prove Albert Mann and his cronies are responsible for the electric wires? If so, we could get Frank in on this, after what you told me happened last night."

Maggie shrugged. "I don't know. We can't prove who did it. Mark was here, but I didn't see him go in back and cut the wires. You know that's what Frank will say."

"Maybe the police could help anyway." Garrett slurped some coffee and ate another piece of pie.

"How?" Maggie asked.

"Albert Mann was there trying to intimidate you into selling the property last night." Garrett wiped his lips with his napkin. "The police might be able to expand on that after they hear about the vandalism. Maybe offer you some protection. You could even sue for damages, if you can prove Mann's involvement."

Ryan looked at Maggie. "It's worth a try. Maybe they could check into some things that would be hard for us to find. There might be fingerprints on the electric box, or they could see if Mark had a text or phone call from Albert telling him to cut the wires."

"Okay. I'm game, I guess." She smiled at him. "Can you take some time and come with me?"

"I think we should all go." Aunt Clara glanced at her watch. "We won't have many other customers today after the outage. It's already four thirty. Let's lock up and go down there. We can straighten up here before we go home."

It seemed like a good plan. Frank was even at the police station when they arrived. He showed them into his office after shaking hands with Garrett. It seemed the two had known each other for a while.

"What can I do for you?" Frank asked when they were all seated at his desk.

Since Frank knew Garrett, it was silently decided that Ryan's father should tell him about their theory. Frank listened and nodded as he doodled on a pad of paper.

When Garrett was finished, Frank said, "I can tell you've

thought this out and I know it seems to make sense, but it's unlikely that Albert Mann would go to such lengths to get the property. I know he and his friends have been annoying. Doing something more physical probably isn't on the roster."

"Did the mayor call you about last night?" Maggie wondered if that was why he was refusing to look into the problem.

"No. I told you, I'm not worried about that. What you're talking about is more than a hard sales pitch. I need more proof before I can do anything investigate it. Was there a threat from this lawyer or from Mann himself that something of this nature would happen if you didn't agree to sell?"

"No," Aunt Clara responded. "Albert's always been a perfect, though annoying, gentleman. And Mark has always been a polite customer."

Frank shrugged. "I'm sorry. There's nothing I can do."

Garrett wasn't happy with that. "While we're here, anything new on the Goldberg killing?"

"No. We're not making much headway, sad to say. I still think our best bet for finding Louis Goldberg's killer is sticking to the announcement he planned to make, revealing the thief at the bank. NYPD is going over his business records, including his laptop from the bank. Once they get back with us, we should have a better idea of what happened that brought him down here."

"Well, we appreciate you hearing us out anyway, Frank." Garrett got up and shook his hand. "You've seen for yourself that Mann is trying to push Mrs. Lowder into selling her property. I hope you won't wait too long to look into that problem."

"As far as I know, there's no proof Mr. Mann has done anything except offer money for the property. If you have evidence to the contrary, I'll be glad to look at it. Or if Mann gets physical with Mrs. Lowder. Otherwise, my hands are tied legally. You know how it is."

Garrett agreed that he understood. Maggie tried to be the first one out of Frank's cramped office. Before she could get out, he asked her to stay for an extra moment without the others.

"Don't say anything without a lawyer," Ryan whispered as he left.

"Don't worry. I'll be fine."

Frank closed the door behind the others. He asked Maggie to sit down again.

"I'd rather stand, if you don't mind."

He nodded and sat down behind his desk. He opened a file on his desk. "Look, Maggie, there's been more information about your friend being poisoned. We know now where the poison came from." Frank gave back her cell phone. "We won't need this anymore. I'm sorry this has been so hard on you and your aunt. Sometimes it's hard to find the truth."

Maggie was really happy with that development, though she tried to keep her expression blank as she put the phone into her pocket.

"I was wondering what you could tell me about the whole embezzlement case," Frank continued. "If you could take a moment and write down exactly what happened and the people you think could be involved, I'd appreciate it."

"May I send you an email?" She was conscious of the people waiting for her and not sure this was something she should do until she had a chance to think about it.

"Sure." He reached to hand her his card. "Whatever you can tell me could help."

Maggie already had one of his cards but she took it anyway. "I'll try to come up with something."

"This doesn't mean I want you and your friends out there to go around trying to figure out what happened to Mr. Goldberg. People get hurt that way."

She couldn't promise to stop since she had no intention of it. She smiled and said, "Thanks for the warning."

"I know that's what you've been up to," he continued as she opened the door to leave. "You can be arrested for obstruction of justice, you know."

Maggie closed the door between them.

Ryan, his father, and Aunt Clara were all waiting outside. They hurried out of the police station together, the other three waiting eagerly for Maggie to tell them what Frank had said to her.

She told them what Frank had said and what he'd asked for.

"Does this mean we're giving up trying to figure out who killed Lou?" Ryan asked.

"Of course she's not," Aunt Clara said. "He was a close friend. We're still going to sort it all out."

Aunt Clara and Maggie agreed to meet Ryan and Garrett at the Bombay Grill in an hour after they'd finished cleaning up and closing the pie shop.

Despite their rocky start, Aunt Clara and Garrett

seemed to be getting along very well on the way back from the police station, walking in front of Maggie and Ryan, talking about everything under the sun.

"It looks like nothing spoiled in the fridge while the power was out." Aunt Clara changed the subject, ignoring her niece's teasing about her and Garrett when they were alone.

"You can't sidetrack me after the way you almost threw me into Ryan's arms," Maggie said. "You and Garrett have a lot in common. You both opened businesses at about the same time. You're both alone now."

"Have you had a chance to look into that insurance policy for the shop yet?"

"I get it. You want to talk about my boyfriend, but you don't want to talk about *your* boyfriend. Unfortunately, you don't have a choice. If you meddle in someone else's life, you have to expect the same in yours."

"I haven't kept up with things the way I should have," Aunt Clara continued on her own subject. "When your uncle died, everything changed."

Maggie hugged her, despite wearing plastic gloves, forgetting her teasing. "I'm so sorry. You should've told me."

"It wasn't like it happened all at one time," Aunt Clara explained. "It was more like a slide, I suppose. I kept making pies and running the shop. Everything else slid away from me."

"Well, we won't let that happen again."

"What if the bank wants you to come back when they figure out you weren't the thief?"

"I don't care," Maggie said. "I'm not leaving again."

"Don't be silly, honey. You have your own life to lead, your own dreams to follow."

"I followed my own dreams already and look where it got me." Maggie squirted cleaner on a tabletop and rubbed a cloth over it. "I'm going to find a new dream right here, Aunt Clara. I don't need to go anywhere else."

As if the universe was trying to test her resolve, Maggie's cell phone rang. It was her old friend Claudia Liggette with a job offer.

• • •

"This is a fabulous opportunity," Claudia gushed. "Pack your bags and get here as soon as you can."

"I don't think I'm interested." Maggie cleaned another tabletop as she glanced at Aunt Clara, the cell phone on speaker.

"Of course you're interested. I got your email. No one sends a pathetic email like that if they aren't desperate for a job. I'm telling you—this is the opportunity of a lifetime."

Claudia had promised the same thing about the bank job when she'd convinced Maggie to take it ten years ago. She'd been right, of course, but Maggie was looking for something different now. At least she was pretty sure she was looking for something different.

"Things have changed," Maggie said.

"I know. I heard about Lou Goldberg. What a tragedy that was, huh? I know his sister. She said he was in some trouble. Who knew it would kill him?"

Maggie frowned. "When did she tell you he was in trouble?"

"One—maybe two—weeks ago." Claudia paused and shifted gears. "Never mind them. This is your ticket home. You could be back on top with this one."

"Did she say what Lou's problem was?" Maggie persisted.

"Are you listening to me? I'm offering you the job of a lifetime and all you're asking me is questions about the dead man who fired you."

"I know—"

"Take a day," Claudia finally said. "Twenty-four hours. It won't wait for longer than that. Think it over. I'll call you back. This is it, kid."

Maggie could imagine Claudia shaking her mane of tawny blond hair, huge gold earrings flying around her heavily made-up face. She was a headhunter with good contacts around the world. She was also a good friend.

As she put her phone back into her pocket, the life she'd had flashed before her.

Instead of talking quietly with potential bank customers in exotic, elegant surroundings, she was wearing plastic gloves and cleaning tables in her aunt's pie shop. She was only in her thirties. She'd be a fool not to take Claudia's offer.

"What did she say?" Aunt Clara had taken off her apron and was heading for the front door.

Maggie put away her cleaning supplies and made sure the back door was locked. "She has a job for me."

"How did it sound?" Clara asked in an excited voice. "This could be your chance, honey. You shouldn't let it pass you by."

"I don't think so." Maggie turned off the lights in the shop. "I don't think I want that life again."

"If this is about me," Aunt Clara walked out of the shop, "don't worry. I'll be fine. I always have been."

Maggie looked at her aunt in the glow from the overhead light. She was five-foot-nothing, with a big smile and her weird fringe of red hair around her impish face. She'd seen pictures of her aunt when she was younger. Clara had been a pretty girl with soft features and flowing red hair.

Maggie knew her aunt would never be fine again running the pie shop on her own. Either she had to stay and help her or she had to convince her to sell the property and retire. There seemed to be no other way. The decision had to be made now.

# Sixteen

Ryan and Garrett both got to their feet when they saw Maggie and Aunt Clara. The restaurant wasn't crowded. It looked like the two couples would get all the attention they wanted plus some.

The Bombay Grill was opulently decorated in bright red and gold. There was pleasing, soft sitar music playing in the background and the lights were low. There had once been an ice cream store here. Maggie remembered sneaking over for small tastes of different flavors when she was a child.

She hadn't been in the Bombay Grill since she got back.

Maggie wasn't a big fan of Indian food. She liked Thai better. She had to admit that her meal was delicious, though.

Aunt Clara ate very little. She didn't particularly like anything spicy or hot. Ryan and Garrett ate heartily. Their hosts lingered, asking if they needed anything, for the first thirty minutes. After that, they went to check on new guests who had come in.

It was a relief to Maggie, who wasn't used to that much attention while she ate. Raji had asked her a dozen times if the food was good.

"So what's the next move?" Garrett asked when they were drinking tea after their meal.

"I'm waiting to hear from Sarge," Ryan said. "He's getting me Lou Goldberg's cell phone records."

Garrett nodded his approval. "He's a good man. I'm sure he'll come through for you."

"I don't know what that will tell us," Maggie said. "Even if Lou talked to people, that doesn't mean they had anything to do with what happened to him. He used to call me every day when we were working together."

"It might give us someplace to start." Ryan shrugged. "Otherwise, you knew him better than anyone. What do you suggest?"

Maggie told him what Claudia had said about Lou being in trouble. "When I talked to his sister, Jane, she didn't mention that to me. Maybe we should go and talk to her again. I know where she's staying. There might be something she knows that we're missing."

"I'm up for that," Ryan agreed. "Even if she doesn't know who killed him, she might be able to clue us in on what led up to it. Maybe if we knew how Lou got the information proving who'd stolen the money from the bank, we could figure something out from that."

"Exactly." Maggie didn't tell him about the subtle and not-so-subtle hints that she might have been having an affair with Lou. Garrett offered to take Aunt Clara home. Maggie and Ryan took his car to the Hilton Hotel where Lou's sister was staying. The large structure was highlighted by floodlights against the dark sky. Cars were waiting in line to drop off their luggage at the front door.

"I'm really sorry about the newspaper today," Ryan said again. "I don't know what people will think when they read my article after reading my dad's. At the very least, I think it will be confusing. I think they deserve to know the truth. I hope we don't lose a lot of subscribers. This isn't exactly a rapidly growing business."

"I don't know. Even the *New York Times* and the *Washington Post* make mistakes and print corrections and clarifications. Honestly, I'm not as worried about what people who read the paper think. I was beginning to feel like I couldn't trust anyone if I couldn't trust you. I know it's your livelihood and you feel differently."

Ryan pulled the Honda into a visitor parking space at the hotel. "I appreciate the difference. This is your life, Maggie. I'll try not to let you down again."

She smiled. "I'm sure you won't."

They kissed for a few minutes then held hands as they walked into the hotel lobby.

The interior was nicely furnished, not opulent. Maggie had stayed in elegant, expensive hotels around the world.

This one looked like Durham to her—clean, friendly, and home.

The clerk at the front desk rang the Islebs' hotel room after Ryan had asked for Jane. Maggie tapped her fingers impatiently on the arm of the chair while they waited. She looked at all the people going by, wondering about them and the business that brought them here.

Jane finally came down a few minutes later, looking like she'd been asleep. Her eyes were red and she was sniffing into a handkerchief. Her hair and clothes were mussed. It looked like she'd smeared on too much lipstick and hadn't noticed. The woman was a complete wreck.

"I'm sorry it took me so long. I fell asleep." She smiled and apologized. "I don't mean to rush you, but Stan is due back anytime. I-I don't know how he'd feel about you being here."

Maggie introduced Ryan and the three of them sat in the coffee shop. She wasn't sure how to bring up what she wanted to ask Jane—how could she say, "I think your brother was in trouble before he came down here to bail me out. What do you know about it?" Most people were protective of their siblings.

She didn't have to ask. Ryan posed the question in almost the same words.

At first, Jane paled and drank her coffee silently, not looking at them. When she finally spoke, her voice was hesitant. "I think what Lou said about knowing who'd stolen the money was true. At least at first. He started poking into things, looking around. There may have been threats against him because of it."

She sighed and wiped her eyes with the handkerchief. "He took a leave of absence from the bank. It seemed as though his whole life was falling apart. He was scared the last time I spoke to him. I think he knew someone was coming for him."

"You have no idea who that could be?" Ryan asked. "He never gave you any hint of what he'd learned or who he thought was the real thief?"

"No. I told Maggie that when we talked. I was hoping she might know. I don't think Lou told anyone because he wasn't sure who to trust."

"Except for the person who killed him," Maggie said. "I think he told the wrong person."

"You might be right. I don't know. I hope the police can figure it out. My nerves are shot with all these questions and everyone wanting to know why Lou didn't tell me what was going on. We were close, but he wasn't himself the last few weeks."

"Did your brother have any dealings with local real estate?" Ryan asked her.

"Local? You mean *here*?" Jane said it like Durham was the most unlikely place her brother could possibly have dealings with anyone. "I don't think so."

Ryan glanced at Maggie. "Just trying to link the two possibilities together."

"What two possibilities?" Jane questioned.

Maggie explained about her aunt's property and Albert Mann's desire for it.

"Lou wasn't into real estate, as far as I know," Jane said. "He may have known this Mann person—it's possible he was a client of the bank. I've never heard his name before. Have you, Maggie? You probably still know more about any business Lou might have been working on than I do."

Maggie had to admit she'd never heard of Albert Mann while she'd worked for the bank. "It was just an idea. We're not really sure which direction to look in."

Jane nodded. "I appreciate your enthusiasm. If the police were like you two, they'd probably already have Lou's killer in custody. I'm sure they'll eventually figure out what really happened."

She glanced at her cell phone. Her face became even paler and her eyes looked worried. "That's Stan. He's on his way back. I-I have to go upstairs. I hope you understand."

Maggie and Ryan said good night and left the coffee shop after watching Jane get on the elevator to go back to her suite.

"She seems to be taking it hard." Ryan shook his head. "I'm an only child. I can't imagine how bad it must be for her."

"I'm an only child too," Maggie said. "I always wanted to have a brother or sister. Mostly a brother. I was kind of a tomboy growing up. Girls always seemed too prissy."

"I wonder why Lou talked to her about finding the real thief but didn't tell her who it was," Ryan said. "She's different from a business associate like you or Stan. He could've confided in her without having to worry if she'd tell someone."

"I guess he didn't want to involve her. I know that feeling. I wish Aunt Clara could've been spared the last few days."

"Now she and Stan are stuck here until the medical examiner releases Lou's body," Ryan mused. "People don't expect their loved ones to be murdered."

As though thinking of Stan Isleb made him materialize, Ryan opened the glass door for them to leave the hotel, and there he was.

He frowned when he recognized Maggie. "What do you want? Are you looking for me?"

"No." Maggie glanced at Ryan thinking she could understand why Jane was reluctant to have Stan know anyone was there talking to her about Lou. They needed to protect their "source." "We were here for . . . a meeting."

"That's right. The city council holds their meetings here sometimes." Ryan put out his hand. "Ryan Summerour, sir, owner and publisher of the *Durham Weekly*."

Maggie could see Stan didn't want to shake Ryan's hand. He did finally unbend enough to do it, a grimace on his face.

"And you were here for a city council meeting?" Stan speared Maggie with his cold gaze. "Why would you care what happens at a city council meeting? You're a waitress at a pie shop!"

"It involves my aunt's pie shop." She'd almost forgotten how rude he could be. He was famous for it at the bank. "She needs—rezoning."

Maggie went on to explain, in terrible, boring detail, about the medical office building and how Albert Mann wanted to take her aunt's property. Anything to keep him from guessing the truth about their real mission and keep him from confronting Jane.

That seemed to do it for Stan. His furrowed brow wasn't

quite as furrowed. What was left was his normal expression of displeasure with the world.

"I see," was his only remark. "Well, good night, then, Ms. Grady, Mr. Summerour."

Maggie was glad to walk out and would have done so.

Ryan spoke up, pushing it one step further. "Since you're here, Mr. Isleb, would you care to comment on your brother-in-law's death for the paper?"

Stan's frown deepened again. "No. No comment. Excuse me." He pushed by them and stalked into the lobby, not looking back.

"He's a pleasant person." Ryan watched the other man head toward the elevators as his wife had done moments before.

"I never had much to do with him, thankfully. Lou never had much to say about him. I guess that's why I never even knew they were related."

They walked back to the car, talking about what Jane had said—or really hadn't said. The parking lot was full with people coming and going to the hotel. Traffic was still heavy despite the later hour. The threat of rain hung heavy in the air along with the smell of onion rings and fried chicken from the nearby fast food restaurant.

"I guess that's all we can do until we get some kind of lead," Ryan said. "I hope that will be from the cell phone records. I'll give Sarge another call tonight and see if I can speed him up."

Maggie had been staring out the window, lost in her thoughts, as Ryan started the car and left the parking lot.

"Maggie? Are you okay?"

"I'm fine." She told him about Claudia's job offer. "It's what I've been living for the last few months. I've dreamed of nothing else since I was fired. It feels like the opportunity to prove to everyone that I'm not a thief and that I can handle working a tough job again."

Ryan was silent until he stopped at a red light on the corner. "You know, you don't have to prove anything to anyone. I'm sure your aunt never believed you were capable of theft, much less murder. I know I couldn't believe it right after I met you. I don't think anyone would."

"Thanks." Maggie sighed. "I'd really made my mind up not to go back before I got this call. Aunt Clara needs me to help her run the pie shop. I realize that. I don't think she can take care of everything by herself anymore. She doesn't want to give it up—which is why she won't take Albert Mann's very healthy offer."

"Now you're not sure?"

"Would you be? If the police wanted you to take a job with them, wouldn't you at least *think* about it since it was your first dream?"

"I don't know. I'm not the same person that I was ten years ago when I took over the paper. I like getting information the way the police do, without the threat of constant danger. I'm not sure I'd want to actually do the work now."

She smiled at him. "I guess that's me. I'm not sure either. Aunt Clara has always been there for me, no matter what. I feel like I owe her something."

"You can't build your whole life on that. I understand."

He parked the car in front of Aunt Clara's house and turned off the engine. It was dark and quiet in the car.

"Of course, I have a stake in this decision." He smiled and kissed her. "I'd hate to lose you after just finding you."

"I won't be lost. Durham is only a short flight from New York."

"And how many of those short flights did you take in the ten years you worked for the bank?"

"Not enough." She smiled and kissed him. "I know what you mean. I'll talk to you tomorrow."

Maggie went inside and found that Aunt Clara had put all of her insurance records in a box on the desk in the living room for her. She sat down at the desk and waded into them, glad to have something to occupy her mind.

Most of the paperwork went into the trash can since it was twenty years old or more. She read notes Uncle Fred had handwritten to his insurance agent in his slanted, left-hand script. She separated the insurance policies for the house from the policies for the pie shop.

When she'd finished sorting through everything, there was no current insurance policy for Pie in the Sky. There hadn't been since Uncle Fred had died. Maggie said a little prayer of gratitude that the worst that had happened to the pie shop was the electric wires being cut. Aunt Clara wouldn't have been covered for any major loss.

Her aunt came downstairs when she heard Maggie come in. She'd sat beside her as Maggie searched through the box of paperwork.

She shook her head when she heard Maggie's verdict. "I can't believe I can be so forgetful, especially about something so important. I can remember perfectly how to make any kind of pie without even glancing at a recipe. Why can't I remember these other things?"

"Maybe you remember the things you want to remember, like everyone else," Maggie said with a smile. "You were lucky anyway. Nothing bad happened. You won't be able to use it to pay for the electric wires being cut, but at least no one was hurt. It could've been much worse. I'll call first thing tomorrow and get a new policy. I'll also check to make sure the other shops have up-to-date policies."

"You're such a help." Aunt Clara hugged her. "I'm glad you came home and were able to help me sort through everything. I should be right as rain before you have to leave again."

Maggie gazed at her dear face, losing all her doubts about taking Claudia's offer. "I'm not going to take the job. I'm staying here and helping you run Pie in the Sky."

"Nonsense! Just because I'm a little scattered and behind? That's no reason not to live your own life, Maggie Grady. Don't use that as an excuse not to get back in there and fight for what you want."

Maggie considered her words. "It's not an excuse and this is my life now, Aunt Clara. This is what I want to do—for you and for me."

Tears crept into Aunt Clara's green eyes. "I wanted to hear that from you before I gave you this."

"What's this?" Maggie looked at the legal documents she'd given her. "Partnership? Are you sure that's what you want?"

"I'm sure. I've spent more time running Pie in the Sky with a partner than without. If we're going to do this, let's do it right."

"Okay." Maggie signed the papers that made her half owner of the pie shop. "I guess that's it, partner."

The two women hugged, then Aunt Clara said it was too late to celebrate anymore that night. "We have to get up early, you know. Those pies don't make themselves."

Maggie turned off the lights downstairs and locked both doors. She was tired, but she knew sleeping would be hard with all the questions running around inside her head. Too bad there weren't a few more answers.

• • •

Maggie was getting used to staying up half the night going through her mother's treasure trove of clothes and personal items. It helped her think.

She finally sorted all the clothes into two piles, one for washing and one for dry-cleaning. She'd start that project in the morning.

She found a wonderful old locket with an enameled rose on the front and a picture of her mother as a child in one frame, her grandmother in the other.

It was comforting thinking back to the women in her life. Her grandmother had been a professor of economics at Duke, one of the first female professors to teach there.

Maggie knew she didn't have the right temperament to teach. But since becoming an adult, she had thought occasionally about having a child or two of her own.

The man who would be part of that equation had always remained faceless. She'd never been serious enough about any man to consider him suitable for the task.

Was Ryan that man?

She shook herself and yawned. She must be overtired. She hadn't known him long enough to even think about that.

What she knew about him, she definitely liked. It was a start.

She finally turned off the light and went to sleep, dreaming about pie and spilling hot coffee on customers.

• • •

Professor Simpson was their first customer the next morning. He came in with a colleague right after Maggie got off the phone with the insurance company.

She breathed a sigh of relief knowing the pie shop was covered again. The same agent who'd worked with Uncle Fred was still at the insurance agency. He was glad to be involved with the shop again.

The professor was all smiles, very courtly with his much younger friend. The lady couldn't have been more than twenty. She seemed very shy and sweet.

It made Maggie smile to see them together. She wondered if, despite the age difference, they were having a romantic relationship. *Funny how it is when you have a special person in your own life. Romance is always on your mind.*

Garrett brought them a few copies of revised *Durham Weekly,* fresh off the press. He apologized for botching the first article about Lou's death.

Maggie read the article between cutting slices of pie and pouring coffee. There was a huge difference between what Ryan had written and what his father had done.

Still, she was in a forgiving mood. She assured Garrett that everything was fine. She was over her initial anger and disappointment. That had only been because she'd thought Ryan had written about her that way. Once she'd learned it wasn't him, she'd felt a lot better. It was nice that some people would read the new story and possibly see her in a different light.

"I hope we've got that settled now." Garrett winked at her. "I'd like to pay my respects to your aunt before I go."

Maggie wasn't surprised. Maggie had noticed he seemed to like her aunt. "She's in the kitchen. I'm sure she'll be glad to see you."

It amazed Maggie that she could see something of Ryan in the article about Lou and the other stories that filled the paper. He had a lighter, sometimes almost whimsical style compared to his father's terse, dry one. She'd never known a writer before and hadn't realized there was so much personality in the words they wrote.

Ryan came into the pie shop. She smiled and waved at him as she freshened Professor Simpson's coffee. He didn't look her way, as though his mind was miles away. Maggie went to meet him with a coffee cup. She wanted to thank him for the story he'd written.

The shop was packed with students studying for exams when he came in. Other patrons were enjoying their Chocoholic Cream pie, the flavor of the day. Maggie had already helped Aunt Clara make a dozen of them.

"I met Sarge finally," Ryan told her in the kitchen area where he'd dragged her away from listening ears. He looked surprised to see his father there, continuing with his news anyway. "You're never going to believe who Lou spoke to before he died."

# Seventeen

"Who?" Maggie put on gloves to take pie shells out of the hot oven for Aunt Clara to fill. Her aunt was mixing chocolate pie filling and had Garrett whipping cream. He was wearing one of her green aprons.

"Stan Isleb," Ryan announced with a flourish. He nodded to his father.

Maggie shrugged, disappointed with those results. "Well, Stan *was* his brother-in-law and he worked with him. It might be odd if he hadn't spoken to him."

"I suppose that's true," Ryan continued in an excited voice. "Guess where he was?"

"Stan or Lou?"

"Maggie!"

"All right." She closed the oven door. "Where was one or both of them?"

"They were both right here in Durham."

She had to agree that was a surprise. Aunt Clara even put down her whipped cream bag that Garrett was filling. She used it to make the rosettes on top of the cold chocolate pie.

"So Stan was here, in Durham, before Lou died?" Maggie said.

"Yes. He didn't come here because Lou died."

"And why was he here?" Aunt Clara asked.

"Sorry." Ryan's smile faded. "I don't know that yet. It's very interesting, isn't it?"

"It is," Maggie agreed. "Why would Stan have been here *before* Lou died?"

"How can we find out the answer to that question?" Aunt Clara added.

"I'm not sure about that." Ryan glanced at his father.

"Don't look at me." Garrett finished filling the whipped cream bag. "I never did that kind of digging for a story when I wrote the paper. I think you should leave that part to the police. You can always point them in the right direction. That's what I used to do."

"We could ask Stan what he was doing here," Aunt Clara suggested.

"After his behavior at the hotel, I'm not planning to ask him anything," Maggie said.

"I don't mind asking him. We'll have to be careful, if

we're considering him a person of interest," Ryan cautioned. "We don't want to spook him and have him run back to New York. That could mean all our work would be for nothing. It would be a lot harder getting NYPD to listen to us."

"Maybe we could sneak into his hotel room and look through his drawers." Aunt Clara blushed then went on. "Well, not his drawers. That would be too personal and I doubt he keeps any information there. Maybe his file cabinets."

Garrett chuckled. "Clara, you're getting a little racy!"

Maggie smiled. "I think you mean his laptop. He's bound to have one with him. Or at least his assistant has one."

"Where does this leave Albert Mann in the equation?" Aunt Clara asked.

"He's probably not involved at all." Ryan shrugged.

"That's hard to believe." Aunt Clara shook her head and started putting rosettes on the pies.

Maggie agreed with Ryan. Despite Albert Mann seeming ruthless enough to do whatever was needed to take the property, she didn't believe he was involved in Lou's death. Long hours of thinking about him had made up her mind about it.

She could see why Aunt Clara would want him to be the killer. Frank had made it clear he couldn't do anything to stop Mann's harassment. It was scary, even if it wasn't life threatening. If he'd killed Lou, he'd go away for a long time. No more harassment.

Maggie didn't think that was going to happen. Maybe there was some other way to convince Albert Mann that they were serious about not selling the property. It might help if he knew Maggie was a full partner now. Like Angela, he seemed to be basing a lot of his assumptions on Aunt Clara being alone.

"I think we may be barking up the wrong tree on that one," Ryan said. "I've looked through everything I could find on Mann Development. I'm sure they want this property. On the other hand, Mann has got so much going on right now that it seems to me that he could wait without much effort. I couldn't find any evidence that he needs the money from the medical office building project. I think he might be a sore loser. But not a killer."

Maggie added, "He's in a different spot from the person who took money from the bank and doesn't want anyone to know he did it. Once that person's name is revealed, his career will be over and his life will be ruined."

Ryan nodded. "You're thinking Stan Isleb, aren't you? That's what I'm thinking."

"Why else would he be here before Lou had a chance to have his press conference? Jane likely told Stan about Lou looking to find the real thief. He probably wanted to talk shim out of it." Maggie sliced pie. "Lou might even have confronted him with it. Who knows? Maybe he thought he could convince Stan to turn himself in. Once Stan knew he was going to be found out, he had to kill Lou before the press conference."

"Makes sense to me." Aunt Clara shrugged. "I still wish it was Albert Mann, though. I'd rather see him behind bars where he can't keep pestering us."

Maggie frowned, glad that they had a suspect, but uncertain how to proceed. "How are we going to get proof that

Stan was here, had access to the arsenic, and gave it to Lou? How can we get Frank to check those things out?"

"We can't," Ryan said. "We need something else. Stan being here before Lou was killed is circumstantial. The cell phone records might help, but I don't want my friend to lose his job. That's what would happen if the police got their hands on these records. We have to find something that will make them research the cell phone records on their own."

"Something like what?" Maggie glanced out the door to see how her customers were doing.

"We might be able to convince the desk clerk at the hotel to confirm that Stan has been there for longer than he told you," Ryan said. "It would be a start anyway."

"Or you could ask him," Aunt Clara said again.

"I have to go freshen coffee and tea," Maggie said. "I'll be right back."

"I have to go anyway." Ryan stopped her. "I have a meeting with the mayor. He wants to talk about his reelection. Can you have lunch with me?"

"Not unless you want to eat pie," Maggie replied. "We're still really busy after being closed. How about dinner?"

"Sounds good." He looked at Aunt Clara. "You should come too, Clara."

"I don't think I should." Her aunt frowned. "You two go on. I've got a good book waiting for me at home."

Garrett stepped close to Aunt Clara. "I'd consider it an honor if you'd allow me to take you out for dinner. We could go out by ourselves, you know. I don't think we need anyone's permission to do so."

Aunt Clara was sweet in her acceptance. "That would be wonderful, Garrett. Thank you for asking me."

"Okay." Ryan smiled and lightly kissed Maggie good-bye. "I'll pick you up at seven."

She calculated the time between closing the pie shop at six and going home to get dressed. "That should work. See you then."

Garrett said his good-byes and apologized again for the newspaper article. "I'll also pick you up at seven, Clara, if that's all right?"

"That would be fine." Aunt Clara's face was flushed—Maggie couldn't tell if it was from the heat from the oven or the idea of a date with Garrett.

Ryan and Garrett left together. Maggie filled her customers' tea and coffee requests and rang up a few whole pie sales.

She went in the back again and watched Aunt Clara filling pies. "So—a hot date tonight, huh?"

"I only agreed to go out with him to get him out of the way." Aunt Clara bustled around the kitchen, avoiding meeting Maggie's gaze.

"Sure. That's the only reason I'm going out with Ryan too. He's always underfoot."

"You're getting cheeky now, young lady. I think you should mind your own business. Going out to dinner with Garrett doesn't mean anything. I'll never think of another man the same way I thought about your uncle."

"It's okay for you to have romance in your life again, Aunt Clara. Uncle Fred has been gone a long time. I'm sure he wouldn't have wanted you to be alone. He'd want you to date other men."

Aunt Clara stared at her for a moment before she broke into peals of laughter. "You didn't know your uncle, then!"

Maggie had no answer for that. She went back up front and got some new customers set up.

As soon as the morning crowd thinned out, she walked back to the house and put her new clothes in the washer. She'd have to walk back at around four to dry them. She wanted something new to wear to dinner that night. Dry cleaning was going to have to wait until she had some money.

Walking to the house and back, Maggie thought about what Ryan had said about finding other evidence that pointed to Stan being in Durham before Lou's death. She knew it would require more than that to prove that Stan had anything to do with killing Lou, but it was the only place they had to start.

She thought about calling Jane and asking her if Stan had left New York before her. Jane wouldn't want to implicate her husband, though, since it would mean ruining her life too. She even seemed a little scared of Stan. Maggie didn't want her to get hurt.

Maggie thought about the other woman's nervousness when she'd talked to her at the hotel. It was possible Jane was already suspicious. It was even possible Stan had realized that others might be asking questions about him.

Short of paying people at the hotel to tell her what she needed to know, Maggie couldn't think of any other way to get information about Stan. She didn't have the resources to throw money around and hated for Ryan to keep using his connections, as he had with the cell phone information.

What else could she do?

A man was walking out with pies in cardboard boxes when she got back to the shop, and she realized that she could pretend to be delivering pies to Stan and Jane. That way she could get into their hotel room and possibly take a look at Stan's laptop and his calendar.

But not if they were there. She needed Ron, Stan's personal assistant, to be there alone. He'd be forced to deal with the surprise delivery, and that would be her opening.

She decided to call Stan and Jane's suite at the hotel.

Maggie checked on all the customers who'd come in while she was gone. She let Aunt Clara know she was back from the house. Then she went behind the counter and called the hotel, asking for Stan Isleb's room.

The courteous hotel clerk put her through. Ron answered the phone.

"I have a delivery for Stan and Jane Isleb." Maggie tried to make her normal voice deeper. Not that she thought Ron would remember what she sounded like, but why take chances?

"I'm afraid Mr. and Mrs. Isleb are out for the day. They won't be back until late tonight," Ron said. "I'll be here to take the delivery."

Maggie thanked him then tried to think what she could do to distract Ron while she took a look around the Islebs' suite.

Nothing came to her right away. She was inspired, however, about an hour later when one of her customers dropped a piece of Chocoholic Cream pie on the floor. It went everywhere. Not so much a problem for her, cleaning the tile floor.

At the hotel—on carpet—would be a different story. Ron wouldn't want to leave that kind of mess for Stan to see.

She had to wait until they closed down the shop for the day. They were too busy to leave Aunt Clara alone.

"I never expected to run out of pie this way." Aunt Clara locked the front door behind them. "Usually twelve of the featured pies of the day is plenty. I don't know if people are hungrier or what."

Maggie laughed. "I guess you were right about the publicity being good for business."

"Well I'm very glad you're here to help. I should tell you though that you overworked your piecrust a little this morning. It was breaking apart on some of the pies. Not an emergency, mind you. Just remember to use a lighter hand."

"Sorry. I'll try not to do that tomorrow. How's the mystery pie coming?"

"I think we have enough people signed up to name it. I usually wait until at least twenty-five names are in the jar. It's always fun to see what they've come up with—and sometimes a challenge to figure out how to make it." Aunt Clara smiled at her as they walked home. "I thought I'd let you have that honor."

"Me? I don't think I'm ready for that—I barely know how to make the tried-and-true variety."

"Of course you don't. That's part of the fun. You're a very creative person, Maggie, and I have several very good cookbooks at the house. You'll look through them and figure it out, like I always do."

Maggie was a little daunted by the task. She wasn't sure her version of the mystery pie would sell. What if she made one that no one wanted to eat?

It started drizzling before they reached the house. The night was going to be cold and damp. Maggie had tried to call Ryan and make their date for dinner later so she'd have time to go to the hotel with her pies. He didn't answer or text her back. Even worse, he was waiting in his car at the house for her.

"I got done with everything early and thought I'd come over here." He got out of the car when he saw them. "We could go to dinner early or we could sit and talk for a while before we go."

Maggie had been hoping that she'd not only have fresh information about Stan but she'd be dressed in something special when he came to get her for dinner. She'd imagined Ryan being bowled over when he saw her.

She realized it had been a fantasy. There wasn't enough time to go to the hotel and get back in time to change for dinner. She didn't want to make him wait. Waiting for people was one of her pet peeves. She'd have to make the best of it.

"I have another idea," she told him. "Let's deliver some pies to the hotel."

She outlined her idea for Ryan, who thought it seemed feasible. "I can't believe you were going to do this without me. I thought we were a team."

"You got the cell phone records. I was trying to do something useful too."

He finally gave in. "Okay. I can keep watch in the lobby in case the Islebs come back too early. Otherwise, it's your baby. Then we can go out afterward and talk about it. I'd appreciate it if you didn't leave me out of the loop again."

Maggie assured him that she wasn't leaving him out of anything, surprised that he'd think so. "I think this will work. I wasn't purposely trying to leave you out. I came up with the plan to get into the hotel suite and wasn't sure how that would work out. I don't want you to take all the risks either."

Ryan seemed satisfied with that explanation, and their talk turned to implementing Maggie's plan.

She'd brought two Chocoholic Cream pies home with her in separate boxes. Her plan was to accidentally open the bottom box and let a pie slip out on the carpet. While Ron went to get something to clean up the mess, she'd look around for a laptop. She even had her old flash drive to take information with her.

"I think it'll work," she said as they drove to the hotel. She held the pies carefully on her lap. It would ruin the plan if she dropped them too early.

"What's the downside if it doesn't? The Islebs will never order pies from you?" Ryan asked. "As long as you don't actually get caught taking information from the laptop, everything should be fine."

She laughed. "Not that I can imagine Stan or Jane ordering pies from me no matter what."

"True. The key here is not to get caught stealing the information. Ron knows you. He'd probably have you arrested."

"So I shouldn't get caught. An important part of the plan."

She and Ryan got to the lobby of the Hilton and split up at the door. Ryan planned to sit in a chair and pretend to read the newspaper, explaining that it was a good cover as well as good promotion for the paper.

Maggie asked for the Islebs' hotel room and told the desk clerk that she had a delivery for them. The man there sent her to the elevator with the suite number. She walked to the elevator, precariously balancing her pie boxes as people rushed out toward her when it opened.

Then she went to suite 236 to spill her pie.

Ron recognized her as soon as he opened the door. "It's you." His eyes narrowed a little as he took in her boxes. "Was Mr. Isleb expecting you?"

"Yes." She smiled brightly. "He wanted me to deliver these pies. He said you'd pay me when I got here."

Ron looked a little less suspicious. "What kind are they?"

She hoped Stan liked chocolate as she told him.

His expression cleared. "Oh, chocolate. That's his favorite. Let me get the cash."

Maggie gave him a price and hid her surprise. Stan didn't strike her as a chocolate eater. She smiled and stepped into the Islebs' beautifully carpeted hotel suite.

She felt a little guilty as she prepared to work her plan. It was going to be a mess, made more so by her crusts that fell apart too easily. Ron might clean some of it up. The majority of it would have to be cleaned up by the hotel staff. She felt bad about that.

Not bad enough to give up on the idea.

She had already worked the light string open a little on the white cardboard boxes. These were thin pastry boxes that ripped easily. There wasn't much holding them closed.

She watched as Ron took cash from a box on a desk set against the far wall in front of a window. Probably some petty cash set aside for things like this.

She waited patiently until he'd started walking back toward her with the cash. The plan worked beautifully as she released the pie in the bottom box. It slipped out and smashed on the once spotless green carpet. The pie went everywhere with the impact.

"Oh, I'm so sorry!" she said.

As she leaned over to show her concern, the second pie slipped out as well. She hadn't planned on that happening. The two pies together on the floor were a terrible mess. She could see the almost comical look of horror written on Ron's face as he reached her.

"Oh my God! How could this happen?" He glared at her. "What should I do? I mean, is there a special way to get this off the carpet? I can't leave this here for Stan to find. He'll kill me. How could you be so clumsy?"

Maggie apologized again. "Let me help you. I can use the cardboard to scoop up a lot of it. We'll still need some wet rags, maybe wash cloths or towels from the bathroom."

"Yes. Yes, of course. Where's my brain? I'll get them." He brought her a lined trash can. "Put all of it in here. Be careful not to spill any more."

As soon as he left the room, Maggie ran over to look at the desk by the window. There were papers all over it, some of them she recognized with the bank logo on them. Her eyes immediately tried to focus on the writing.

*Concentrate.* She needed the laptop, not the papers.

She saw a laptop. It wasn't what she was expecting. She stopped cold.

*Is that—?*

It was *her* laptop. The used one that had been stolen from the house.

# Eighteen

Maggie picked the laptop up, glancing to see if Ron was coming back. She opened it. There was her butterfly sticker that a customer from the pie shop had given her. It was definitely her laptop.

That meant Stan, or probably Ron on Stan's behalf, had broken into Aunt Clara's house and taken her laptop. It was crazy to even think about.

Stan had to be guilty. It was the only thing that made any sense. He wanted to know what she knew, either about the money that was taken from the bank or about Lou's death.

Either one of those things might make him guilty of being a thief or a murderer. Maybe both.

She looked at the open doorway again. There was still no sign of Ron. Should she simply take the laptop with her?

This might finally be enough to get the police interested in asking Stan some hard questions before he went home. She didn't need Stan's laptop, which didn't seem to be on the desk anyway. The fact that he'd stolen hers should be enough to bring Frank in on it.

Maggie whipped out her cell phone and took pictures of the laptop. She made certain the pictures included items that would make it obvious that it had been in Stan's hotel room—he had business and personal items all over the desk.

She planned to leave it there and call the police. But what if Stan had Ron get rid of it? She'd be out a laptop and lacking the only evidence that could prove Stan's involvement. What if her photos weren't enough?

She could call Frank and wait until he got there, daring Ron or Stan to throw her out of the room. But what about hotel security? She couldn't fight off armed guards.

She was going to have to steal her laptop back. She'd have the photos to make her case. Frank probably wouldn't like that. But what choice did she have?

"Here are the wet towels—what are you doing? Put that down. I'll call security." Ron stumbled into the room. "Where are you going? You're supposed to help me clean up the mess you made."

"Later." She ran out of the hotel suite with her laptop. "Sorry about the mess. Use the cardboard to scoop up most of the goo. It'll help."

She didn't feel guilty about leaving him to clean it up. She was pretty sure he'd been the one who broke into the house and made that awful mess she and Aunt Clara had to clean up. She could easily imagine Stan giving Ron the order to get the laptop and the loyal employee doing his master's bidding.

Her heart was beating fast as she approached the elevators. She expected Ron to run out and tackle her at any moment. She hoped he'd resorted to using the cell phone, explaining the situation to Stan.

Or calling the police.

Stealing her laptop back wouldn't prove that Stan was guilty of murder—not the way his laptop might have. It proved that he was willing to break into a house and steal something from her, however. Maybe Frank could use that to show the lengths Stan would go to because of the theft.

Maggie knew taking her laptop wasn't as bad. Maybe it wasn't the best idea, but she was in panic mode.

What was done, was done. She had to worry about getting away with it. She hoped Ryan had some ideas on where to go from here. She seemed to be fresh out of them.

Her cell phone buzzed and she jumped. It was a text from Ryan. *Islebs on their way up. Get out now.*

Her heart started pumping even faster. She ignored the elevator coming up, possibly with Stan and Jane on it, and ran for the stairs. She could go down a floor and get on another elevator to evade them—and possibly the police who might already have been called.

Once she was in the stairwell at the next floor, she found she couldn't get back into the hotel without a card key. Maggie ran down the next flight of stairs and found herself in the same predicament.

A couple opened the door from outside as she was about to run back upstairs. They smiled and held the door for her. She thanked them and got out as quickly as she could, hugging the laptop to her chest.

She texted Ryan that she was in the parking lot.

*Hurry.*

The police could be there at any moment. Maggie didn't know if Stan would bother with hotel security. He'd know what it meant for her to have found her laptop in his suite as well as she did. The faster she was caught, the faster the possible damage to his reputation would be averted. If she had a chance to turn it in, explain the situation, Stan's goose was cooked.

"You got it?" Ryan ran out of the hotel and found her at his car. "I don't mean to sound astonished, but I am. I wasn't sure if the plan would work."

"It worked. Not exactly like I thought it would. But it worked. Let's get out of here."

They got in the Honda and Ryan left the parking lot, heading for Aunt Clara's house.

"We can't go back to my house," she said. "We have to take this right to Frank. Once Stan finds out it's missing, he's going to either come after it or call the police."

"He'll have to figure out it's missing first, right?" He smiled at her. "Right?"

"Ron saw me leave with it. I couldn't help it."

His smile rapidly turned to a frown. "You didn't mention

that part. Maybe you should turn it on and let's take a look at it first."

"We don't need to. This isn't Stan's laptop. This is my stolen laptop, the one that Aunt Clara bought me at the thrift store. It was in his hotel suite. You know what that means."

"I know what I hope it means," Ryan said. "This could go either way. He took it from you and you stole it back. You're right. Let's take it to Frank and see what he has to say about it. I hope it doesn't involve both of us going to jail."

They found out Frank was off duty when they got to the police station. Ryan managed to get his address from the desk sergeant who was an old friend of his. He didn't tell him why he needed it and the sergeant didn't ask. He'd done favors for Ryan before and Ryan had reciprocated.

"Did you ask him if the police had been dispatched to the hotel?" Maggie asked when he got back in the car.

"No. That would be asking him to investigate *if* that had happened. In order to ask him that question, I'd have to tell him why I was asking. We don't need to do that right now. Let's get this to Frank and hope he sees our side of the story."

Maggie wasn't sure if she agreed with that. She wanted to know what was going on. She went along with it anyway, assuming that Ryan had a lot more experience dealing with the police than she did.

It struck her that he'd said *our side of the story*. He was putting it all on the line, even though he didn't have to.

"Thanks for your help." She touched his hand on the

steering wheel. "I hope I can make this up to you later when things quiet down. I wouldn't have gotten this far without you."

Ryan smiled and took her hand in his. "You're welcome. I wouldn't have missed any of it."

She still clutched her laptop to her as though someone was about to rip it out of her hands. Her heart was racing and her head hurt. She wasn't cut out for this kind of work. Ryan seemed as cool and calm as though he did this every day. He didn't even seem nervous.

They jumped out of the Honda when they got to the address the sergeant had given Ryan. It was a squat, brick apartment building, slightly out of range of student housing for the university. Lucky for them, last names were listed on the mailboxes inside the doorway.

Maggie buzzed Frank's apartment, hoping he wasn't out for the night.

"Yeah. Who is it?" His gravelly voice came out clearly over the intercom.

"It's Maggie Grady. I need to talk to you right away."

"I'm not on duty right now. Can't it wait until tomorrow?"

"No, I don't think it can. Please. I need to see you." Maggie glanced behind them, even though there were no sirens coming up the street. She could feel the police in hot pursuit.

"Okay. Fine. Let me put some clothes on. I'll come down to you."

She and Ryan stood in the shadows of a large fir tree, waiting.

"Are you *sure* it's your laptop?" A little doubt had crept into Ryan's voice. "They kind of look alike, you know?"

"It's absolutely mine. I can't believe Stan stole it from me. What was he thinking?"

"Maggie, someone murdered Lou, possibly to keep him quiet about a large amount of money that had been stolen from a multinational bank. It's the stuff movies and novels are made of. What's a little breaking and entering?"

"I suppose that's true."

The light came on in the foyer of the building. Frank, wearing jeans and a partially buttoned blue shirt, opened the door for them. His hair was almost standing on end and he smelled like pizza.

Maggie remembered that his wife was out of town and his mother-in-law had his kids some of the time. She shuddered to think what his wife would come home to.

A distant police siren reminded them that time was short. She and Ryan scooted into the foyer quickly.

Maggie hardly made it through the door before spilling the whole story. It all came out in one long breath. Frank listened without comment.

When she was finished, he groaned. "Are you seriously here to tell me you took a laptop from Stan Isleb's hotel room?"

"It's mine," she tried to explain.

"I like you, Maggie. Why would you want to put me in a spot like this? I can't look the other way. Even if he took it from you first, you're not entitled to steal it back. You should've called the police."

"It's *my* laptop," she repeated, bewildered by his misunderstanding. "Don't you see what this means? He needed it to find out what was going on. He wanted to protect himself, maybe enough to have killed Lou."

"I get it, but . . ." He paused and seemed to let the idea roll around in his head. "Are you sure about this?"

She opened the battered laptop and showed him the butterfly sticker. "Mrs. Conner's granddaughter gave me this sticker one day at the pie shop."

Frank took it one step further. He had her turn it on as he watched. Her familiarity with the device was obvious. It was very clear that the laptop belonged to her. She knew the password for it and the emails were coming to her name.

"Let's think about this for a minute." Frank took the laptop, closing it and sitting on the steps. "I think I need some coffee. I must still be asleep in front of the TV because this is starting to make sense to me. Let me get my shoes and we'll talk about it over a cup."

Since the pie shop was closed, they drank coffee at Biscuitland. Drinking coffee here seemed to have become some kind of terrible ritual.

There was only one other person in the place and employees were mopping floors and cleaning bathrooms. The smell of Pine-Sol didn't add anything to help the flavor of the coffee.

Maggie watched Frank butter a biscuit that looked a little stale. She and Ryan were too nervous to eat anything.

"So, let me get this straight. You pretended to be delivering pies so you could get into the Islebs' hotel room and steal the laptop that he stole from you." Frank summarized after he'd had a few bites of his biscuit and sips of coffee.

"Well, I was going to take a look at Stan's laptop. I wanted to see his calendar so we'd know for sure that he was in Durham before Lou died. Ryan and I had some information that Stan was here. Then I saw my laptop and I took it."

Frank covered his ears with his hands. "Please, don't confess to anything else. It's bad enough that you took this laptop."

"But it's mine. He shouldn't have had it."

"I know. I know." His cell phone rang and he answered it, nodding and saying okay a few times. When he turned it off, he said, "Looks like Stan Isleb is already at the station waiting to press charges against you for breaking and entering and who knows what else, Maggie."

"There's got to be something we can do," Ryan said. "She didn't break into the hotel room. Isleb's assistant let her in. He's trying to cover up his mistake."

"There's something we can do." Frank grunted as he got up from the table. "We have to give it back and tell Isleb you're sorry it happened."

"Give it back?" Maggie demanded. "But—"

"It doesn't matter," he said. "We give it back. You apologize with a pretty, but dumb smile, and make up some BS about taking it."

"What about Stan lying about how long he's been in Durham?" she asked. "Why don't we get to ask him about that?"

"I didn't say we weren't going to ask him about that," Frank said. "First we get them to drop charges against you. You drop any idea of charges against him for stealing it in the first place. Then we ask important questions. Get it?"

Maggie agreed, even though she didn't get it. There was no sense of wrongdoing on her part. Stan had broken into Aunt Clara's house and stolen her laptop. She'd taken it back.

"He has a plan," Ryan assured her as they followed Frank to the station. "He knows what he's doing."

Maggie wasn't sure she agreed with that. It hadn't been so long ago that Frank had questioned her because he thought she'd killed Lou. That wasn't particularly confidence inspiring.

It became even more debatable when they'd reached the station and saw Stan and a red-faced Ron waiting there. Maggie could imagine that he'd received a stern talking-to from his employer. She'd known assistants at the bank who'd been dismissed for less. She felt sorry for Ron. She didn't care. She was sticking to her story.

Frank herded all of them into his office. There were only two chairs in front of the desk—Stan and Maggie sat down.

"Okay. I want to hear from Maggie first, and then we'll get the other two stories." Frank sat down behind his desk. "You'll each get a turn so please don't interrupt."

Maggie took a deep breath and explained again what had happened at the hotel. She left out the part about wanting to see Stan's laptop. There was no point in muddying the water. Frank had made that clear.

"Okay, Ron. You were there too," Frank said when she'd finished. "You're up next."

Ron drew a deep breath and glanced at his employer before speaking. "I walked into the room as Ms. Grady had picked the lock on the door and was walking in pretending to deliver pie—"

"There's nothing in the report about the lock being tampered with," Frank said, interrupting.

"I didn't really see what she did," Ron admitted. "She was standing there suspiciously. The door was locked the last time I'd checked it. She tried to convince me that Mr. and Mrs. Isleb had sent her to the hotel with pies. I knew something was wrong. They don't indulge in sweets very often and then only the first quality."

"Watch it," Maggie warned. "Our pies are as good as anyone's. Better than most."

Ron ignored her. "I knew something wasn't right. I went along to see what game she was playing. As I went to get money for her from the petty cash reserve, she dropped both pies on the floor, snatched the laptop, and ran out of the room. She left me to clean up chocolate cream pie from the carpet."

"Do you know who owns that laptop, sir?" Frank asked him.

Ron looked at Stan again. "The bank, I suppose."

"You brought it with you from New York?"

"No, sir. We—I—uh, appropriated it. I, uh, saw Ms. Grady with it at the pie shop and knew it didn't belong to her. It's standard issue from the bank to its employees. She was stripped of all bank-related paraphernalia and shouldn't have had it. She signed a waiver so the bank wouldn't prosecute her."

"You broke into her aunt's home, at your employer's behest, and took it?" Frank stared at him calmly. "Is that right?"

Stan abruptly sat forward in his chair, as though he couldn't stand anymore. "If I may explain—"

"Okay. Let's say it's your turn, Mr. Isleb. Explain how you came to have this laptop in your possession."

"The laptop is issued by the bank for its employees." He glared at Maggie. "When an employee is dismissed, especially under circumstances like Ms. Grady's, the bank takes the laptop back. Ms. Grady understood that she was to keep no bank property upon her dismissal. Because of this, we could change our minds at this point and decide to prosecute her for theft."

The veins in his temple and neck were standing out and his face got very red. Maggie was worried Stan was going to have a stroke before she could accuse him of killing Lou.

Frank nodded. "How could Ron here look at this laptop from the outside and tell anything about it?" He turned the laptop over. "It looks like any other black laptop of this brand to me."

Ron swallowed hard. "It's of the same brand and type issued by the bank. I knew it immediately."

"Except this one is mine," Maggie argued. "I have the receipt for it. It never belonged to the bank. You broke into my home to get it. You didn't say anything at the pie shop to me about it—if you were *really* there."

Everyone looked at Stan. He cleared his throat and looked annoyed that he was being forced to defend himself. "We believed it belonged to the bank, Detective Waters. We have a great deal of trouble with former employees using their laptops to hack into bank files. That's why we retrieve the laptops from our employees, especially those who have been terminated."

"Has Ms. Grady done anything of that nature with this laptop?" Frank asked.

"We haven't been able to verify that as yet," Stan said. "The laptop will have to go back to the bank and be checked by our IT experts."

"That's not happening right now, sir." Frank put the laptop on a side table and added a large red evidence sticker to it. "This laptop is now part of an investigation into a breaking and entering at Mrs. Clara Lowder's home. It can't be released to anyone until the case is closed."

Stan's mouth tightened. "I believe there has been some misconduct on Ron's part. He was a little overzealous about procuring the laptop."

"Good. Now we're getting somewhere," Frank said. "So Ron will admit to breaking into Mrs. Lowder's home and stealing the laptop?"

Unhappily, Ron looked at his employer and nodded. "I was only doing what I thought was right for the bank."

Frank nodded at Maggie. "Your turn. You admit to stealing the laptop from the Islebs' hotel room?"

"What? No. I didn't steal it." She was shocked that Frank would ask her that after Ron's confession.

Frank glanced at Stan. "You want to press charges against Maggie?"

"Yes. I certainly do." Stan was defiant.

"Fine." Frank shrugged. "I'll put you both in jail right now."

That resulted in a loud argument with everyone denying any wrongdoing.

Frank whistled loudly between his teeth. When the room was quiet, he said, "Or you can both forget pressing charges against each other and we can settle this the easy way."

"How's that?" Maggie demanded.

"Let's take a look at the laptop," Frank suggested. "If it isn't bank property, it goes back to you, Maggie. You don't press charges against Ron. Stan doesn't press charges against you for taking back your property. Everyone goes home and I don't do any paperwork tonight."

They finally agreed after a whispered conversation between Stan and Ron and a thumbs-up from Ryan to Maggie.

Maggie and Frank stood beside Ron and Stan as Ryan turned on the laptop. Frank had designated Ryan for this task since he was an outsider.

A few moments passed as they all got to look at part of Maggie's personal journal and some pictures of good-looking male models in her email. Her face was hot and red when Ryan winked at her. She vowed never to keep personal information on a laptop again.

When it was over, Stan had to admit it wasn't bank property after all. He didn't even demand that Maggie go back home and get the receipt for it.

"The bank purchases better quality laptops than this one for their employees." Stan was dismissive as he walked around to the other side of the desk.

Maggie was relieved it was over. She agreed not to press

charges against Stan and Ron and close the case so she could have the laptop.

Stan agreed to forget that Maggie had taken the laptop from his hotel suite. He and Ron were ready to leave.

Frank got up. “Now that we have that settled, Mr. Isleb, maybe you could tell me why you were already in Durham before your brother-in-law died.”

# Nineteen

"Pardon?" Stan drew himself up proudly.

"You were already here before Lou Goldberg was killed. You didn't hop a plane and head down this way after you got the news. Isn't that right, sir?"

"I had business." Stan didn't deny the accusation.

"Was this business with someone who can give you an alibi for the time Mr. Goldberg was killed?"

"I don't know what time that was, Detective Waters. I assure you I was either with my wife or with Ron."

"Forgive me for wanting an alibi from either someone you aren't married to or someone you don't own. Got any other ideas? Our medical examiner figures the poison was administered at about eight a.m."

"Poison?" Stan glanced at Maggie. "I thought *she* was your suspect."

"No. She spoke with your brother-in-law hours after that. He was already dying. She was at the pie shop when he was poisoned."

"You think I had something to do with it?"

"Did you?" Frank asked.

"You'll have to ask my attorney, Detective Waters. That's all I'm saying on the subject. Ron, we're leaving. Good evening to you all."

After the door closed behind Ron and Stan, Frank shook his head. "I don't like that man."

"No one does," Maggie assured him. "Thanks for helping me get my laptop back."

He shook his pencil at her. "Don't ever do anything stupid like that again. I might not be able to bail you out next time."

"I won't," she promised. "What about Stan? What are you going to do about him?"

"The first thing I plan to do, since I'm already here, is to make you sit down right now and write out that list of people from the bank that you promised me. I don't know what they're doing in New York about the bank theft. We still have a homicide to solve."

Maggie sat down and wrote the names of everyone she could think of from the bank who could be involved in either the theft or Lou's death. Or both.

It wasn't a particularly long list. She didn't know many

people outside of her department. She didn't mention her flash drive. She didn't have it with her anyway. Besides, she felt sure Stan was the killer.

"Do I want to know how you found out Isleb was in Durham before Goldberg died?" Frank asked Ryan.

"You could find out yourself by checking his cell phone records," Ryan suggested.

"Not that you did any such thing, right?"

Ryan shrugged. "Where would I get that kind of information?"

Frank rolled his eyes. "Both of you get out of here. Let us figure the rest of this out, okay? Even though you're a reporter, Ryan, you don't have any business sticking your nose in this for a story. And you"—he pointed at Maggie—"need to worry about making pies. Is everyone clear on that?"

Ryan and Maggie both nodded solemnly. Both knew they would break their vows to Frank if it was necessary.

Maggie handed Frank her list of bank employees. "I'm sorry I can't be more helpful. I didn't work inside the bank a lot. These are people I knew and people I remember Lou mentioning. I think we both know that the only name we need is Stan's."

"I think we need more evidence before we can say that. And by we, I mean *me*. This has nothing to do with you anymore, Maggie. We'll find out what we need to know about Stan."

"I'm sure you will," she agreed.

Frank looked at the names. "What do you think Isleb was looking for on your laptop?"

She shrugged. "I don't know. Even if it had been the laptop I got from the bank, I can't imagine what he thought he'd find."

Ryan added. "We both thought Stan wanted to know what Maggie knew about Lou's death."

"There isn't anything like that on the laptop," Maggie assured Frank, hoping he wouldn't want it back again.

"Maybe it was that strong sense of duty Ron confessed to," Frank said. "Something about it doesn't smell right to me. I guess I'll have to chase Mr. Isleb down and ask him that question."

Ryan shook Frank's hand before they left. "Thanks for all your help."

Frank glared at him. "I'm not helping you. This is my job. Stay out of trouble. Next time, I'll lock you both up if you get in my business."

Maggie and Ryan didn't argue. They walked out of the almost-empty police station and got into his Honda.

"Now what?" she asked. "That was kind of a letdown as far as solutions go. I was hoping Stan would confess and that would be it. My name would be clear."

"Now we let Frank do his job." Ryan started the car. "Your name is clear as far as the murder is concerned and mostly clear about the embezzlement."

"What if Stan leaves before Frank can figure out he's the killer?"

"Then they'll track him back to New York," Ryan said. "I don't think there's anything else we can do at this point without making Frank really angry. I wouldn't want to do that for several reasons."

Maggie wasn't as convinced, but she was out of brilliant ideas for the moment.

Realizing they were both starved since they'd skipped dinner, they made a quick stop at the McDonald's drive-through. Hamburgers, shakes, and fries had never tasted so good as they did in the parking lot that night.

They drove through the late-night traffic to Aunt Clara's house after they were finished, both silent as they went through what had happened in their minds.

When they reached the house, Ryan turned off the car and faced her. "He's bound to slip up somewhere. Maybe there'll be something on Lou's laptop that the NYPD is going through right now. I think we're getting close. And what a story!"

Maggie opened the door and got out. She was a little annoyed that Ryan thought of the things happening in her life as stories. She supposed he was hardwired that way. It was his job, after all.

Ryan kissed her good night at the front door and she went inside, deciding not to say anything about it.

After making sure both doors were locked, Maggie went to bed. She couldn't believe her aunt had gone to bed with both doors unlocked. Obviously, she wasn't as affected by people breaking into the house as Maggie was.

Maggie stared at the dark ceiling for a long time, going over everything in her mind.

It bothered her that Lou had probably been killed because he'd wanted to make what had happened to her right. Didn't she owe him something for that effort?

She was still convinced finding the killer might also mean finding the thief. That was what she really wanted—to clear that part of her life too.

There had to be a way.

• • •

The next morning a steady, hard rain pummeled the city. Maggie's head felt like it was stuffed with cotton. The sooner she and Aunt Clara got to the pie shop and got the coffee going, the better.

The large pile of her mother's dressier clothes was gone from the foot of the bed. She hadn't even noticed the night before. In its place was a small wooden box painted with flowers.

Maggie got dressed in her usual jeans and T-shirt. She brushed her teeth, combed her hair, and washed her face. Then she sat down and looked in the little box.

The box was filled with recipes for all kinds of foods, from pie fillings and crusts to meat and potatoes. Each card was carefully filled out in a neat, flowery script that was easy to read.

"Your mother's recipe box." Aunt Clara came to check on her. "I found it under that pile of clothes I took to the cleaners last night. I didn't even realize we had that."

Maggie hugged her. "I didn't want you to pay to have the clothes cleaned. Thanks."

"I didn't." She handed Maggie a check and a piece of paper. "You've worked very hard the last six weeks and haven't even asked for a paycheck. I'm not a slave driver, you know. This is for your time."

Maggie looked at it in surprise. "You're supporting me with food and a place to stay. You bought my laptop and my phone and pretty much everything else since I got back."

"You'll find the paper I gave you is an itemized list of money you've spent. We'll work out a payment plan, eventually. In the meantime, a girl has to have some money in her pocket. Now, let's get going. Rainy cold mornings are good for coffee and pie. We'll be busy today."

They each had a slice of toast with peanut butter for breakfast then set out for the pie shop, Maggie holding a big black umbrella over them both as they walked.

The streets and sidewalks were drenched with the rain that had fallen all night. Puddles splashed up as cars went slowly by them on their way to work and school. A brisk wind made sure the umbrella didn't keep them completely dry.

Once they were at Pie in the Sky, Maggie tried to be more careful with her piecrust. It wasn't easy. She watched Aunt Clara's patient, gentle hands as they worked the crust lightly yet got the job done. Her fingers didn't seem to want to do what she was asking of them.

She thought about her mother's recipe box—the recipe for coconut cream pie in particular. It was the pie Aunt Clara never made, never ate, because no one could make it like her sister.

Maggie contemplated what seemed like the impossible. She wanted to make that pie for her aunt. She wanted to show her how much she meant to her. She realized if she botched it, it might be worse than not making it at all.

She felt a little presumptuous even contemplating the task. If Aunt Clara felt like no one, including her, could make the coconut cream pie as well as her sister had, what were Maggie's chances?

She wasn't sure. It seemed like the right thing to do. She supposed that was going to be the mantra for her new life. She'd have to try and make sure she didn't overwork the crust.

She and Aunt Clara made a dozen crusts for the pie of the day, Pumpkin Pizzazz. Aunt Clara had decided they were close enough to the holidays to get people interested in the spicy pumpkin flavor.

Maggie fluted the crusts, pleased with the results. As soon as her aunt began to fill the empty shells, she went out to start the coffee and get the shop ready to open. That included setting up the cash register, something Aunt Clara had stopped doing once she saw Maggie could handle it.

After working for the bank, Maggie couldn't imagine allowing someone else to take over her finances. It was a personal choice for her. Aunt Clara must not have felt that way in her youth, since Uncle Fred had handled everything financial.

The shop was half an hour from opening as Maggie looked out at the gray streets in the misty morning light. She was drinking her second cup of coffee, pondering how much it would cost to put in an espresso machine. She could have really used a triple-shot latte that morning. She'd have to talk to Mr. Gino about it.

Only this time, she'd haggle over the price. Aunt Clara wasn't much for haggling.

The refrigerator they'd bought from Mr. Gino's nephew was too expensive—she'd looked it up online. Still, they were paying for convenience, she had to admit, and same-day service. She had to figure that into the cost too. Maybe it wasn't so bad. She was going to have to get much smarter about the restaurant business.

The world was waking up and she felt like she was waking up too, for the first time in a long while.

Before the first customer came in and the day got crazy, Maggie emailed Claudia Liggette and told her she wouldn't be taking the plum job she had offered.

She thanked her longtime friend and promised to call soon. Then she sat down and thought about what she'd done and what her future would be as partner in the pie shop.

But not for long.

There was a faint rap at the front glass door. Maggie looked out. It was Jane Isleb. She looked like she'd been out in the rain all night without an umbrella. Her brown hair was plastered to her head and her face was pale. Her clothes and shoes were dripping with moisture, probably ruined.

Maggie hurried to open the glass door and let the other woman in the shop. She wondered if Jane and Stan had a fight, or if something even worse had happened.

"Are you okay? Can I get you some coffee?"

"Thank you." Jane's response was a ragged whisper. Her shoes squelched as she walked across the tile floor and carefully sat down.

Maggie got her a cup of coffee and wished she had a towel to offer. She even tried not to mind that a large puddle of water was forming that would have to be mopped up before they opened. She offered Jane something to eat, but she didn't want anything.

Aunt Clara looked out of the window between the kitchen and the shop. Maggie shrugged at the question in her sharp, green eyes.

"I suppose you've already heard the news." Jane took an unsteady sip of coffee.

"We've been kind of busy setting up," Maggie replied. "What's happened?"

"Stan has been arrested." Jane let out a long sigh that seemed to come from deep inside her. She shook her head and pushed the coffee cup handle away from her. "It happened early this morning. Right after midnight. The police came to the hotel for him. It was horrible."

"What?" Maggie was surprised to hear that and wondered if they'd arrested him for the theft or the murder. She hoped it was both. "How did it happen?"

"It was the police in New York, apparently. They broke into Lou's computer at the bank. That information led them to Stan. He's being accused of stealing millions."

Unconsciously, Maggie let out a sigh of relief. She couldn't help it. This news meant her name would be cleared for everyone to see, with Lou's help and his sacrifice.

She'd always wonder if he'd known the truth when he'd fired her. Had he felt guilty? Was that why he couldn't leave it alone?

It had cost him his life to prove it to the world. No matter how it had come about, Maggie couldn't help but feel grateful to Lou for what he'd done.

Jane smiled in a forlorn way. "That's right. You're off the hook. At least for embezzlement. There will probably be a nice settlement coming your way from the bank. Don't take the first amount they offer you. They're bound to do better with the second one. Remember, you're the wronged party here. Don't let them cheat you."

"Thanks. I'm so sorry about Stan." Maggie tried to think of a nice way to ask if Stan had also killed Lou as he tried to cover his tracks.

She looked at Jane's face and couldn't say the words. As much as Maggie had lost, Jane had lost so much more. Even if Stan didn't kill Lou, her brother was dead and her husband was going to prison.

That didn't stop Aunt Clara, who'd wandered out of the kitchen. "Do the police think Stan killed Lou?"

Maggie wouldn't have thought it was possible for Jane's face to become a worse shade of gray—it did. It was hard to say if she was crying or if it was still the rain streaming down her cheeks.

"I don't know. Surely not. They were family. We were family before all of this. Even with knowing what Lou meant to do—"

"Stan knew that Lou was going to expose him?" Maggie asked with a gasp.

Jane nodded. "Lou called him. He called me too. I tried to reason with him that morning. But you know Lou. He was like a bulldog. Nothing I said made any difference. He was determined to do whatever he had to do to clear your name, Maggie. That's why I was so sure the two of you were romantically involved. He was willing to ruin his life, other people's lives too. I never realized my brother had such an overdeveloped conscience."

"At least he tried to do what was right, bless his soul,"

Aunt Clara said before going back into the kitchen as the oven timer chimed.

Maggie had left the front door open and two customers came in, almost as soaked as Jane. She went to take their orders and when she looked back, Jane was gone. After getting pie and coffee for the men who'd come in, she sat down behind the counter.

For the first time since she got back, she felt like she could take a deep breath. She wanted to stand back and think about her future. She wanted to cry and scream in her relief. She didn't have that luxury, though, as more customers came in out of the rain. She felt as if her old life was over and something new was finally beginning.

Ryan came in about twenty minutes later with the news of Stan's arrest. He bemoaned his fate that the newspaper wouldn't be out for another week. "That will make Stan's arrest old news, I'm afraid. I'll have to come up with something fresh for my readers."

Maggie poured him a cup of coffee. "Maybe you'll get lucky and they'll announce that Stan killed Lou in time for the next edition."

Ryan was immediately contrite. "Sorry. I can't help it. It's what I do."

"I know. I probably wouldn't mind as much if it didn't involve me. Seriously, do you think they'll be able to put the two together?"

"Frank doesn't expect that. They thought so to begin with because of Stan's ties with a company in this area that makes arsenic pentoxide. It looked good to begin with."

"Then?"

"They couldn't find any trace of the arsenic on him, in the hotel, or in his car. Also, Stan has an alibi for that eight a.m. time frame when Lou was poisoned. He was out jogging with some other bank president."

"And that's that." Maggie nodded. It still wasn't over.

"Maybe not. Frank said he plans to seriously question Ron since he loved the bank enough to steal your laptop."

"That would be a whole new level of dedication," Maggie agreed.

"Frank said the police task force in New York thought this wasn't the first time Stan has taken money from the bank. He'd been experiencing losses in his stock portfolio for the last five years. They think he might have stolen more than fifty million dollars and blamed it on other people." Ryan smiled at her. "People like you."

She nodded, almost too choked up to speak. "I know. Jane said to expect the bank to compensate me. She said not to take the first offer."

"Sounds like good advice," he said. "Have you made a decision yet on that job opportunity?"

"I'm not going to take it. I'm not leaving Aunt Clara again."

"You're sure?" He took her hand. "You're staying?"

The door chimed and Clara called out that there was a customer coming in.

"I'll be right back," she said.

It was Albert Mann with Mark Beck right behind him. They didn't sit down. They stood in the middle of the shop, looking around.

*The king surveying the peasants,* Maggie thought.

He still made her nervous even though she realized it was unfounded. She'd never been more careful with anything in her life than she was with her aunt's finances in this matter. There was nothing he could do to them. Now that she wasn't leaving Durham, he'd have to deal with her too. Aunt Clara wasn't alone anymore.

"Can I get something for you?" Her tone was a lot less friendly than it would have been if he had been anyone else.

"We're not here for coffee and sweets." He waved her away with his cane. "I want to speak to Clara. This is the last opportunity she's going to have."

# Twenty

"She's busy," Maggie said. "You'll have to make an appointment."

She certainly wasn't going to bother her aunt for one of Mann's many threats.

He snarled at her. "Get her out here now, young woman. I'm tired of your attitude."

All the talk that had been going on in the pie shop slowly died away. That made Mann's words seem unnaturally loud in the quiet that was left behind.

"I also think your aunt should question *your* intentions." He continued raging at Maggie. "You're going to leave again now that you've been cleared of stealing from the bank. Have you told her? Are you planning to leave a helpless old woman alone again to fend for herself?"

No one said anything. Maggie simmered. She was torn between not making the situation any worse in front of their customers and cutting Albert Mann down to size.

Aunt Clara wandered out of the kitchen into that uncomfortable silence. She was wiping her hands on a clean towel. Her blue-and-white-checkered apron was covered with flour. There was even a white smudge on her cheek. She pushed a stray lock of her hair from her face and got down to business.

"If you're not here for pie, Albert, you should leave," Aunt Clara told him. "We don't have time to sit down and talk with you about your crazy schemes. Shouting at my niece, who by the way is now my legal partner, won't change anything. We're not selling the shop to you and that's that."

He took off his fedora and nodded to her, his demeanor changing completely as he faced her. "I think you should know that your niece is indeed leaving you again, Clara. No matter what she's told you. A friend of mine in New York got a résumé from her. Now that she has been exonerated of wrongdoing in the bank theft, she won't think twice about leaving you alone again. I want to give you one last chance to sell this place before the deal is off the table."

Aunt Clara didn't even glance at Maggie for confirmation of his words. "This is our place, Albert. I don't care what you found out. It's not for sale. Now go away. I'm very busy."

He frowned. "You know, I promised Fred I'd look out for you before he passed. I'm only making good on that promise. He wouldn't want you to lose the shop because you forgot to pay your taxes, would he?"

Aunt Clara's mouth was set in a tight line in her pretty face. "Don't try to bamboozle me, Albert. You promised Fred no such thing. It does you an injustice to be standing here saying this in front of all these people. Find someplace else for your building. Maybe you can have this property when I die and Maggie sells it to you."

"Very well." He drew himself up proudly and put his hat back on. "You leave me no choice. Don't expect me to change my mind when your niece is gone and you're alone, Clara. I wash my hands of you."

He turned sharply, almost colliding with Mark. They stormed out of the pie shop together—a little like the Batman and Robin of the development market. A thunderous applause followed him as everyone there congratulated Aunt Clara on her victory.

Her face pink with embarrassment—and a little pride—Aunt Clara went back to the kitchen.

Maggie followed her there. She understood how Albert Mann knew about her innocence in stealing from the bank. How did he know she was sending out her résumé? The man obviously had friends in low places, one of them being Claudia. It made her wonder if the job was actually legitimate or a hoax to get her to leave.

Either way, she was glad she hadn't fallen for it.

"I'm sorry about that." Maggie hugged her aunt. "You know I'm not leaving."

"I know. I hope you aren't sorry. I hope you don't lose your dreams."

"I'm going to find them right here. I love you, Aunt Clara. We have to stick together. I have to be able to tell the secret piecrust recipe to another generation, right? It's all going to work out."

Clara smiled through her tears. "All I've ever wanted was for you to be happy, honey. If you can be happy here, I'm thrilled."

They were still hugging each other when Ryan ventured into the kitchen. "I poured some coffee for a customer up front and spilled some on the floor. Sorry. I was trying to help. I thought you two could use some time alone together. I'll mop it up."

Maggie smiled and wiped away her tears. "That's okay. I'll get it."

After the coffee spill was contained, Maggie checked with her customers for refills, then sat behind the counter with Ryan again.

"You know, I was so sure that when we found the person who took the money, we'd find the killer," she said. "I feel kind of let down. Who killed Lou if Stan didn't?"

"Maybe Ron." Ryan shrugged. "I don't know. Frank will find out. He's done a good job so far."

"I guess you're right."

"So, if you're planning to stay in Durham, does that mean we can keep seeing each other?"

"I hope so." She smiled at him. "I'd like that."

He kissed her quickly. A customer had come up to pay her bill at the counter. She giggled when she saw them.

Maggie took the student's money and rang up the next customer. Ryan had to leave. There was a special city meeting he had to attend.

That left Maggie cleaning tables and wondering how much money the bank would give her for compensation. She hoped it would be enough to do some renovations to the pie shop and the house—and maybe buy an espresso machine.

She couldn't help but think about Lou again as she cleaned the table where they'd sat on the day he had died. He'd known he could be in danger. He'd even said they would both be safe after the press conference.

Someone had already taken that safety from him. He hadn't known it yet when they were together. She wished there would've been some way to save him.

Aunt Clara's prediction about the pie shop being busy all day because of the rain turned out to be accurate. At lunchtime, they had to make twelve more Pumpkin Pizzazz pies. They ran out of whipped cream and Maggie offered to walk down to the grocery store and get some. Mr. Gino was a good supplier, but his price for extra deliveries could be quite high.

"I'll pick up something special for lunch while I'm down that way," Maggie volunteered. "I'm craving Italian and there's that little restaurant next door to the grocery store. How does that sound to you?"

"That sounds fine." She gave Maggie her bank card. "I should've given you cash for your salary. You don't even have a bank account."

"That's okay. I'll open one. There's that bank kiosk next to the newspaper office. I'll have to go to a branch and open the account—that should be a convenient location in the future."

Aunt Clara laughed. "Especially since you'll be spending a lot of time at the newspaper office."

"Maybe. Ryan is here a lot too. And what about you and Garrett? How's that working out?"

"I don't know yet. He's a very stubborn man." Aunt Clara leaned against the cabinet and winked her eye. "I may have met a new gentleman at the library. Only time will tell."

Maggie was thrilled that her aunt had taken her advice about dating. She wanted her to be happy.

Saying she'd be back as soon as she could, Maggie started toward the grocery store a few blocks away, a smile on her face as she walked. Everything seemed so right. She knew what she was doing, and had plans for the future again. Life was good.

When she reached the intersection, the pedestrian crossing was displaying the Do Not Walk sign. Since there were no cars coming from the side street, and traffic was slow on the main road, she stepped into the road and started across.

An approaching car revved its engine loudly and she looked down the street, surprised as it raced toward her.

She moved quickly across the street, but the car followed her—and she realized that it was deliberately coming right at her!

Panicking, she ran for the sidewalk as fast as she could. The pavement was badly broken at that spot and dipped down, giving Maggie the precious few seconds extra that she needed.

Spotting a narrow passage between a small building and a large metal fence, she jumped into the space and ran through it, losing her footing and falling to the ground as the car bumped up over the curb.

The car rammed the entrance to the space a second later, unable to fit inside it. After gunning the engine uselessly a few times, the driver finally backed out and raced away.

Her teeth chattering with shock and fear, Maggie couldn't move. She'd skinned her knees and torn her jeans; her palms and the side of her face were cut too.

Someone had deliberately tried to run her down!

Realizing that, she forced herself to move. She was terrified to leave the temporary shelter she'd found, but what if the driver returned?

What if the person came back without the car?

She wasn't safe here.

Holding her cell phone under one of the eaves from the old store to keep it dry, she dialed Ryan's number. There was no answer. Of course, he had his phone off during the meeting.

Maggie still had Frank's phone number in her pocket. She prayed that he'd answer.

"Detective Frank Waters."

"Frank. It's Maggie. I've had an accident. Well, I don't really think it was an accident. I think someone just tried to kill me. Ryan's at a meeting. Could you send someone?"

"Have you tried 911?"

"No. Sorry. I didn't think of that."

He grunted. "Sit tight. I'll be right there."

A few minutes later, Frank was getting out of his car. "What the hell happened here, Maggie? You should've told me this was a hit-and-run." He took out his phone to call an ambulance. "People need to learn the codes."

"Sorry." Her teeth were chattering almost too much to speak. "I didn't know what to call it. It was crazy. I tried to get away. The car kept following me."

"Never mind," he growled, offering her a hand up. "Did you see where the car went or the license plate?"

"No. Sorry. I was too scared."

The paramedics arrived a few minutes later, along with another police car.

They bandaged her knees, hands, and head while she explained what had happened to Frank and the uniformed officers. She refused to be transported to the hospital.

"I'm fine. Just a little banged up. Thank you anyway." She signed the form they gave her agreeing that she had refused the trip.

Maggie sat with Frank in his car as he filled out paperwork about the incident. He'd sent the other police car away. A crime scene van had taken its place. Workers were taking paint samples from the fence and the side of the old store, hoping to figure out what the car looked like that had tried to run her down.

"I know you said the car was a dark color," Frank said. "You think it's a late model. Not sure on the make. How about the driver?"

Maggie thought back to the frightening experience. "I don't know. I couldn't see who was driving, even though they were close to me."

"Probably tinted windows. It makes it hard to see inside. Anything else you might have noticed?"

"No. I guess I was too scared. First I was surprised when I realized it was coming after me. I wasn't sure what to do."

He wrote down what she'd said. "Any ideas on who might want to kill you?"

"Maybe Albert Mann or Mark Beck. Mark is as devoted to Mann as Ron is to Stan." She told him about their visit to the pie shop that morning. "Although that wasn't Mann's car."

"It would be doubtful that someone like Mann would do it himself anyway," Frank said. "I'll see what I can find out. I hate to say it, but it might've been some crazy who's been following your story in the paper too. People get odd ideas about what they see and read."

"That's a scary thought."

"Tell me about it." He finished his notes. "Let me give you a ride back to Pie in the Sky."

"I have to go to the grocery store for whipped cream and I promised Aunt Clara Italian food for lunch."

He rolled his eyes. "I'll take you. My wife hates when I eat Italian for lunch. She says I get too full. She wants me to eat salad or something. She's home now, you know. She might be the next one trying to run you down."

Frank was a little more cheerful as a chauffeur, especially with Italian food involved, compared to when he was being official. Maggie was amazed that he was willing to help her out this way.

As soon as Aunt Clara saw Maggie's scratched and bruised face, she ran out of the kitchen. "What in the world happened? Are you all right?"

They went back in the kitchen to talk—Maggie thought their customers had seen and heard enough drama for one day.

Frank stayed and ate lunch with them, meatball subs. He asked Aunt Clara if she wanted to have a restraining order posted for Albert Mann so he'd have to stay away from her, the business, and the house.

Aunt Clara laughed at that. "Imagine going to court to keep that old so-and-so in his place. When I can't defend myself against men like him, it's time for me to retire."

Frank shrugged as he finished his sub—no salad. "Okay. Just offering. If you change your mind, let me know."

"I hope you'll speak to him about this other incident." She nodded at Maggie. "It's wrong for people not to be able to cross the street safely in this town."

"Yes, ma'am. I'll check into it. If I know Albert Mann though, he'll have an alibi."

"Are you saying it's not safe for me to go out?" Maggie asked.

"I don't know," he admitted. "Just be careful."

Aunt Clara made a *humph* sound. "It seems to me that if Albert really wanted to accomplish something, he'd try to run over both of us tonight on the way home. What good would it do to just run over Maggie?"

# Twenty-one

Frank had offered to have a police officer take Maggie and Aunt Clara home that night.

Ryan called before they were ready to leave and offered to drive them home, upset when he heard her story.

"It's hard to believe Mann would be this stupid. He knows people saw him at the pie shop. This isn't how he works, according to what I've read about him. He's more subtle—more like a spider than a raging bull. I don't think he'd put himself in that position."

"The police already have Stan in custody," Maggie said. "He couldn't have been there."

Aunt Clara went out with friends that evening, leaving Ryan and Maggie at the house alone. He had a pizza delivered while she worked on creating a perfect coconut cream pie for her aunt.

Maggie had changed clothes and was wearing a pretty spring-green wool dress, one of the new ones she'd found in the attic. It was lightweight and dropped a little below her injured knee so the bandage didn't show.

The smile on Ryan's face when she came downstairs told her it was a good choice.

"You look great! I'm sorry we're not going out so I could show you off."

"Thanks." She smiled and kissed him. "It's nice to wear something besides jeans for a change."

The coconut cream pie—she was thinking of naming it Coconut Charisma Cream pie—was giving her a hard time. It wasn't the crust. The filling was too loose on the first one and too hard on the second.

Then she ran out of milk. She didn't want to send Ryan out in the rain for more, though he offered to go. She'd have to try again later.

Instead they sat together talking and listening to music after cleaning up the mess in the kitchen.

"I don't understand why anyone would attack you," Ryan said. "Unless Mann has upped his game. You should be out of the picture for what happened with Lou."

Maggie had been thinking the same thing. She hadn't wanted to bring it up. So much of their time together involved talking about Lou's death. She wanted to talk about

Ryan and what he'd been like growing up, what he was interested in, besides the paper.

She shrugged. "I know. It doesn't make any sense. There doesn't seem to be any explanation for it."

"You must know something about the killer," he said.

She started to protest.

"Hear me out, Maggie. I know you don't know what you know." He smiled at his words. "It could be something that could reveal whoever killed Lou. Eventually it'll come to you."

"Then I guess the killer is safe. The only thing I know about Lou's killer is that it isn't me. That's not much."

Ryan hugged her. "We'll figure it out. It's only a matter of time. Sometimes you hear or see things that don't register as being important. When you do—bam!—it hits like an earthquake. It happens to me all the time after interviews."

Maggie didn't really care at that moment if the truth hit or not. She was happy where she was, about to have her name cleared of any hint of embezzlement. It didn't hurt that having Ryan close was nice too.

Aunt Clara made it home finally around nine. Ryan left soon after.

Maggie made hot chocolate for them, needing to use packets of hot chocolate mix. Aunt Clara commented on their surprising lack of milk.

"I used a little for dinner. I guess we were almost out," Maggie said. She didn't want Aunt Clara to guess her secret yet. She felt bad not being honest with her about the milk.

"I must be more absentminded than I thought." Aunt

Clara sipped her hot chocolate as Maggie volunteered to pick up more milk tomorrow.

"How was the evening with Ryan?"

"Great. Every time I see him, I like him more. I wish we could move past Lou's death and all the other problems that brought us together."

Aunt Clara yawned. "I'm sorry. That was no reflection on our conversation. I'm tired. I'm sure you'll get past all this other nonsense. Many times, unusual circumstances bring people together. It's what's left behind that counts. I'm going to bed. I'll see you in the morning, honey."

• • •

The next morning, Maggie went to open a bank account and pick up her dry cleaning after making plenty of coffee and Blue Devil pies at Pie in the Sky. Bountiful Blueberry always had a name change on Fridays when there was a home game, in honor of the team.

She kept a watchful eye on the road and cars around her. Her trip was accomplished with no mishaps this time. She gave a grateful sigh of relief when she was back at the pie shop again. She couldn't be afraid to go out. What kind of life would that be?

There were only two customers when she got back. She let Aunt Clara know she was back and refilled coffee cups. Everything felt as it should.

Aunt Clara had taken an order for three Pumpkin Pizzazz pies while she was gone and they had to make four more Blue Devil pies.

A short, thin man, who looked young enough to be a

serious-faced teenager, came in around 10:00 a.m. He gave Maggie his business card and asked if she could sit down for a minute.

"The bank sent me with their most sincere apologies for the mix-up regarding your termination," Brad Andrews told her. "I have some paperwork for you to sign and a check that should cover your severance plus some. You'll have to agree not to pursue this any further and not to hold the bank in any way responsible for what happened."

Maggie looked at the check he slid toward her across the table. Her eyes lit up. This was great. The things she could do with this money.

She had a few doubts. She could certainly sue the bank for wrongful termination and defamation of character. She'd thought about that.

On the other hand, lawsuits had a way of hanging around forever.

She wanted this out of the way—not hanging around her neck anymore. The money was fair, even good, if she didn't think too much about what she'd gone through.

Despite Jane's urging that she hold out for a better offer, she signed the documents and took the check. Now that she was leading a more modest lifestyle, the money would go much further. She might even buy a car for her and Aunt Clara. To her knowledge, her aunt had never owned a car.

Brad Andrews thanked her and put the documents she'd signed into his briefcase. He shook her hand and walked out of the pie shop.

It was the end of that life that had meant so much to

her. Not the end she'd expected, but a better one. Maggie had a feeling her life was taking a good turn.

Frank came in shortly after Brad had left and ordered a piece of Blue Devil pie, waiting patiently until Maggie could talk.

"You're looking better today," he said with his terse smile. "No lasting side effects from almost being run over, I take it?"

"No. I was lucky, I guess. Anyone come in and confess to trying to run down a pie shop waitress?"

"No. Sorry. We're still working on it. I can tell you that we've completely ruled out Stan Isleb as Mr. Goldberg's killer. His alibi held up. He'll probably go away to one of those fancy Club Med prisons up north for embezzlement. He won't be working for another bank in his lifetime."

"No clues about Lou's killer?"

"We're checking out his assistant. I personally don't think the boy has it in him. It's one thing to lie or even steal for your employer and another to kill for him. I don't think Ron did it."

"So we may never know who did it." Maggie glanced around at her customers. They all seemed to be doing fine. "The killer could be back in New York by now."

"Could be. Or it could be that's what that hit-and-run was about. You could still be a loose end, Maggie. He could be waiting to get rid of you before he leaves town. Is there anything else, anyone else, you might have missed telling me about?"

She shook her head. "I don't think so. Ryan and I talked about this last night. If I know who the killer is, his secret is safe with me. I keep drawing a blank every time I think about it."

Frank stood up and put some money on the table for his pie and coffee. "I assigned someone yesterday to keep an eye on you for the next day or two. Sorry. That's all I can afford. Maybe we'll get lucky and the killer will come after you right away."

"I don't think that sounds like luck. Thanks for thinking about me anyway."

"All part of the service, ma'am."

Maggie watched him leave, hoping he was wrong about anyone trying to kill her. It wasn't part of her perfect new world.

She wanted to put Lou's death, and everything else that had recently happened, behind her. She needed a new, fresh start.

Life was suddenly very sweet. She had Aunt Clara back in her life. She had Ryan, and a big check to spend on the house and the pie shop. The tide had turned in her favor. She didn't like that the person who'd killed Lou was still out there, but she didn't see what else she could do to change that. She hoped the police would find his killer.

Study groups of students trickled in between 4:00 and 6:00 p.m. Even Maggie's rude student showed up again. This time he was in a better mood. It probably had something to do with the pretty dark-haired girl who was with him. No doubt she was part of his improvement.

Angela Hightower came in and walked directly to the counter. "Hi, Maggie. I ordered the pumpkin pies to go. I guess Clara calls them Pumpkin Pizzazz. We've had a few nice sales at the office this week and I thought I'd have a little celebration with my associates."

"Sounds like a good idea." Maggie smiled as she totaled up what Angela owed.

Angela was chatty, as usual. "I heard Mann Development is looking at another piece of property for the medical office building. It won't be as good as this one. Bad luck for Clara."

"Not really," Maggie said. "Aunt Clara wants to keep the shop. She doesn't want to sell. Albert Mann was wasting his time."

"Everyone is willing to sell for the right price, honey." Angela handed Maggie her card to pay for the pies. "Albert didn't offer her the price she was looking for. If he had, it would've been a different story."

"I don't think that's true in this case," Maggie said, handing her card back with a receipt for her to sign.

"It's always been true in my years of experience." Angela signed the receipt and smiled. "I'm not saying it's always money. There are other things people want. To close a tough sale, you have to figure out what that is."

Angela sounded a little ruthless. She was pleasant enough to be a good customer. Maggie knew she didn't want to see her other side.

She smiled and gave up trying to convince Angela that Aunt Clara didn't want to sell the pie shop. There was only so much she could say and a line was beginning to form behind her.

Officer Jack Harding came in and identified himself. He was a slightly older, rounder version of Frank, dressed in uniform. He pulled at his cap. "I've been assigned to keep you safe, Ms. Grady. Please don't make that job any harder by trying to go off by yourself, okay? I'll be right out front when you're ready to go home. Any errands you have to run, we'll run them together."

He talked her into riding home in the police car with Aunt Clara. Every time Maggie looked out the front window, she saw the cruiser conspicuously parked there.

It made her wonder if she'd done the right thing calling Frank for help after the hit-and-run. True, she was scared at the time and didn't know who else to call. Maybe it was a little overboard.

Looking back on it, she felt sure she was a victim of misplaced road rage. She probably made someone angry when she was crossing the street. People did crazy things when they were driving and other people got in their way. It probably wasn't an attempt on her life at all.

It had been easy to fall in with Frank's suggestion that someone might have been trying to kill her because of everything that had been going on.

Maggie forced herself to relax and waved to Officer Harding. She picked up coffee cups from the table. It would all blow over in a few days. Aunt Clara was excited about riding home in a police car. What harm could it do?

Ryan had texted a few times to check in and let her know what he was doing. He'd been tied up with meetings all day. He'd also asked her out for dinner.

Maggie had the perfect outfit in mind. She hummed as she thought about the turquoise sweater and tight black skirt. One thing about being depressed, even working at the pie shop, she'd managed to lose a few pounds. Ryan was going to be surprised when he came to pick her up.

She put out the Closed sign at six and started cleaning up. Forty-five minutes later, Aunt Clara said everything was in good shape and she was heading for the front door.

"Let me put the trash out back. I'll be right there," Maggie said.

"Hurry. I don't want to miss *Dancing with the Stars* tonight. I think they're going to vote Carmen and Angel off the show. I have to see that."

Maggie chuckled as she took the trash through the kitchen to the back door. She unlocked the door and pushed it open, wrestling the bags down the stairs to the trash bin.

It was darker than usual in the alley. One of the overhead lights had gone out. It was always something. No wonder Aunt Clara couldn't keep up with all of it. Maggie marked that down on her to-do list.

As she dropped the bags into the Dumpster, the heavy, metal back door slammed closed behind her. She looked up.

Someone was standing on the stairs.

Maggie thought it was her aunt. "I'm fine, Aunt Clara. And I'm hurrying. You didn't need to come out."

A husky voice answered, "Don't worry. I won't be here long."

It was Jane Isleb.

# Twenty-two

Maggie's heart beat a little faster. She looked around the dark alley. Except for Jane, she was alone back there. There was nothing but the Dumpsters.

"Hi, Jane. What are you doing here? We're closing up for the night."

Jane laughed in a way that made Maggie's stomach tighten. "Why do you think I'm here?"

Suddenly, Maggie understood. Jane had tried to run her down yesterday.

And she knew why.

Ryan had been right. So had Frank. Jane had given herself away when she'd talked to Maggie about Stan. She'd admitted to being with her brother that morning before Lou had come to visit the pie shop. No doubt that was when she'd fed him the poison.

"You don't have to do this," Maggie told her. "I haven't said anything to the police."

"So you realized what I'd told you? Did you recognize me yesterday when I screwed up trying to kill you? Why didn't you tell your cop friend?"

Maggie was trying to look around inconspicuously for anything she could use as a weapon. She had no doubt Jane was there to finish the job. In the meantime, Officer Harding and Aunt Clara were up front waiting for her.

Maybe if she could keep her talking a little longer her erstwhile protector would realize this was taking too long.

"I didn't say anything to Frank because I understand that you did what you had to do. Lou was about to tell the world that Stan had been taking money from the bank for years. You would've lost everything."

"My brother was such a fool," Jane said. "He would've done anything to clear your name. I think he was in love with you, no matter what you say."

"He was trying to do what was right."

"Well, he messed up my life doing it. Now Stan is going to prison and he'll never have anything again. I'm too old to start over. I'm sorry you were caught in the middle. I'm even more sorry I got carried away and told you something I shouldn't have. I want this to be over now, Maggie. I guess it is for you."

Maggie heard the distinctive click of a pistol. Jane wasn't taking any more chances. She darted behind the Dumpster and tried to keep her talking.

"Hiding back there won't help," Jane said.

"Look, Jane, if I was going to say something, I'd have done it by now, don't you think? I realize that you've been through a lot. So have I. Can't we move on from here and forget this ever happened? I'll keep your secret."

"You won't. I know you won't. Something will come up and you'll feel compelled to tell the truth. I don't want to kill you, Maggie. I like you. I loved Lou. We only had each other. I did what I had to do—not that it helped. Stan was stupid enough to get caught anyway. And now what? I can't think about where to go from here. My life is over. I probably should kill myself after I kill you."

"You know, Lou loved you too, Jane. He was always talking about you. He wanted what was best for you." Maggie didn't know if any of this was true. She was just stalling.

Lou had never mentioned his sister. That's why Maggie had been so surprised when Jane had introduced herself.

"I know. I suppose you think I'm a terrible person. I mean, who murders their own brother to keep up a standard of living? A very good standard—but still—he was my brother. It wasn't easy. Lou was soft. Once he found out you weren't really guilty of stealing that money, he wouldn't rest until he put it right. I begged him to leave it alone that morning. I didn't give him the poison until he made it clear he wouldn't back off, but I was ready for it."

That must've been as much a surprise to her as it was to Maggie that Lou wouldn't stop until the true embezzler was revealed. "We can work this out, Jane. I know we can. What can I say that will convince you?"

"There's only one thing left to say." Jane sounded like she was crying. "Good-bye."

Maggie knew Jane couldn't see her well in the dim light. She'd have to come down off the stairs to shoot her. As soon as Jane started down, Maggie planned to run around the front of the building. Her breath came fast, like she'd been running, and her heart was pounding.

The next instant the back door flew open, knocking into Jane. Light came from inside the pie shop.

"Maggie? What's going on back here? I thought you said you were going to hurry."

Maggie didn't waste another moment. She could see Jane's slender form on the ground where Aunt Clara had unwittingly pushed her off the stairs.

"Let's get inside." Maggie grabbed hold of Aunt Clara's hand as she shut the door tightly behind them and locked it.

She immediately went to the front of the shop and told Officer Harding what had happened. He called for backup then took out his pistol and walked around to the back of the building.

Maggie grabbed Uncle Fred's old baseball bat he'd always kept behind the register in case someone tried to rob him.

She tried to convince Aunt Clara to stay in the pie shop. Of course Aunt Clara insisted on going outside with her.

Maggie walked carefully around the building. She didn't need to bother. It was all over by the time she got there. Officer Harding was handcuffing Jane, who hadn't completely revived from her close encounter with the back door.

A few minutes later two other police officers and Frank had arrived. Ryan wasn't far behind them with his camera. He'd also brought a gun. He kept it hidden since the police seemed to have everything under control.

They took photos of everything—the police and Ryan. Maggie told two officers what had happened, as well as an assistant DA. She'd assured everyone that she was fine.

Aunt Clara was smart. After seeing that Maggie was all right, she had Officer Harding take her home. "There's nothing else I can do here."

Maggie agreed, hugging her. "I think you did plenty! You saved my life."

"No need to be dramatic," her aunt waved away the praise. "I'll see you at home."

Maggie also told Frank everything that had happened. "Jane was waiting for me. She was going to finish the job."

"You were lucky, like I said. She came right after you again. Maybe that doesn't seem like a good thing, but because of it Officer Harding was here to save the day. He might not have been if she'd waited too long."

"I'm glad Aunt Clara was here too," Maggie said. "If she hadn't come out at that moment, this story would have another ending."

Frank looked around. "Where is she, by the way? I'll need a statement from her too."

Maggie laughed. "I imagine she's home watching *Dancing with the Stars*. I hope her statement can wait until tomorrow."

"Sure. That's fine," he said. "*Your* statement can't, though. Let's go down to the station and you can tell us once more what happened and how it happened. This time I promise that someone will write it down."

Ryan drove them to the station after getting as much information as he could. "Aunt Clara must have really walloped her with that door. I never realized she was so dangerous."

"Only when you get between her and *Dancing with the Stars*. She loves that show."

He looked at her when they stopped for a red light. "You're okay, right? No bruises or bullet holes? I'm glad Jane was finally caught. Now you know what happened to Lou."

"Yes. His sister was afraid of losing everything and poisoned her only brother. How sad is that? If I had a brother, I can't imagine wanting my three homes, yacht, and country club more than him. I guess it takes all kinds."

"You know I want a full exclusive for the paper on this." Ryan smiled. "I hope you're up for it. We have a few days. I guess I don't have to ask that you freeze out the other media?"

"I don't know. They might offer me stuff. Do you have anything to offer for that exclusive?"

He pulled the Honda into the police parking lot. "Dinner? Free rides in my car?" He finally kissed her. "Anything else you have in mind?"

Maggie smiled. "I think those will do for starters." She glanced at the well-lit police building. "This could take a while."

"I can wait. There's always time for dinner."

She agreed, lamenting that they would probably go out again with her in jeans and a Pie in the Sky T-shirt. The black skirt and turquoise sweater would have to wait for another time.

• • •

Her interrogation took even longer than Maggie expected. Frank questioned her first. Captain Lance Mitchell, Frank's boss, questioned her as well. Then the assistant district attorney questioned her, again. Each asked her if she wanted to have a lawyer present. Maggie didn't care about that. She knew what had happened and wanted to get this last part over with.

When it was finally finished, she stepped out of Frank's office. Ryan was waiting for her.

So was Stan Isleb. She hadn't expected to see him there.

"Mr. Isleb," Frank said. "Back so soon? I take it you made bail."

"That's right." Stan was still defiant. "I'm here to help my wife."

Maggie shook hands with Officer Harding and thanked him for his help. She wanted to leave without talking to Stan. He was a past chapter in her life and she wanted to move on.

Stan had other plans.

"Ms. Grady," he called her name as she and Ryan were about to slip out the door.

Maggie turned back, not sure what she could say to him. He and Jane had lost everything, including each other. She was involved, but not really part of it. She hoped he'd see that.

If not, they were in a police station. He couldn't do more than give her a hard time.

"Yes?" She steeled her jangled nerves to take whatever he meant to dish out.

"I want to apologize for both your problems at the bank as well as your problems with my wife." For a brief moment, he appeared humbled, looking at the floor as though searching for inspiration. "I'm sorry your life was disrupted by ours. I hope you'll be able to move ahead now."

Maggie was completely shocked by what he said. She certainly hadn't expected an apology. "I know you didn't mean any of this to happen, Mr. Isleb. I hope things work out for you."

In the quiet of the room, Maggie turned and left.

# Twenty-three

Early the next morning when the news broke about Jane Isleb's arrest, a flood of visitors arrived at Pie in the Sky. There was barely enough pie to feed everyone, even with the twelve Amazing Apple pies Aunt Clara and Maggie had made that morning.

"I'd better get in back and get some new ones started," Aunt Clara said when she saw the crowd of reporters, stunned regulars, and curiosity seekers.

"No. Not now," Maggie replied. "There won't ever be a better time to announce the winner of the mystery pie contest. This is a huge audience. Thousands of people will know. Let's pick one out of the jar."

Aunt Clara agreed. It took Maggie a few minutes to get the shop quiet enough so everyone could hear what she had to say. The TV reporters got their microphones and cameras ready.

Maggie stuck her hand into the oversized jar and pulled out a name. She gave the torn piece of yellow legal pad to her aunt.

Aunt Clara read the paper out loud. "Evie Hansen is a student at Duke and she wants the mystery pie to be Evie's Elegant Eggnog pie. Congratulations, Evie! You'll get Elegant Eggnog pie until the new year for free!"

Everyone applauded. Maggie wished Evie had been there. It was a little anticlimactic without her. Still, it was a great opportunity to show off the contest. Even as they emptied the jar to start the new contest, customers began putting their names in.

Between the new publicity from Jane's arrest, and some surprises she had in mind for refurbishing the pie shop, Maggie thought the shop would see a big increase in revenue.

Maggie had plans for the X-Press It owners and Donna Davis from Triple Tan too. She was going to talk to them about paying rent from now on. She was willing to be reasonable, but they needed to realize that paying at least a modest rent was part of running a business.

After about an hour, the excess group of visitors had gone, leaving behind a smaller crowd of regulars with a ton of questions. Maggie wondered if she'd have to start giving tours of the alley and garbage area. Everyone was interested in where Lou's body was found and Jane was arrested.

Maggie had to admit there was a certain poetic justice in Jane coming there to threaten her, only to find herself in custody.

Ryan had called her late last night, after he'd dropped her off, to tell her that Jane had already made bail. She and Stan were on a plane home after certain agreements were reached with the Durham District Attorney's Office.

It certainly put a crimp into her idea of justice to know people got arrested for murder and attempted murder then left to head for their vacation home until the trial. Of course, she couldn't complain. If the bank would've had her arrested for embezzlement, she'd never have been able to prove her innocence. She'd still be in a cell somewhere awaiting trial.

There would be more to it than that, Maggie realized. No doubt Stan and Jane would lose most of what they owned. It might even be more devastating for them than it was for her since she didn't have that much.

The pie shop stayed busy all morning with no quiet time. It was all Maggie and Aunt Clara could do to keep up with pie making. Coffee poured faster than rain from a downspout. Maggie encouraged her customers to drink iced tea. There weren't a lot of takers on that. The chilly weather made everyone want something hot.

Ryan had been there with the crowd early in the day. After hearing how busy they continued to be, he brought lunch for Maggie and Aunt Clara. He even took some pie out to customers and poured coffee so they could sit down and eat.

"Did you have a chance to deposit your check from the bank?" Aunt Clara asked her.

"Yes. And I have some really good ideas about ways to spend it. What would you think about new tables and chairs, a paint job, and new tile? I think Pie in the Sky could use a face-lift, don't you?"

Aunt Clara smiled. "I think that would be wonderful. I can't wait to see how it turns out."

Maggie didn't tell her about the money she planned to spend on the house. That could come later. She didn't want her aunt to be too surprised.

"I have good money news too." Aunt Clara drew a letter from her pocket. "The money from the rents on the shops is enough to pay off the lien on the house. Isn't that wonderful?"

They both watched Ryan run around the pie shop serving customers.

"He's a good person," Aunt Clara observed. "He could use a little practice pouring coffee. Otherwise, I think he's a keeper, don't you?"

"I like him a lot," Maggie admitted. "What about you and his father?"

"It doesn't seem like Garrett and I are going to work out. He only wants to talk about politics and golf. I only want to talk about pie. We can't seem to find any common ground. There may be someone else. We'll have to see."

"Well, I'm sorry he's not what you were looking for. I

have a little surprise for you." Maggie got up and went behind the counter to take a box out of the glass case. She opened it on a perfect coconut cream pie.

"For goodness' sake. Did you make this all by yourself?"

"It's from Mom's recipe. I started thinking about you not eating your favorite pie because she was gone. I know it probably won't be as good as hers, but I made it with lots of love."

Aunt Clara had tears in her eyes as she tried a piece of pie. "This is very good. You added exactly the right amount of coconut. That's always a hard part. What are you going to call it?"

"Clara's Coconut Cream pie," Maggie announced. "What do you think?"

"I like it. Stay right here a minute." Aunt Clara hurried into the kitchen and came back with a pie box. "I was thinking the same thing about the deep-dish cherry pie I used to make for your mother. I made one last night while you were out with Ryan."

Maggie smiled. Would anyone else in the world understand their family's association with pie? Probably not.

She opened the pie box and looked at the cherry pie inside. "And what are you going to call it?"

"I'm thinking about Delia's Deep-Dish Cherry pie, in honor of your mother. What do you think?"

Maggie cut a piece of the pie and put it on her plate. "I think I'd better join a gym if I don't want to gain so much weight that I won't fit through the front door. Thank you, Aunt Clara."

# Epilogue

Pie in the Sky had been closed two days over the weekend for remodeling. Aunt Clara wasn't happy about it. Maggie felt that there was no other way to get the bulk of the big work done—painting, new light fixtures, tile, and a new counter.

They went in on Monday morning and saw that it had been worth the effort.

The pie shop still smelled of fresh paint and glue, but it looked fantastic. The walls that had been dingy were now a bright, clean white. No spots of missing or peeling paint anywhere.

The new tile was a vivid dark blue for all their Duke fans. It looked so new and clean that Maggie almost hated that customers would come in later and spill coffee on it.

The new blue counter and coffee-cup-shaped lights were everything she'd hoped for. The old tables and chairs would have to do for now. New ones would be delivered Tuesday.

"Oh my stars!" Aunt Clara said when she saw the fresh interior. "It's wonderful. Well worth the wait. Where did you get those old Blue Devil photos? I love them up there."

"I got them from Ryan. His dad had taken them for the paper years ago. I have a surprise in the kitchen too."

Aunt Clara gasped when she went into the kitchen and saw the new, larger oven Maggie had installed while the shop was closed. "Where did you find it?"

"In a supply catalog." Maggie smiled as her aunt ran her hand lovingly across the ceramic finish. Until now, Aunt Clara had worked with a small oven even older than the refrigerator that had stopped working. "It can bake twelve pies at once."

"That's completely amazing. Just think of all we can do with it. You know, I've been thinking about introducing a new pie—Killer Key Lime. It would go with the whole theme of our latest publicity. What do you think?"

Maggie mulled it over. "It could work. Knowing what happened here sure hasn't stopped anyone from coming in."

"It's settled then." Aunt Clara nodded. "We'll add Delia's Deep-Dish Cherry, Clara's Coconut Cream, and Killer Key Lime to the menu. I'm afraid we'll have to wait to do the lime until Mr. Gino brings supplies this week."

"Okay. Let's get started. People must be pie hungry since we've been closed."

Maggie and Aunt Clara worked on dozens of piecrusts since there were no pies made after being shut down. The pie of the day was going to be Delia's Deep-Dish Cherry, since they'd already purchased supplies for that.

After the pies were set and a dozen were in the oven, Maggie started the coffee and added the new pies to the large, new erasable whiteboard that would carry the menu from now on.

Ryan rapped at the front door about thirty minutes before opening. "Any coffee ready yet? I've been up since three a.m. doing research."

Maggie closed and locked the door again behind him. "Good morning to you too. Yes, there's coffee and you can have a cup. What are you researching?"

"Hey!" He looked around. "The place looks great! What a difference." He spread out a notebook on one of the tables. It was filled with old newspaper clippings.

"What's this?"

"Bad news, I'm afraid. This man." He pointed to a picture of a handsome older gentleman. "His name is Donald Wickerson. He's originally from Atlanta. He's spent the last few years in North Carolina. The last time he visited the Raleigh area, his wife accidentally fell down a flight of stairs and died."

Maggie looked through the other newspaper articles that highlighted other accidents that had befallen unlucky women married to Donald Wickerson. "So he's like a black widow, except he's a man. What do you call that?"

"I call it a killer," Ryan said. "Six women have died and left him money during his lifetime. I happened to get the scoop that he's in Durham. That can only mean one thing."

Maggie nodded. "He's looking for another wife to kill."

"Number six died the end of last year in a swimming pool accident."

"Why haven't the police arrested him?" she asked.

"He always has an alibi and they can't pin anything on him. I'm thinking about running a series of articles about this kind of thing—nothing about Wickerson himself, since he's never been caught. It might be enough to scare him away. Or it might be enough to get the police to look into it. Either way, great newspaper stories."

"I hope that helps," she added. "What's his type?"

"Usually wealthy, widowed business owners who are unlucky enough to have come to his attention. The more successful, the better."

Maggie heard the back door to the pie shop open and close. Aunt Clara rarely used that entrance because of the sticky door. Not having very good memories of the back door, she went toward the kitchen.

Before she could see what was going on, Aunt Clara, her pretty pink face smiling, walked into the front of the shop. There was a tall, broad-shouldered older man in an expensive suit on her arm.

"Maggie, Ryan, I'd like you to meet someone I met at the library a few weeks ago. This is Donald Wickerson. He's a book lover and a pie aficionado. How could anyone ask for more?"

New Pie Recipes from

*Pie in the Sky*

Now that everything has settled down at Pie in the Sky, Aunt Clara and I will be working on our newest pie recipes for the shop. We'll also be baking the old favorites: Lotsa Lemon Meringue, Delia's Deep-Dish Cherry, and Clara's Coconut Custard.

We'll make all three of these pies with our family's secret recipe for the best piecrust.

Enjoy!

—*Maggie*

# Flaky Piecrust

Be sure to chill all mixing utensils and ingredients first.

2 cups all-purpose flour

1 ½ teaspoons salt

1 cup vegetable shortening

1. Stir flour and salt together, then quickly work shortening into the mixture until the particles are as small as BBs.
2. Sprinkle in a sparse amount of cold water, only enough until the dough sticks together in a ball. It should be dry, not moist. Chill for at least 30 minutes.
3. Preheat oven to 350 degrees. After dough is chilled, place it on a pastry board or other flat, nonstick surface. Dust surface lightly with flour. Flatten the dough a little, then use a lightly floured rolling pin to make smooth, even strokes from the center to the edge of the dough.
4. Turn the dough frequently to keep it round. Use an ungreased 9-inch metal pie pan for flaky crust. Don't turn the crust over when putting it into the pan. Leave rolled side up. Use your fingers to lightly press together any cracks in the crust. Flute crust, if desired.

5. Bake at 350 degrees for 10 minutes or until golden brown. Cool for about 5 minutes before adding cold, unbaked filling. Refrigerate at once. Otherwise bake with filling according to type and recipe. Precooked fruit requires less time than raw fruit.

- *Makes one 9-inch piecrust*

# Lotsa Lemon Meringue Pie

This recipe is an old favorite.

One baked 9-inch pie shell

1 cup plus 4 tablespoons sugar (or alternate sweetener)

¼ cup cornstarch

1 cup boiling water

3 eggs, separated

1 tablespoon butter, salted or unsalted

Grated rind and juice of 1 lemon

¼ teaspoon cream of tartar

1. In the top part of a medium-size double boiler, mix 1 cup sugar and cornstarch.
2. Add boiling water slowly and cook on low heat, stirring constantly.
3. Beat egg yolks slightly. Add yolks and butter slowly to mixture in pot.
4. Cook until thick, stirring constantly.
5. Add lemon rind and juice then let cool.

## *Meringue*

1. Preheat oven to 350 degrees.
2. Beat egg whites with cream of tartar until frothy. Mix in 4 tablespoons of the sugar. Continue beating until stiff.
3. Put lemon mixture into the baked pie shell. Swirl meringue over the top into peaks.
4. Bake at 350 degrees for 7 to 10 minutes, or until meringue is slightly golden.

• *Makes one 9-inch pie*

# Delia's Deep-Dish Cherry Pie

You will need two unbaked 9-inch piecrusts for this one. Use fresh cherries when you can. Or you may use one can of cherry pie filling. Adjust baking time accordingly.

1 pound tart red cherries, pitted
½ cup cherry juice
6 tablespoons sugar or alternate sweetener
2 tablespoons cornstarch
½ teaspoon salt
1 tablespoon butter

1. Preheat oven to 375 degrees.
2. Mix pitted cherries with juice, sugar, cornstarch, and salt.
3. Place one of the unbaked piecrusts into an ungreased 9-inch metal pie pan.
4. Pour the cherry mixture into the piecrust and dot with butter, salted or unsalted
5. Cover with the second piecrust. Make slashes in it so steam can escape.
6. Bake at 375 degrees for 30 minutes or until crust turns golden brown.

• *Makes one 9-inch pie*

# *Clara's Coconut Custard Pie*

3 eggs, separated
½ cup sugar or alternate sweetener
2 cups scalded milk
½ teaspoon salt
⅔ cup shredded coconut, sweetened or unsweetened
1 9-inch unbaked piecrust

1. Preheat oven to 300 degrees.
2. Beat egg yolks with the sugar.
3. Gradually add the milk, salt, and coconut, stirring gently until well mixed.
4. Beat the egg whites until stiff and add these to the egg yolk and milk mixture.
5. Fill the uncooked pie shell and bake for 30 minutes at 300 degrees. Filling is done when it is firm.

• *Makes one 9-inch pie*